SASSENACH IN STILETTOS

Love Regency Style

ROSEMOUNT MANOR
BOOK II

LOUISA CORNELL

Amazon ISBN: 9798308002604

Ingram ISBN: 978-1-953100-66-5

Cover Design: Dreams2Media

Editor: Penny Brandon

First Trade Paperback Printing by Scarsdale Publishing. Ltd. February 2025

10 9 8 7 6 5 4 3 2

www.scarsdalepublishing.com

Trademark Acknowledgments

Maserati
Hummer
Kate Spade
Jimmy Choo
Louis Vuitton
Ken doll – Mattel
Oscar
Mattel (Ken doll)
Kool-Aid
Google
The Hangover
Alexa
People
Maglite
Kama Sutra
Astro Turf
Clorox
Ralph Lauren
Karen Rose
Kardashian

Outlander by Diana Gabaldon
The Quiet Man
Netflix
G.I. Joe
iPad
Land Rover
The Brown Betty Teapot

Who went to war at the age of sixteen. He served six years in the United States Army and twenty-five years in the United States Air Force. He served in two wars, won honors for bravery, some of which we had no knowledge until after he died.
He seldom talked about his tours in combat. When asked about the honors we knew about he simply said "I was just doing my duty. That's what I signed up for."

He was my first and forever example of what a hero is both in war and in the everyday life of a loving husband, a devoted father, an honorable man, and one of the most generous, compassionate, and giving people I have ever met.
The horrors of war made him strong. The way he dealt with them on a daily basis all his life made him the bravest man I have ever known.

Love you, Daddy.

Chapter One

❧

28th February
Los Angeles, California

THE CAR SERVICE WAS LATE. PAR FOR THE COURSE AS FAR AS Lily Randolph was concerned. One last disaster in a month-long series of disasters. The way things were going, she might not make that plane to Scotland at all. Why tempt fate? Or whoever was running the shitshow her life had become.

"We could drive you, sweetie," Derek said from behind the kitchen island where he cleaned up the remnants of the fruit smoothie he'd made for her breakfast.

He'd started out as her personal chef, but now served as chef, housekeeper, personal shopper, and friend. When she'd had to cut back on staff, Derek and his husband, Raphael, had stayed. They told her they had nowhere else to go. A lie, but one the three of them had tacitly agreed never to admit, at least not to one another.

"You just want an excuse to get behind the wheel of my Maserati." Lily checked the driveway of her Hollywood Hills home for the tenth time. Nothing. Dammit, her credit was bad, but not that bad. She had enough to pay for car service to the airport.

"There is that," Derek said with a grin.

His lithe body and blond surfer good looks made him appear much younger than forty. He'd hooked up with body-builder and personal trainer Raphael, eight years his junior, six years ago—about the same time Lily had hired them both in the hope of giving her failing career one last try.

"And how would you suggest we load all my luggage and the three of us into the 'Rati? Raphael would have to ride on the hood."

"He would make a show-stopping hood ornament." Derek gave the island's marble top one last swipe then draped the dishcloth over the edge of one of the sinks. "Or I could run down to the gatehouse and hotwire *he-who-shall-not-be-named's* Hummer."

"Only if you promise to park it at the airport and leave the keys in it," Lily said as she dropped onto one of the cream-colored couches in the great room and rummaged through her carry-on.

She dragged out her copy of *A Matter of Honor* and tucked it into her Kate Spade purse. The most anticipated film of the year was about to start production. Based on a novel by an obscure romance writer, the female lead role had been fought over like the last pair of size six Jimmy Choo's the night before the Oscars. And somehow, Lily had come up Cinder-fucking-ella. She still had trouble believing it.

"Ouch!" Derek flopped down on the oversized ottoman in front of her. "Tell me how you really feel."

"Doesn't matter." She pretended to check the tags and locks on her Louis Vuitton carry-on. "They picked up the Hummer last night." She handed Derek an index card. "New security codes. I sold the car, along with everything else he left in the gatehouse. And I changed the gate and house codes so he can't come on the property."

"Wasn't he supposed to come back tomorrow and pick up the Hummer and his possessions?"

"Was he?" Lily checked her phone with her patented expression of pretend innocence.

"That's my bitch," Derek said with a laugh.

"I learned from the best. Where is that damned car?" She sprang from the couch and stalked back to the front door, phone still in hand.

"He didn't deserve you, Lily," Derek said in that firm, *I-know-what-I'm-talking-about* voice. Not to be confused with his *I'm-trying-not-to-sound patronizing-because-you're-sad* voice.

"I don't know about that, Derek. But I do know I didn't deserve to walk into *my* sauna and find him banging *my* personal assistant." Oddly enough, saying it out loud only hurt a little today. In a month or so it wouldn't hurt at all, especially now.

"Do you want me to have Raphael kill him? There's room in the rose garden for at least one more scumbag ex before we have to start burying them under the jacuzzi."

"Before I kill anyone, there's a limo out front," Raphael said as he sauntered in shirtless, with his sweatpants riding low on his hips. "And the driver does *not* look like the type who loads luggage." He hefted two suitcases under each arm and headed for the door, which Lily held open even as she stood on her toes and kissed his cheek.

"You are so lucky," she told Derek as he grabbed her carry-on and handed her the Kate Spade.

"So are you, sweetie," Derek replied as they trekked out to the limo. "You just landed the biggest role in the biggest film of your life. This is the one. I can feel it. Everything is going to be wonderful from here on out."

"From your lips to God's ears, my friend." She stood next to the open limo door while Derek situated her carry-on and purse inside. Raphael made two more trips from the house, then finally closed the trunk of the long, black stretch.

"You're all set," Raphael said as he hugged her and kissed her on both cheeks. "Maybe you'll meet some handsome Highlander in Scotland and bring him home as a souvenir."

"I have no idea why Wentworth is insisting on us spending all this time in Bumfuck, Scotland before filming starts. And I have no interest in men in skirts, thank you very much."

Lily's nerves hummed like a thousand stage lights. Derek saw this role as the start of a revived career. He didn't realize it could be the end of one. Or if he did, he didn't say so.

"Don't knock men in skirts until you try one." Derek helped her into the limo. "And I do recommend you try one."

"I love you both," Lily said as Raphael put his arm around Derek. "I'll call you when I land. Take care of each other."

She knelt in the seat to peer out the back window as the limo rolled slowly down the drive. Once her friends disappeared from view and the driver merged onto the road into the heart of LA, she settled onto the soft leather seat and checked her phone again. She'd missed a call.

From her mother.

How the hell had she gotten this number?

She deleted the call and blocked the number. Mommy Dearest probably got it from Lily's latest ex. Now that she'd booted him out, he was desperate for money. He'd sell his own mother, let alone Lily's private cell number. She could count on one hand the number of people who had it and whom she hadn't blocked—Erik Wentworth, the director who had given her the role of a lifetime, Derek, Raphael, her agent of the last five years, and her hairdresser. Pathetic if she thought about it, which she tried hard as hell not to do.

She had bigger fish to fry. The flight from LA to Aberdeen might give her just enough time to fire up the grease.

THREE HOURS LATER, LILY HAD TO ADMIT GRATITUDE FOR TWO things. The first? She had restrained herself from getting shitfaced while she waited in British Airways' VIP lounge. The second? Her agent hadn't only booked her a flight on British Airways, but he'd booked her in first class. She was in her own luxurious little pod of a seat and there were only three other passengers in this section of the plane. They had all recognized her, as had the flight attendants. So, either they'd decided to show some class and not disturb her, or they all knew her career was a dumpster fire and wouldn't lower themselves to associate with, let alone fawn over, a now B-list actress who hadn't had a major movie role in years.

Whatever the reasons, Lily now had time to think through this latest turn her life had taken. Rumors about the casting of *A Matter of Honor* had been circling Hollywood like the mechanical shark from *Jaws* for months. Even now, Erik Wentworth, the hottest new director of period films, hadn't made an official announcement, though he'd told Lily the entire cast was pretty much a lock at this point. That was the source of her angst and irritation at the moment—one of the sources at least.

It was a good thing she'd already signed the contracts before Wentworth told Lily who her leading man was going to be. Of all the actors in the business, of all the actors in the world, what the hell had possessed this supposedly brilliant director to cast an action star in the lead role of the most anticipated period film of the decade? Not just any action star. No, in keeping with the shitshow theme her life had adopted of late, Wentworth had cast Danny Arneaux as Captain Rothgate.

Lily had read the damned book twice. If Danny I-Don't-Screw-Children was a Regency romance hero, her mother was Mother Teresa. And Lily's mother was no damned Mother Teresa. Danny Arneaux was no saint either. He'd hooked up with every starlet in Hollywood six years ago. She'd been eighteen years old and not a child by any stretch of the imagination. He'd turned her down anyway. His last two films had crashed and burned spectacularly, which meant she was going to have to carry him in this film.

Like hell she would.

They were both flying to Scotland to participate in some kind of Regency boot camp, but Wentworth had hired a special Regency tutor for Arneaux. That meant the director *knew* the Cajun Ken doll didn't have the chops for the job. Lily intended to make sure Wentworth never forgot it. With luck, he'd dump Arneaux and hire a real actor for the role.

"Are you reading *A Matter of Honor*?" the flight attendant with the cute British accent and sort of old-fashioned uniform asked as she delivered Lily's elegant meal tray. She indicated the book Lily had been trying to read again. "I love that book. I've read it three or four times."

"Why?" Lily fiddled with the contents of the tray—draped her napkin across her lap, organized her silverware, then buttered the fluffy roll. "Why do you love it?"

She didn't normally engage with the people who waited on her. Most saw it as her being too snobby and self-absorbed to bother, which was fine with her. Over the years, she'd come to understand that if people hated a celebrity, they tended to leave them alone. However, she really wanted to know the appeal of this romance novel that had come out of nowhere and become a bestseller so monumental Erik Wentworth had snapped up the movie rights.

"Really?" The flight attendant sounded suspicious, as if Lily were either making small talk or looking for a reason to tease her.

"I really want to know." Lily put down the silverware and gave the woman her full attention.

The flight attendant stepped closer and said in a low voice, "Because he does the right thing. Captain Rothgate. He has every chance not to, every chance to escape a terrible situation. He's been hurt, betrayed, traumatized by war, and he still does the honorable thing. He has no idea if it will work out for him and his wife. Neither does she. Life has been awful to them. But in the end...." She shrugged. "I guess I like the idea of someone doing the right thing even if they don't have to, and in the end it's the one thing that works out. Because of love. Silly, when I say it out loud like that."

"Not at all," Lily replied. "Life never works out like that, but it's nice to think it might."

"Exactly." The woman smiled and went back up the aisle to the first-class galley.

Well, that was monumentally not helpful. The flight attendant's reasons for loving *A Matter of Honor* were the same as those in every review of the book Lily had read. Hundreds of them. The same as those of everyone she'd asked from her hairdresser to the girl that did her nails to... hell, even Derek had rattled off words like *right thing* and *honorable man* and *love wins*. Lily didn't get it. She truly didn't. Intellectually, her lack of understanding made her a cynic. Emotionally, it scared the hell out of her. Lately everything about acting scared her.

She'd won an Oscar at the age of twelve. In a period film, no less. That was why she'd latched onto *A Matter of Honor* as her chance to revive her career after a couple of years of lackluster young adult films followed by ten years of television movies and offers of projects one step above porn. The role she'd played at twelve had been easy because she understood the character and the story. She wasn't one of those actors who could portray a role she didn't understand through technique, method, or talent. She had to…step into the character's soul.

She glanced at her worn copy of the novel and shook her head. Time to eat. She could do that. It was instinctual. When it came to opening herself up enough emotionally to deliver an Oscar-worthy performance in the part of a woman like Captain Rothgate's wife, she didn't know where to start. Those instincts had taken one helluva beating in the past five or so years. Her biggest fear of all? That those instincts might never come back.

Chapter Two

Lachlan Innes leaned against the worn stone corner of the west wing of Rosemount Manor and folded his arms across his chest. The perfect spot to watch his brother's worst nightmare unfold in the front drive of their ancestral home. Then again, since their father's death six months ago, Knox had dealt with a whole series of nightmares, each one worse than the last. It had started with him inheriting the title of Duke of Turra and had sped downhill ever since. Lachlan tried to muster a bit of sympathy for his older brother. The man damned sure didn't make it easy.

"Think Himself will make an appearance?"

Urquhart, Rosemount's wiry horse master, eased up next to Lachlan without so much as disturbing a blade of grass. The man would've made a damned fine assassin had MI5 been clever enough to lure him away from the Highlands. Nothing short of a Holy Edict or a ducal command would do that.

"Not so far," Lachlan said. "Is he supposed to?"

"'Tis said that Miss Witherspoon ordered him to be there to welcome the Sassenachs to the manor."

'Tis said meant someone on Rosemount's staff had over-heard Knox arguing with Miss Witherspoon, or Elle, as she'd asked Lachlan to call her, and had delivered a blow-by-blow description of said argument at the staff dining table. Elle would also have words with Urquhart if she heard him call their visitors Sassenachs—his word for anyone not born in the Highlands, and not a particularly flattering word at that.

"I'm sure that went over like Irish whiskey at a High-lander's wake," Lachlan remarked. Whoever these people were, they traveled with enough luggage for a general's staff setting up headquarters. The familiar twitch that image evoked only lasted for a second this time. Lachlan was having a good day for a change.

"Don't know about that." Urquhart nodded toward the front of the house. "There he is."

"Well, I'll be damned."

"Never happen. Mrs. Wallace lights a candle for the both of us every Sunday. Not even the Almighty would cross that woman. We're doomed to an eternity of playing harps and singing hymns."

"You need to shag that old woman and get it over with, Urquhart." All hell had broken out on the front lawn. Two large black and red dogs wreaked havoc with the footmen. This whole Regency boot camp might be a bit of fun after all.

"I will if you will," the old man shot back.

"'Fraid I'm not man enough to shag Mrs. Wallace."

Urquhart laughed and elbowed Lachlan in the side. "You've been wandering these hills too long, lad. You need a bonny lass to keep you warm in that hut you've holed your-self up in and no mistaking it."

"Now you sound like my brother. He's the one that needs a woman so he can breed an heir for all this. Though little good it's done him to take on Rosemount. Little good it did our father."

"Your father didn't take on Rosemount. Himself is the only duke in my memory to try and save this place."

"Despite hating every minute of it?"

"He doesn't hate Rosemount, lad. He'd not be letting the American lass do all of this if he hated it."

"Time will tell." Lachlan straightened and took a step closer to the front drive, closer, but not close enough to be seen. "Who is that?"

A dark-haired woman in a bright green monstrosity of a coat launched herself out of the ridiculous luxury coach looking vehicle and appeared to give the other two passengers what-for. She had the pale sort of skin that would look incredible in moonlight. God only knew what her shape might be, but those legs. Lachlan had never seen legs like those in his life. Or if he had, maybe he just hadn't noticed. He damned sure noticed them now. His cock was hard enough to jump out of his kilt and cross the lawn all by itself.

"Humph." Urquhart pulled an ancient pipe out of the pocket of his tweed jacket and lit it up. He looked Lachlan up and down.

"What?"

"Didn't say a word." He nodded toward the fountain in front of the manor's double doors. "This don't look good."

Knox stood in front of the fountain. Miss Legs in the ugly coat sauntered toward him. She curtsied for God's sake. Lachlan rolled his eyes. Another American looking to become a duchess. Knox extended his hand about the time the two huge dogs arrived and reared up to….

"Bloody hell," Lachlan choked out.

"Aye," Urquhart said solemnly.

Lachlan snorted. He couldn't help it. It hurt too. He planted his fists on his hips to keep from covering his mouth with his hands. Didn't help. Suddenly he was bent double laughing his arse off. His throat hurt. His ribs hurt. It had been so long his entire body seemed to say *What the hell do you think you're doing?* In a few more minutes, he regained his composure, though it still hurt to breathe.

"I don't know whose dogs they are, but I'm having Cook serve them two of our finest game hens for dinner," he said.

"For knocking your brother into yon fountain? Shame on you, Lachlan Innes."

"For knocking His Grace, the Duke of Turra, on his arse into yon fountain in front of the entire household, Elle, and a coachload of Yanks." Lachlan brushed a tear from his eye. "I'd give my left nut to see Knox's face."

"You might have seen his face if you weren't staring at that lass's legs when she went arse over teakettle into the fountain."

"And you didn't look, old man?"

"Didn't say I didn't. Said you did."

A gust of wind whipped around the corner of the house—wind that smelled and tasted of heather, lavender, and earth as the footmen helped Knox and the woman in question out of the fountain. Elle hurried everyone into the house.

"Well, I'm not dead yet," Lachlan said as the two of them turned and strolled toward the stables.

"Couldn't prove it by me these two years since you got back."

Lachlan had no intention of starting this conversation with Urquhart yet again. It served no purpose and triggered nightmares. Nightmares far worse than anything the Duke of Turra suffered.

"You don't need to be worrying about me. You need to worry about teaching the Sassenachs how to ride horses and drive carriages. Seamus said Miss Witherspoon has you signed up for this little charade as well."

"I'm more than a match for the Sassenachs. You're the one who needs to be worried." Urquhart touched the brim of his cap and opened the gate to the garden in front of his little cottage next to Rosemount's impressive stables.

"Me? What have I got to worry about?"

The horse master's rusty laughter followed Lachlan like a Highland mist as he strode down the unpaved lane from the stables across the sheep fields and on to the gamekeeper's cottage, which he'd called home since he'd returned from Afghanistan. He opened his door, but an odd sensation kept him from going inside just yet. There was that scent again of heather, old lavender and newly turned dirt. He turned back toward Rosemount Manor.

Elle, the American event planner who his brother had hired to come up with ways to use Rosemount Manor's ancient house and remote location to attract high-priced clients, had said the Regency boot camp would last at least three months, and if the Hollywood director who'd set it all up had his way, these first people and others would invade Rosemount for as long as a year or more while making a film. Knox hated the whole idea, but thanks to their father, they needed the money to keep the estate going and to pay off inheritance taxes and debts. Lachlan hated the disruption of the peace he'd found in this place that hadn't changed a great deal in the last hundred or so years.

He'd have to avoid the house and the guests, that was all. An image of dark hair, pale skin, and long slender legs came unbidden to mind. His cock stirred.

"None of that," he said as he entered his cottage. "Keep that up and we'll be going for a swim in the loch, March or not."

THIS WAS LACHLAN'S FAVORITE TIME OF NIGHT, NOT QUITE midnight, but late enough the manor had settled. His only companions as he hiked the fields, his staff for aid, were the night calling birds, some sheep, and the scrap of fur he'd brought back from Afghanistan with him. Black and white like the estate's sheepdogs, but no bigger than one of his late mother's lap dogs, Leonidas thought he was a mastiff.

Lachlan refused to argue with him. The dog had survived at least a year in a country where dogs were seen as vermin, unclean, and targets for marksmen's practice. Even after he'd attached himself to Lachlan and the other men in his unit, Leonidas had dodged roadside bombs, artillery fire, and military regulations.

"Come on, lad," he called as the dog's white flag of a tail disappeared behind a hedgerow. "I'm for home and a toddy. Freezing my *magairles* off out here." With luck the past few hours roaming the hills would wear them both out enough to sleep. Sleep without dreams.

Where the hell had the dog gone?

A flash of white caught Lachlan's eye. Headed toward the manor. Leonidas had honed his begging skills on the streets of Baghdad. He needn't have bothered. Rosemount's cook was a soft touch when it came to dogs and young boys whose parents' only talent was for hurting each other or their sons.

Lachlan shifted the heavily carved seven-foot staff in his hand and headed down the hill toward the ditch they called a ha-ha between the fields and the formal gardens at the back of the manor. If he hurried, he'd head Leonidas off before he crossed the bridge over the ha-ha.

"For pity's sake, 'Nidas, you've been eating all day." Lachlan started around another hedge and stopped in his tracks. He took a step back.

"She took my phone, Derek. Seriously. These people definitely drank the Regency Kool-Aid."

Derek? Lachlan didn't see anyone with the woman seated on the stone bench on the other side of the hedge. She *was* an

American. Maybe she was like Knox's *imaginary friend* when they were children.

"Well, of course I had a spare phone. I'm not stupid, I just play stupid on TV." She paused, he assumed to listen to this Derek person. Boyfriend? Husband? "Oh, don't even ask," she continued. "Arneaux is being a horse's ass and then some. I slapped the hell out of him to remind him who he is dealing with. At the airport in front of his Regency coach. I'll fill you in later. I'm freezing in this idiotic costume. Kiss your hubby for me and I'll talk to you soon."

Aha! Most definitely not a boyfriend or husband.

Lachlan peered through the branches of the neatly trimmed boxwoods. It was her, the woman who'd landed in the fountain with his brother. She wore a costume evening gown with no sign of a coat or shawl. He'd been right. Her skin took on a mother-of-pearl glow in the moonlight. Her hair was so dark and thick piled on top of her head the light glinted off it in little sparkles.

His breath grew thick. His vision began to curl at the periphery. Perfect time for a panic attack. He needed to get back to his cottage. Leonidas would find his way home, he always did. Something brushed across his forehead, a gentle sweep of his hair like a mother's touch. Lachlan straightened and turned to leave.

"Great. How the hell am I supposed to get back across this ditch?"

The sound of the woman slapping against the hedge and stumbling on the pebbled path along the ha-ha made Lachlan turn and edge back to the end of the row of boxwoods. She mumbled some very unladylike curses and stalked up and down the edge of the deep, wide ditch that separated the fields from the grounds of Rosemount Manor. The more she paced the more creative her language became and, unfortunately, the closer she got to falling into the—

"Oh, shit!"

Lachlan dropped his staff, crashed through the hedge, and in two strides grabbed the woman around the waist just as she started to slide down the embankment. He earned a flailing elbow in the nose in the process. Stung like hell.

"Hey, watch it, buddy."

Once Lachlan set her back away from the ha-ha, she wiggled out of his grip and batted at his hands.

Lachlan backed away arms raised. "Maybe I should have let you fall in the ha-ha. Good night." He gave a sharp whistle. "Come, Leonidas." Out of the dark, a white streak flew from the direction of the bridge, circled Lachlan's ankles, and ran back toward the woman. Lachlan looked over his shoulder to see his furry friend sitting at her feet, his head cocked to one side.

"Wait a minute. Is this yours?"

"He is, and the bridge across the ha-ha is up that way. Come on, lad. Home with you." Lachlan strode on in the hope the woman would cross the bridge and leave him alone.

The wind kicked up and pushed against him. *What the devil?*

"Is everybody in this country rude as hell?" she demanded.

Lachlan turned just as the woman stepped into a wide swath of moonlight. *Damn!* She had the face of a fairy queen from one of the stories Mrs. Wallace used to read to him and Knox when they were boys. High cheekbones, a delicate nose, dainty ears, full lips, and eyebrows like birds in flight. Her eyes were dark in the moonlight, perhaps brown? And while he was staring at her like an idiot, she rubbed her arms and shivered.

"Is everyone from the States stubborn enough to freeze to death just to make a phone call?" He shrugged out of his coat and wrapped it around her. She waste no time in slipping her arms into the sleeves and buttoning half the buttons. "This way." He took her hand and tugged her toward the bridge. He loosened his grasp, terrified he'd crush such tiny fingers.

"Excuse me? Hello? My name is Lily Randolph, and yours is?"

"Lachlan Innes. Here you go." He stopped at the foot of the bridge and dropped her hand. He clenched his fist around the place in his palm burned by her touch. "Cross this, and you'll be in the gardens. Go straight up the path between the rows of gas lights."

"You want your coat, Lachlan Innes?" She started to unbutton the black wool overcoat that nearly drowned her.

"Keep it. One of the footmen can bring it to me tomorrow. Next time, wear that green puffer. If it's dried out by then."

By the light of the gas lights at the far side of the little footbridge, it was obvious her eyes were brown—big brown eyes like a doe. This particular woman, however, wouldn't like the comparison. He was nearly certain of it, especially as those lovely brown eyes narrowed and currently had murder in them.

"You saw that."

He gave a curt nod. "I did."

"I didn't see you there."

"You were rather busy at the time."

"Busy?"

"Shrieking. Falling. Legs in the air. Head in the fountain. Shrieking some more. Dripping all the way to the house."

"I suppose you thought it was really funny. Seeing someone like me humiliated that way."

She was a great deal more upset about the entire episode than her stony expression let on. He'd learned to mask his own emotions well enough to recognize that state in another person.

"Someone like you?" he said.

Her brow folded into a series of wrinkles, which made her look confused, and cute. "You don't know who I am, do you?"

"Should I?" Probably not a good answer, but these days he tended to speak first and think about it later. Much later. Most days his brain had trouble making connections.

"Well." She paused as if to give him time to come up with an appropriate response. Whatever that may be. "I'm glad you enjoyed the show. Thanks for the coat." She stepped up onto the bridge.

"Miss Randolph?"

"Yes?" Her response reeked of suspicion.

"I was standing at the far corner of the manor. That's why you didn't see me. And the only part of the show I enjoyed was seeing His Grace get a good dunking."

Leonidas stopped beside her and she surprised Lachlan by bending and scratching the dog behind his ears. "You're not the first person to say so. That far away at least you couldn't see well enough to get in on the bet the footmen had."

"Bet?"

"The color of my panties."

He waited until she'd crossed the foot bridge. "Lime green," he called after her. "To match your skirt."

He walked to the hedge, picked up his staff, whistled for Leonidas, and trekked back across the fields toward his cottage. The complete outrage on her face kept him warm all the way to his front door. Well, that and the brilliant way she wove *rude, asshole,* and *in a skirt* into a tapestry of profanity every one of the regulars down the pub would stand up and applaud. There were United States marines who didn't curse like this woman.

Once he'd built up the fire in the sitting room, and

Leonidas had burrowed under the quilts and sheepskin rug on Lachlan's bed, he fired up his computer. While it booted, he made himself a hot toddy with a hefty dose of the local whisky, some honey, and some mulling spices.

Elle had warned him not to allow any of the guests participating in the present event to use his computer. Something about ruining their Regency experience. Silly warning as not even Knox had been in the gamekeeper's cottage for the last two years—which was exactly the way Lachlan wanted it.

He dropped into his desk chair and pulled up Google. "Let's find out who your latest lady love is, shall we?"

Leonidas thumped his tail but didn't bother to open his eyes. There wasn't a housemaid, shopkeeper, or barmaid in the county who could resist Lachlan's little furry lothario friend. Miss Lily Randolph was no exception.

The windows rattled under the sudden onslaught of the March breezes from the hills. Lachlan scrubbed his face with his hands to rid his nose of the latent aroma of heather and lavender. This was not happening. The enigmatic scent of lavender only happened to Knox, usually when Knox was dead drunk or close to it, which was not very often.

Leonidas yipped in his sleep. All he had to do was roll over, snuffle, and sleep returned to the fuzzy beast immediately. Lachlan should be so fortunate. The long walk in the cold was meant to wear them both out to the point they'd collapse into bed and not wake up until the fire went out and the room grew too cold to sleep. Tonight, his encounter with the American beauty had his nerves humming and his mind racing. Among other things.

He turned back to his computer. His monitor screen was filled with an image of *Lily Randolph – America's Sweetheart, All Grown Up.*

"Jesus, Mary, and Joseph." He'd seen sticking plasters bigger than the bikini she wore in the photo.

She stood on the bow of some millionaire's yacht and smiled like…a woman who'd rather be anywhere else. He recognized that smile in an instant. It was the one he wore anytime he had to go up to the manor and hold it together for the sake of the clan.

In addition to her glorious legs, she had a lithe, but athletic build, except for a pair of beyond memorable breasts. Her hair was longer than he realized, but it was the smile that got him. The smile that wasn't a smile, *and* her grip on one of the mast ropes of the yacht.

Bloody fucking hell.

The blurry sound of feminine laughter wafted past the closed cottage door.

Nothing for it. He'd have to stay holed up in his hermit hole for as long as the Yanks invaded Rosemount. He glanced at the bed where Leonidas now sat up, head tilted, looking at him with a question in his liquid brown eyes.

"We're screwed, my friend. There is no way in hell I'm going anywhere near Lily Randolph ever again."

Chapter Three

❧

Lily reminded herself to slip the footman, Robbie, a five pound note the next time she saw him.

Over the past several days she'd tried everything to gather information about Danny Arneaux and his little Regency coach—which included befriending the weapons expert hired to train Arneaux and to advise the director once filming started. Big. Mistake. Oh, Teddy Rousseau had proven useful enough. He hated Dr. Samantha Higgins almost as much as Lily hated Arneaux. Lily didn't know why and frankly could give two shits. But Teddy was a tool of the first order. He assumed Lily's friendship came with benefits.

As if.

Teddy had more hands than a Vegas poker tournament. He'd taken to trailing after her like a lost puppy. A lost bloodhound puppy. Lily had had a miserable morning, and Teddy had homed in on her frustration with a suggestion they go for a "walk in the gardens." Translation? "Let me drag you into the bushes and try to kiss you, feel you up, and anything else I can get away with before you knee me in the nuts."

Robbie, thank God, had seen her exasperation and hurried down the main staircase to "remind" her of her carriage driving lesson this very minute with the duke's stable master, Urquhart. Even better, when Teddy offered to join her, Robbie had told the jerk of a swordmaster the duke was looking for him. Teddy had trotted off like the good little Brit brownnoser he was in search of His Grace. What Lily and Robbie both knew was the duke had been driven into the village to some sort of council meeting and would be gone all day.

Hell, she needed to give the kid a ten-pound note.

The story wasn't a complete lie. She did have a driving lesson in about thirty minutes. She debated skipping it. Teddy had told her Samantha Higgins was a fraud. She'd never served as the historical advisor on a major motion picture, or any picture for that matter. The prim and proper schoolmarm who had Hollywood's biggest bad boy wrapped around her finger was a mere assistant to the guy who was supposed to be the advisor on *A Matter of Honor*. When he passed on the job, this woman had somehow persuaded Erik Wentworth to hire her.

Great piece of information to have until Lily tried to out Samantha to the woman in charge of their little boot camp. Danny had headed her off at the pass and snagged Lily's second cell phone and handed it over to the Jane Austen Nazi. Now she had no way to communicate with anyone, and it was all the Cajun asshole's fault.

Lily picked up the leather satchel she'd started carrying since her arrival at the manor. She stepped out the front doors and wrapped the warm, heavy plaid around her shoulders the way Emma, her assigned maid, had shown her.

"You'll freeze your tits off if you don't start covering them up, miss."

She smiled as she proceeded toward the stables. Lily liked Emma a lot. She was outspoken, pulled no punches, and didn't hesitate to answer any question asked, which was how Lily had found out Lachlan Innes was the duke's younger brother. He'd gone to war at eighteen and came home two years ago after eight years of tours in the Middle East. He wasn't "quite right" and worked as the duke's gamekeeper. Whatever the hell that was.

In all the misery of living without technology of any kind, electricity, a real bathroom, or decent clothes, Lily's memory of her encounter with the rude, but incredibly sexy dog walker had been the one bright spot. He was at least six feet tall and had a build that made Raphael look like a regular guy in comparison. She suspected those rock-hard biceps and broad shoulders didn't come from the gym. This was a man who worked for a living. Whatever shape the military had whipped him into, he'd maintained it and then some. His hair was dark and well past his shoulders, and his eyes were a light eerie gold. She wasn't sure.

Not that it mattered. Everyone she'd asked, at least those that had answered, said he never came to the main house, and he preferred to be left alone. So, except for some very erotic dreams, Lily was stuck plotting her revenge on Danny Arneaux and wondering about the duke's brother. Probably just a well. She'd never—

"Miss Randolph?" One of the footmen from the house opened the stable yard gate for her. "Are you really going to learn to drive that monstrosity?" He indicated the carriage across the yard with two horses hitched to it.

"So they tell me, Dougal. Should be fun."

He blushed bright red, probably because she remembered his name. "Don't know about that, miss. Don't know if I've ever seen a woman drive one of Himself's antique phaetons."

"Do you think it'll piss him off?" she leaned in close to whisper as she grabbed the young footman's arm with both hands.

"Might." Dougal patted her hand. "But if Miss Witherspoon approved it, there's naught he can do about it, or so McGinty says."

McGinty. McGinty. Ah! Angus McGinty. The guy who ran the estate for the duke, his…steward. Gruff old man. Soft touch.

"I guess I'll just have to settle for pissing him off in silence then, won't I?" She winked. "I gave up worrying about keeping men happy a long time ago, Dougal. There aren't many who are worth—"

Across the stable yard, Lachlan stood, head down, as he talked to the short man who checked the harnesses of the two horses. Lachlan wore a white shirt, a blue, black, and gray plaid kilt, and leather boots up to his knees. In the light of day, he was a stone-cold fox and more. Real men didn't look like this one. Not without great lighting, a stylist, a costumer, and a makeup artist.

Damn.

Did she say that out loud? He snapped his head up and looked right at her. And…made some sort of gesture with his hand, grabbed the tall wooden stick that leaned against a stall door, then disappeared out the back gate and up a narrow road toward the fields. Fast. What the hell? She stomped across the cobblestones to the short man who stared after the duke's brother.

"Are you Mr. Urquhart?" she demanded. When the man turned and looked at her, she felt bad for the way she'd spoken to him. He reminded her of her grandfather. She stuck out her hand. "I'm sorry. I'm Lily Randolph. I'm supposed to be having a driving lesson?"

The man smiled and took off his tweed cap before he

shook her hand. "Just Urquhart. Pleased to meet you, miss. I'm afraid we'll have to postpone yer lesson. Yer teacher is… indisposed." He glanced back toward the road Lachlan Innes pounded down like he was leaving a tax audit or an appointment with his dentist.

"That's my teacher?" She pointed at the broad back that got smaller with every minute.

"He was. He said—"

"'Scuse me, Just Urquhart."

Lily brushed past him and took the same gate out to the road. She never thought she'd be grateful for the ugly brown boots they'd given her to wear with her simple burgundy wool dress. The boots did, however, make it easier to run down a rude asshole Scot in a kilt. She lengthened her strides and doubled her pace.

"Hey," she called once she'd nearly caught up with him. "Lord Lachlan."

He stopped and looked over his shoulder. "Don't call me that."

"Fine. Lord Asshole. What's your problem?" She marched right up to him and got in his face. "You want to tell me what that was all about?" She jerked her head back toward the stable.

"What *what* was all about?" The last word came out *aboot*, and she had to fight a grin.

She rolled her eyes instead. "Please. The minute you saw me, you took off like a dog seeing the dog catcher. Why?"

"Are you the dog catcher?" His eyes were light amber in the sunlight. Eerie. He tapped one finger against the wood of the stick in his left hand.

"The men I've dated lately? Apparently. But we're not talking about me." And she damned sure wouldn't talk about the men she'd dated. Not with this man. "Why did you run?"

"I didn't run. I walked away. Like I'm about to do now." He turned and took a step.

Lily wrapped a hand around the stick and snatched it away. "Not without an explanation, you're not."

He reached for the surprisingly smooth and thick piece of wood. She took a step back. He folded his arms across his chest. His sleeves, rolled up to his elbows, revealed thick, toned forearms. The tendons on the backs of his hands stood out as he flexed his fingers.

"You have no business driving that phaeton. You'll break your fool neck," he said.

"That's why you're going to teach me to drive it. I have to drive one for the film."

"That's what stunt women are for."

"Oh, so you don't object to teaching women to drive a carriage, just to teaching *me* to drive a carriage."

"We're not having this conversation."

Lily wiggled her hand through his arm and tried to drag him back toward the stables. "No, we're not. Miss Witherspoon hired you to teach me. Let's go."

"I don't work for Elle." He stood there, a big Scottish lump.

"Elle? Well, according to the footmen, you all work for her. She's running the show to keep this entire place from going bankrupt. So, get with the program."

A blood vessel ticked in a line from his jaw down the side of his neck. His expression turned unreadable. Maybe she'd pushed too hard. Wouldn't be the first time. Still, it stung a little. What was wrong with her? What was it about her he didn't like so much he'd run away from a simple driving lesson? Screw this!

"Forget it." She tugged her hand free, shoved the big stick at him, and marched back toward the carriage and horses

Urquhart had waiting for her. "I'll teach myself. Have a nice day." She didn't look back.

She'd ridden and driven horses since she was ten years old while auditioning for parts in westerns and English period films. She'd never driven anything like this vehicle, but she'd die trying before she asked Lord Hard Body to teach her now.

Arneaux's first riding lesson had been a disaster. The horse had dumped him on his ass, and he'd ended up flat on his back in bed. Lily had no intention of going down like that. She'd push her supposed teacher's rejection aside and get the job done. She'd been doing so since she'd dumped her mom as her agent and pretty much ghosted the woman. The fewer people she depended on, the less she was disappointed —and Lily had had enough disappointment for a lifetime.

"Hello, beauties," she said once she reached the team of horses hitched to the carriage.

She rubbed their noses and scratched behind their ears while cooing nonsense to them the entire time. The old man stepped back and watched her. Lily followed the lines attached to the bridles. The bundle of leather strips—the reins—went over the front of the carriage and were looped together over what appeared to be a footboard in front of the narrow seat.

She took in a long breath, ran her hand down one horse's back, then turned to the stable master. "Are these two pretty steady, Just Urquhart? Used to pulling a thing like this?"

The old man removed his cap and brushed the toe of his boot against the cobblestones. "Aye. They're steady. Don't harness them to this particular carriage verra often, but his lordship tried them early this morning, and they behaved themselves."

"His lordship? Lord Lachlan?" Lily went to the side of the carriage and leaned up and across to grab the reins.

"Aye."

"Good for him." She handed Urquhart the reins. "Hold these while I hoist myself up onto this seat."

"What are you about, miss? Wait." He took the reins she shoved at him and tried to take her arm.

Lily stepped on one of the wheel spokes, gripped two spots on the side of the carriage, and pulled herself up between the footboard and the seat. She hitched up her skirts and flopped like a fish onto the seat. It wasn't until she straightened, wiggled into position, and fixed the twenty yards of wool fabric, which had to have gone into the dress she wore so her feet didn't get tangled, that she saw Lachlan Innes barreling across the stable yard like a pissed off bull.

"What the devil do you think you're doing, woman?" He came to the far side of the carriage.

"Excuse me?" She reached for the reins. Urquhart must have seen something in her face because he handed them to her, crammed his hat on his head, and got the hell out of Dodge. "What did you say?" she demanded of Lachlan again.

"I asked you—"

"You didn't ask me a damned thing. You asked *woman* something. My name is not woman."

She could almost hear his teeth grinding. "What are you about, Miss Lily Randolph?"

"I am *about*"—she pronounced the word aboot as he had—"to teach myself to drive this carriage because the man who was supposed to teach me is either too afraid or too big a snob to teach me. Now, step back before I run over you." Lily threaded the reins over her forefingers and clamped her thumbs down to hold them in place. She gave them a quick snap, and the carriage lurched forward.

So worth it.

Lachlan stumbled back, eyes wide and mouth open. Of course, in the next minute he grabbed the bridle of the horse closest to him and stopped the poor thing so quickly the horse tossed his head and stamped his feet. Lily wanted to do the same. However, the crowd of men she figured worked in the stables that had gathered across the way stopped her.

"You're mad," Lachlan said.

"Not yet, but I'm getting there. Let go of my horse."

"*Your* horse?"

"Fine. Your brother's horse. Let. Go."

"Bloody hell."

He ran his hand down the harness, stepped onto the wheel, and landed on the seat next to her in one graceful move—which set every nerve ending in Lily's body on red alert. She'd met some of the sexiest men on the planet. Dated some of them. Slept with a few. None of them, not even Danny Arneaux, held a candle to the Scot who sat and muttered in some foreign language while trying to wrestle the reins away from her. Sex in a skirt and boots. Lily needed to look for the exit and bail on this whole thing and quick.

She slapped his hands. "I'm not taking any passengers this first time out. Check back next week and I might take you for a ride."

The young guy who had come to hold the horses snickered.

"Really?" she narrowed her eyes on him.

The kid had the good sense to blush.

"Give me the reins before you kill us both." Lachlan held out his hand.

Lily didn't trust him as far as she could throw him. He'd take the reins and call his loyal subjects to haul her off the seat and carry her back to the house. "You tell me what to do, and I will do it."

"That would be a pleasant surprise."

"Screw you. I learn better by doing, and I am not giving you the reins. Start teaching or start walking. Your choice."

Lily looked straight ahead and gripped the reins so tight her knuckles turned white. She didn't dare meet those golden eyes, not when her body screamed, *"Climb this man like a tree."*

A shudder went through him. Lily knew it because he sat so close the vibration pressed him against her thigh, her arm, and the side of her breast. He radiated heat, and he smelled like rain and evergreens. In an instant he changed. He stretched his legs toward the footboard and crossed them at the ankles. He raised his arms and placed them along the back of the seat, one pressed like a carved tree into her back.

"Step back, lad," Lachlan said, his voice quiet and firm, the voice of a soldier.

"My lord." The young man tugged at the front of his cap and stepped out of the way.

"Well, Miss Randolph? There's the road." Lachlan pointed with the hand not behind her back. "Can you take us out without tearing Urquhart's gate off the hinges?"

Lily raised the reins and started the horses toward the gate. She'd never tell him, but this high up and in a vehicle she'd never driven, the terror level pegged at about a nine. She stiffened her spine and scooted forward a little on the seat. She held the horses to a walk, but she could tell they weren't happy about it.

"Loosen up on the reins. You'll hurt the horses' mouths." Lachlan leaned up to speak directly in her ear. His breath was warm and smelled like…cloves? He sat up and reached with both hands to adjust her hold on the soft leather lines. "You should have worn driving gloves."

"I wasn't issued any. The commander of this boot camp provided me with lots of ugly wool dresses and even uglier footwear." She stuck her foot out enough to turn her ankle-high leather boots back and forth for him to see. "But driving gloves were not included in the trunks of fashion don'ts Miss Witherspoon insists I wear."

"Sensible," he replied. "The boots."

"I'd rather wear yours." She finally met his gaze.

He blinked twice and looked down at the boots that came to just below his knee. The tops folded over, and they laced up the sides. They looked like the boots the hero of that time travel television series wore.

"They're sexier." She returned her attention to the road.

He gave her a sideways glance. "Hmm."

Lily huffed and blew her hair out of her face. She'd had better conversations with a casting director stoned out of his mind.

"Here. Rein them in a bit. They're getting away from you." Lachlan planted both feet in front of the carriage bench and grabbed the top of the footboard with one hand.

He was right, dammit. She'd been paying attention to him and not the horses. *Note to self: Carriage driving teachers need to be ugly old men.* The carriage started to rock back and forth. Not a great sensation as high as the seat was. Who the hell drove something like this? What purpose did it serve? The horses broke into a faster trot. She refused to call it a canter. The road was smooth, hard-packed dirt, while high embankments and hedges lined the sides. She hauled back on the reins.

"Not like that, woman. You'll kill us for sure." He tried to take the reins.

"My name is not…woman, asshole. Let me do this."

"Drive or kill us? Jesus!" He wrapped his arms around her and hauled her back onto the bench after the rut they hit nearly bounced her out of the carriage.

"Your choice," Lily snapped. Every bit of blood in her body dropped to her feet. They topped a hill and started down the other side like a bat out of hell. "If you had bothered to teach me instead of walking away with your ass on your shoulders, I wouldn't be wondering what the flying fuck to do to fix the balance of this death trap before it tips over, dumps us, and Frick and Frack up there run over us on the way back to the barn."

Lily shoved the reins into Lachlan's hands. He fumbled. The carriage lurched to one side. It went up on two wheels, and Lily held on for dear life to keep from falling off the side. Lachlan let loose a high-pitched whistle and pulled back on the reins. The horses slid to a stop. Lily's side of the carriage rolled up on an embankment. Her knees slammed into the footboard, and she nearly took a header onto the horses' rumps. Lachlan grabbed the back of her dress and slammed her back onto the seat.

Silence. Well, except for the creaking of the harness, the horses stamping their feet, and the wind whistling down the road. The wind carried a weird scent—lavender, a trace of some other wildflower, and ashes, maybe? Then there was the sound of her carriage driving teacher breathing like a racehorse or some out of shape boyfriend after sex. Lily was about to suggest he put his head between his knees.

"Are you out of your bloody mind?" he shouted. At least he'd caught his breath.

"Bring it down, Lord Lachlan. You're scaring the horses."

"Me? I'm scaring the horses? Do you have any idea what could have happened to you?"

"'Could have', being the operative words."

She took a good look at him. His face was pale, his eyes wide open and kind of wild, he had a death grip on the reins, and his hands shook. Her stomach hurt. She'd actually upset him. This big bundle of muscles and sexy who spoke as if each word cost money was…angry, but more….

"You could have been killed. You could have been thrown from the carriage and dragged under the wheels. From this height you probably would have broken your neck." His voice trembled as he got louder and more strident. He slapped the reins into one hand and latched onto her arm with the other. "What the hell possessed you to do this you silly little—" He gasped for breath and shook her arm. Was Lachlan Innes about to have a panic attack?

"I ought to…I ought to…."

Lily broke his grip on her arm, clasped his face between her hands, and kissed the living hell out of him.

Chapter Four

She kissed him.

Of all the ways to stave off one of his "spells" as Mrs. Wallace, Rosemount Manor's housekeeper, called them, this was the most outrageous. And the most effective because when Lachlan grabbed Lily's arms to shove her away, his only thought was to drag her closer and kiss her back.

So, he did.

Her lips were soft and sweet. She slid her hands to the back of his head, grabbed handfuls of his hair, and proceeded to plunder his mouth with her tongue like a band of reivers on an Anglo-Saxon border raid. A blaze of heat roared up his body from the soles of his feet to the top of his head—which by all rights should have burst into flames.

Saints preserve him, the woman knew how to kiss.

He tangled his tongue with hers and lifted her onto his lap. He crushed her breasts against his chest, and the wool of the shawl wrapped around her teased his skin through his thin cotton shirt. She gasped and drew back, then nipped his bottom lip. A half laugh bubbled in his chest. She stroked his hair and kissed him again.

Lily touched her lips to his with the lightest of pressure—the corner of his mouth, his top lip, his bottom lip. Some primitive instinct came to life in him, and he took charge of the kiss. He cupped the back of her head with one hand and clasped her hip with his free hand. She sucked his tongue into her mouth and held it. He groaned and hauled her back up against him.

The carriage jerked forward. Lachlan froze. Lily raised her head and glanced at the horses. He set her back on the seat and took up the reins. His chest heaved, and he dragged in a couple of breaths to settle himself. They sat there, side by side, while the horses stamped their feet, impatient to move. Lachlan had no idea what to say. His rock-hard cock had some ideas, rubbing against the front of his kilt like a cat against a gatepost.

"Feel better?" she asked without looking at him.

"Pardon?"

She laughed. "The polite Scottish hermit is back. You're fine."

His almost panic attack. She knew, dammit. "What are you going on about, w—"

She turned toward him and stuck her finger in his face. "You call me woman one more time and I will punch you in the nuts, shove you out of this carriage, and drive over your knees on my way back to the stables."

Lachlan stared at her. He couldn't help it. Her brown eyes held specks of gold that glittered when she was angry. Those soft, sexy lips thinned into the sort of line a sergeant major might envy. A sergeant major who was about to put his boot up some poor grunt's arse. She grabbed the reins and held them, although he didn't let go. This was not the smoldering hottie whose photos were all over the internet.

"I realize you're upset, but—"

"I'm upset?" She tugged at the reins. He tugged back. "I'm

not the one screaming like a lunatic and about to have a full-blown meltdown in the middle of a little carriage accident."

"Meltdown?" At least she didn't say panic attack. "You nearly killed us. I knew teaching you to drive a phaeton was a mistake, and you proved me right." He pried her hands off the reins while muttering, "Little carriage accident."

"Oh, for fuck's sake." She threw up her hands. "Did you die?"

He bit the inside of his cheek to keep from laughing. Two years home without a single desire to smile, and all he'd done since he'd met Lily Randolph was fight the urge to do so.

"You did not just quote that ridiculous *Hangover* film at me." He gave a short whistle and backed the carriage off the embankment.

"That is not a ridiculous movie. That is a great movie. Would have been better if it had been four girls, but still a great movie. Or don't you think women can handle that kind of trouble?"

"Women like you? Absolutely. That kind of trouble and more." He handed her the reins, which she took despite the stunned look on her face. Lachlan jumped down from the carriage bench. As he moved from wheel to wheel and checked both axles for damage, he kept one eye on the enigma of a female who rewrapped her shawl one-handed and tapped one boot against the footboard. Now she wasn't shouting at him, he noticed the pale sheen of her skin. She had been afraid.

"Women like me?" she said.

He climbed back onto the leather tufted carriage bench. When she tried to hand him the reins, he stretched his arms across the back of the seat and propped his boots against the footboard.

"Women who eat trouble for breakfast. Drive on, Miss

Randolph." He nodded. "That way." His body vibrated like a tuning fork as her thigh brushed his.

They were *not* going to talk about that kiss. At least he wasn't. Think about it, yes. Dream about it, yes. Fantasize to the memory of it, hell yes. Talk about it? Not on his life.

"What are you doing?" she asked even as she started the horses up the road away from the stables.

"Teaching you to drive a phaeton, against my better judgment, I might add."

"See, you were almost nice there. Almost." Despite her smile, she sat military straight and held the reins in a death grip.

"I am always nice. I may be a hermit, but I was raised to be a gentleman." He sat up and reached around her, caging her between his arms. He covered her hands with his and forced her to loosen her hold on the reins. "Relax. The horses can sense your tension."

"I wasn't tense until you started yelling at me." She moved back slightly.

He sneaked a quick sniff of her hair. Gardenias. That was it. He'd expected all kinds of scents from some ridiculously priced shampoo. Simple. Gardenias. He liked gardenias. He also liked the way she fit in his arms. He sat back so abruptly she turned to look at him.

"Keep your eyes on the road. I make it a policy not to land in a ditch more than once a day." He stretched his arms across the back of the seat once more and told himself he'd imagined the hurt look on her face.

"We didn't land in a ditch. We went up an embankment. Two completely different things." She tugged back on the reins with a light touch, just enough to keep the horses from picking up speed as they descended another hill. She hadn't lied. She'd done something like this before, and she listened to every correction he gave her.

"I love this," she said as the horses moved into a canter and the hedgerows whipped by them. "Why didn't you tell me how much fun this is?" The light in her eyes and the joy on her face gave her the air of some wild fey creature from long ago. "Don't you think this is fun?"

"Hmm."

They tooled along the narrow lane that cut through the acres of sheep fields of the Rosemount estate. The sun did its best to warm the air, but the wind that swept down from the hills had no intention of letting anyone forget it was March in the Highlands. The other thing the wind reminded Lachlan of was the folly of an Innes man who showed the slightest interest in a woman. The scent of lavender and heather when none was in bloom was all in his head. Unfortunately, scenes of violence, death, and loss were in there too. He had no right—

"Someone told you who I am, didn't they?"

"Not exactly," he said so slowly she had to see the lie.

"Bullshit."

"I Googled."

"So that's why you didn't want to teach me."

"Not…exactly." If Lily Randolph kept short-circuiting him like this, he'd have a stroke within days, and he'd be damned if he told her why he didn't want to teach her because if there was a wrong or hurtful conclusion, this woman jumped on it.

"You have something against all actresses or just me?"

"Slow down. Go left at the fork."

She struggled a bit with the turn. He clasped the lines above her left hand and guided her until the phaeton rocked back into position once more.

"This thing is too damned light. How do I keep it from tipping over at high speed?"

"Why do you need to know?"

She made a sound of disgust. "It's in the script. This thing corners worse than my Maserati."

"Maserati?" He had a vision of her at the wheel with her hair loose. Lachlan shifted on the seat and clasped his hands between his knees.

"I thought you Googled me. Remember? That's why you tried to bail on our lesson. You read something you didn't like and decided you didn't want to teach the has-been, slutty actress." Defiance oozed from her every pore. He knew all about that kind of defiance—and where it came from.

"I don't like that word."

"Join the club. Try having it used to describe you in every magazine in the country." She clicked her tongue at the horses and moved them into a trot. "And you still haven't answered my question."

"What question?"

"Why didn't you want to teach me?"

"You're a woman."

"Caught that, did you? You're sharp for a recluse in a skirt."

"Kilt."

"So, it's not slutty actresses, but all women you find unworthy of your time."

"Stop using that word."

Halfway up a hill she reared back in the seat and jerked the horses to a halt. The phaeton rocked back and forth enough they both had to grab at the sides to keep from pitching out.

"What the devil!" he growled.

"Why don't you want to teach me?" She pronounced each word like a cook chopped a carrot. Whack. Whack. Whack.

"I didn't read anything about you. I looked at photos. You're tall for a lass, but you can't weigh more than eight-and-a-half stone. This carriage is dangerous for a grown man to drive at that weight, let alone a woman. Elle didn't tell me who I'd be teaching. I assumed it was the actor. Arneaux." Lachlan broke into a sweat. In the middle of a country lane the world started to close in on him.

"The man who got thrown on his ass at his first English riding lesson? That actor? I am a lot better qualified than he is to—"

"I don't train people to do things that can get them killed," he shouted. "Not anymore." His words seemed to echo in the empty quiet—which oddly enough fascinated him as he had no clue where those words came from or why.

She stared at him with those big, soft brown eyes. He wanted to look away, but he saw something in those eyes that wouldn't let him.

"I'm sorry," Lily said, her tone uncharacteristically quiet. "I forget sometimes it isn't all about me." A slap of the reins and the horses jumped into motion and trotted toward the top of the highest hill on this portion of the estate. "Is there a place to turn around at the top of the hill?"

"Aye." His voice cracked. His throat closed, shredded raw.

"Here." She put the reins in one hand, fished around in the leather bag at her feet, and drew out a bottle of water. "Don't tell Sergeant Witherspoon about this. She'll have me running laps around the fountain in a corset."

He opened the bottle and downed half of it in one long draught. Grateful for the drink, Lachlan took a great deal of care to screw the top back on the bottle. He clasped it between his hands.

"Mind the ruts," he said. "Keep a tight rein on the horses and balance your weight on the seat. Keep a low center of gravity."

"What?"

"To drive a phaeton at high speed. Practice all that until it's second instinct. Then practice some more."

"If I promise not to get killed, will you keep teaching me?"

"Promises you can't keep, Sassenach. None of us can."

"Sassenach?"

"It means—"

"I know what it means. I've read Gabaldon's novels and seen the television series."

Lachlan snorted. It took a minute and a quick body check. His throat didn't hurt. His chest had loosened. His breathing eased.

"You've seen the series," she said as they reached the top of the hill, her words laced with laughter.

"Aye." He gave a one-word answer because he wanted to provoke her.

"Do you like it?"

"Nae," they said in unison.

She threw back her head and laughed, a throaty, erotic sound, and the sensation of water poured over hot rocks soaked into his skin. Lachlan hadn't spent this much time alone with anyone, let alone a woman, since his return to Rosemount. After the first quarter of an hour, his instinct was to beat a hasty retreat either to his cottage or to the vast open spaces of the estate where he could breathe once more. The need still buzzed at his nape, persistent but not at full force, not yet.

"Better?" she asked as they crested the hill. "Oh. Wow."

The phaeton rocked to a fairly decent stop. She stood up, the reins loose in her hands. Lachlan took them from her and intended to list the errors in her actions until he saw her face.

She gazed out over the fields that undulated below them until they reached the mountains in the distance. Her lips parted. Her cheeks flushed under the heavy caress of the winds coming across from the Cairngorms. Tendrils of her hair escaped her old-fashioned hairdo and framed her face.

Her expression, however, was what left him speechless—as if she'd never seen fields the green of emeralds, mountains carved of slate and stone thousands of years old, snow so white as to blind the eye, and skies too blue to be real.

What the actual hell?

His brother was the poet. Lachlan was the blunt instrument, the result of generations of Highland warriors born and bred to fight and defend. And kill. He'd walked these hills and climbed those mountains in the distance all his life. He'd traveled the world and seen mountains and fields and deserts. But not through her eyes.

"It's beautiful, Lachlan. How could you ever leave all of this to go to war?"

She continued to take in the view, completely unaware of the grenade she'd tossed into his morning. Lily reached down blindly and stretched her hand back for him. Still seated on the bench, he took the delicate fingers in his. He turned her question over and over in his mind. He'd had his reasons, most to do with his father and with Knox having fled to university in London. Made perfect sense then. Less so now, especially with everything he'd seen and done in the name of queen and country.

"It doesn't look real. The sky and the mountains. What are all those white dots?"

"Sheep." Lachlan held her hand as lightly as possible in case she decided to pull away. He didn't want her to, not in a million years, but he needed everything to be…about her.

"They look like little clumps of snow."

"Not down here. Isn't cold enough yet."

She sat down but didn't release his hand. In fact, she pulled it into her lap and clasped it between hers, though her hands were too small to cover his completely.

"Not cold enough? Couldn't prove it by me. According to

Emma, if I didn't have this plaid wrapped around me like a Scottish mummy, I'd freeze my tits off."

Lachlan gave a short, painful bark of laughter. Lily cut him a side-eye with a sly grin.

"That *would* be a shame," he said.

"What? And how would you know that? What pictures of me did you look at, oh Lord of Few Words?"

He shrugged. "All of them?"

"Great." She shook her head.

"That's why I didn't want to teach you. You're too skinny." Lachlan winced. Probably shouldn't have said that.

"I liked you better when you didn't talk so much."

"Hmm."

She elbowed him. "I was kidding."

They sat like that, not saying a word, for what might have been minutes, might have been hours. Lachlan took the time to really drink in the beauty of the Highlands, of his home. He also took in the enigma that was Lily Randolph.

"I didn't mean to ask—"

"It wasn't always this beautiful. Being here," he cut in. "That's why I joined the army. My father was a drunk, pill popping womanizer. He brought his mistresses here. My mother ran off to Paris, Monaco, New York. The duke ran the place into the ground. It was one long party even after the money ran out. Parasites, hangers on, women. Even after I finally came home. So, I just hid out in my cottage and out here until the old bastard died six months ago."

"And I thought my parents were bad."

Lachlan couldn't believe he'd told her, a stranger basically, all the dirty details behind his escape into the military. Even Knox didn't know the real reason Lachlan had left.

"We need to get back. Urquhart will think we're dead in a ditch somewhere."

She offered him a sad little smile as she let go of his hand

and took the reins from him. Quick as a blink, she sat up straight and stuck out her chin. "Do all Scots think American women can't drive?"

She worked to maneuver the carriage around in the wide spot at the top of the hill. Lachlan reached in to guide the reins and show her how it was done.

"Not all."

"Very funny."

"I'll be telling Urquhart you are a far better student than Mr. Arneaux, if that's any compensation," Lachlan said.

Once she'd turned the carriage, he sat back and let her drive. Rather than urging the horses into a trot, she let them set a nice walking pace down the hill and along the dirt lane in the direction of the stables.

"It will be if you make certain Danny hears about it. If I'm actually there when Danny hears it, I'll kiss you again." She tossed him a look, half cheek, and half incendiary device.

Lachlan swallowed as the memory of that kiss danced through his mind. A lavender and heather scented breeze swirled around them. If he were a suspicious sort, which he was in his weaker moments, he'd swear his brother's childhood imaginary friend, also known as the Innes Witch, was playing tricks on him. Lily sniffed. She turned her head from side to side and sniffed again. He froze. He was so not in the mood to explain his family's ghostly legend to her. It had to be too bloody cliché even for an American actress.

"Not going to take me up on that kiss offer?" she asked as they made the turn toward the stables.

"How about I have one of the lads take a photo of Urquhart telling Mr. Arneaux and send it to your phone. Then you can keep it and admire it at your leisure." Way to dodge the question, *iongantach*.

"Great idea. But thanks to *Mr. Arneaux*, I no longer have a phone. He narced to Adolph Austen, so I'm stuck here with no way to communicate with the outside world. I can't believe Erik Wentworth cast that asshole in this movie."

A hot flush rolled through him. She had a history with this man, and it pissed Lachlan off. A lot.

"Do you have a cell phone?" she asked as they rolled into the stable yard.

A couple of Urquhart's lads hurried over to take charge of the carriage. Lachlan jumped down and, in less than half a dozen strides, stood at her side of the phaeton. He reached up to help her down. She stood, leaned forward, and he had no choice but to catch her at the waist and lower her down the front of his body. She rested her hands on his shoulders while the press of her breasts and thighs against him set off firework explosions all over his body.

"Um. What was the question?" he asked.

"Cell phone?" She didn't step away.

"Yes, I have one. No, it isn't here because I never use it. And I'll not likely let you use it because Elle threatened me with bodily harm should I allow her Regency boot campers access to my electronics."

"I think you can take her. Arneaux's pansy ass can't, but you can." Lily patted his chest then headed toward the front gate to the stable yard. "Thanks for the lesson, Lachlan," she called over her shoulder. "Same time tomorrow?" She strode toward the manor.

Lachlan shook his head to clear the wrapped-in-cotton-wool sensation he'd had pretty much since she'd climbed up on the phaeton and demanded he teach her how to drive it. Every man and boy in the stable yard stared at him as if he had two heads. He ignored them and hurried after her.

He caught sight of her at the side of the fountain, arguing with Arneaux. He didn't need to hear what she said. The expression on her face was enough. Mr. Action Star didn't say a word, which was a wise decision on his part because Lily looked ready to slap the man. Or kiss him. Fortunately, the actor raised his hands in surrender and trudged into the manor before she had the opportunity to do either. She turned and saw Lachlan.

He met her halfway. "I take it you two have a history?" he inquired.

"Define history."

"As angry as you are with him? He slept with you and didn't call?"

He winced inwardly. *Jesus, Lachlan, what the hell are you doing?*

"So, you *are* like all the rest. Actually, he refused to sleep with me. And he didn't call. Don't bother showing up tomorrow. I think I'll let my stunt double drive the phaeton. It's not as much fun as I thought." She stormed back to the house and disappeared inside in a flurry of wool skirts and hurt.

Should have taken her up on that offer of a second kiss because he doubted she'd make the offer again. He headed back through the stable yard and up the lane toward the fields. This was what he got for leaving his cottage and trying to join humanity again. Trouble was, her last words about Arneaux took up residence in his head and refused to leave.

Actually, he refused to sleep with me. And he didn't call.

Lachlan mulled that over all the way home and wondered why it was so bloody important.

LILY FLUNG THE COVERS BACK AND SAT UP ON THE SIDE OF THE giant antique bed, furious. Mostly with herself. She'd spent the last hour reliving that kiss with Lachlan and wanting to figure out why. She'd had plenty of great kisses in her life, but nothing like the one she'd shared with the hunky Scot.

"Fuck this," she muttered.

She jumped off the bed and swished her feet around to find her feathered mules. Once she'd slid her feet into them she grabbed the flimsy night rail thing from the foot of the bed, shoved her arms in the sleeves, and crept quietly to her bedroom door. A breeze of some kind brushed through her hair. Where was that coming from, as if this room wasn't cold enough.

She cracked the door and peered up and down the hall, dimly lit by flickering oil lamps in sconces placed at five-foot intervals all the way to the end of the wide carpeted passageway. Something touched the top of her head. She ducked and swatted at whatever it was. Flying insect? She hadn't seen any so far, but with her luck the mosquitoes here were the size of crows and played little bagpipes. A small thunk sounded behind her. She glanced over her shoulder, saw nothing, then looked out in the hall again.

Now which room was Danny Arneaux's again? The asshole. She counted the doors and tip-toed down past the first two. Those damned feathered mules were not the best choice for sneaking around trying to find Hollywood's biggest horndog banging his Regency coach. She was about to lose her balance when voices emanated from the room at the end of the hallway before it turned to the left. She flattened herself against a section of wall between sconces.

"Run along, dear. I wouldn't want Mrs. Wallace to discover what we've been up to." Teddy's voice, with its snooty British accent, was easily recognizable even at a whisper.

A girlish giggle followed and Jilly, one of the kitchen maids, slipped past him and ran down the right-hand corridor, half-dressed and barefoot. Teddy stepped into the open doorway, shirtless, in a pair of black silk pajama pants. Bastard was cheating on his wardrobe as well as sleeping with the help. She should rat his ass out to Eleanor on both counts.

Unfortunately, he glanced up the hallway and spotted her. He grinned and touched two fingers to his brow in salute. She rolled her eyes and walked back toward her room. As she passed the door just before hers, she heard what sounded like dogs barking softly in their sleep. Dogs. Danny's dogs, and they weren't in his room. They were in Samantha's room. Lily paused and pressed her ear to the door. Her damned mule chose that moment to turn her ankle and she fell into the hard wood door. *Shit!*

Someone was moving in that room. Lily pushed away from the door and ran back into her room without bothering to see where Teddy was. Something slammed into her head and flew up, dragging strands of hair with it. She raised her hands and batted at the air. She heard fluttering like a bird's wings. *What the fuck?* This time she saw the creature coming straight at her—a bat! The damned thing circled her head and kept dive-bombing her no matter which way she turned.

"F-u-u-u-ck!" she screamed at the top of her lungs. "Get off me! Get off me!"

She fell off her shoes and tripped over one of them. It was in her hair, the bat was in her hair. Her mouth dropped open in one long operatic scream. She spun around in some kind of demented Highland fling, and the bat held on tight.

Suddenly, people were screaming and shouting up and down the hallway. Footsteps pounded down the hallway. Samantha and Teddy burst through her half-opened door. Lily managed to knock the bat away and ran past them screaming.

"Jesus, will someone shut her up?" Teddy asked.

"Does she ever not scream?" That sounded like Robbie, the little shit.

Samantha burst out into the hallways, Lily's shoes in

hand. She handed them to Lily, and Lily dropped them onto the expensive antique carpet and shoved her feet into them.

"Are you all right, lass?" Mr. McGinty demanded.

Lily batted at her hair, certain something was crawling around there. Some kind of commotion was going on at the end of the hall.

"It's in there." Lily pointed at her room. "Kill it!"

A small black something flitted out of her room, swooped over Samantha's head, and flew back into her room. Lily screamed and ducked out of the way.

Mrs. Wallace was suddenly there in her nightclothes ordering the footman, Dougal, who had a fish net in his hand, to deal with the bat. Samantha was saying something about not hurting the damned thing. Teddy, the fiend, held Lily's hand and tried to act like he was comforting her. He probably hoped no one would notice what he was wearing.

The maid shouted something about a ghost at the end of the hallway. The noise of voices, screaming, and running feet made her head throb. The bat kept coming after Lily which meant some of that screaming was hers, though she was long past hearing her own voice.

Suddenly, the duke was there and once he bellowed like a fucking bull everything got quiet. Lily scanned for the bat. She realized everyone in boot camp plus half the staff was out in the hallway. Everyone but Danny Arneaux. Where the hell was he? Teddy made a smart-assed remark about Cajuns eating bats. Samantha, Miss Sweet and Innocent Brit, said she didn't know how Danny had slept through this. Perfect opportunity for Lily.

"Where exactly is he sleeping, Samantha, dear?" Lily managed a dignified saunter down the hallway and headed for the Regency coach's room.

"I assume he's in his room, Lily, dear. Why don't you check?" Samantha sniped.

Lily smiled at Samantha and opened the snotty bitch's door. And landed flat on her back trapped under a couple of pounds of drooling baying dogs. She rolled out from under them and dragged the door shut but caught her robe in it. Lily tugged as Samantha reached around her and opened the door. Lily fell back on her ass and was assaulted by the dogs again.

"Should we help her?" Samantha asked.

"In a minute," Teddy said. "Where's Arneaux? Under your bed?"

"Fuck you, Teddy," Samantha snapped.

"Fuck both of you!" Lily yelled, and got a mouth full of slobber.

"I asked you already," Teddy told Samantha. "You said no."

"I'm going to kill you two. Gross!" Lily shoved at the dogs. "Get off me you fucking drool machine."

"Wanker," Samantha called Teddy.

"Thank you," he replied.

Lily writhed on the floor, getting rugburn on her ass and slobber in her ears. "One of you motherfuckers better help me or—"

"Allow me," a deep rich cultured voice said.

The Duke of Innes lifted her to her feet and glanced at his hand that gripped her elbow, a hand that was covered in dog drool. Lily closed her eyes. Could this night get any fucking worse?

Chapter Five

THE DOOR TO HER ROOM BURST OPEN, AND LILY NEARLY jumped out of her skin. Thank God it was only Emma with a tray balanced in one hand, while in the other, she carried one of those ugly but clean nightgowns Eleanor Witherspoon insisted they wear to enjoy the full Regency experience. If tonight was any example of the Regency experience, Lily would be on the next donkey cart back to the States tomorrow.

"Emma, what are you doing here?" She shifted around on the tapestry upholstered ottoman in front of the fireplace and wrapped the thick quilt tighter around her. "You should be in bed."

"With all that caterwauling and running about going on, you'd have to be stone deaf and dead drunk to sleep." She set the tray on the little tea table next to Lily. The aroma of hot chocolate was too tempting to resist.

Lily shooed Emma's hands away and poured herself a full cup. "You're a treasure, Emma. How'd you know this would hit the spot?" Lily blew on the thick liquid and took a sip.

"From what I hear, you've had one pip of a night, miss.

Cook sent up some of those maids of honor cakes you like as well." Emma picked up the towel Lily had tossed on a chair when all hell had broken loose. She started to dry Lily's hair. "What the devil is in your hair?"

"Dompf fwlobbwr." Lily swallowed the bite of the sweet cake she'd devoured. "Dog slobber."

"Didn't hear about that part of the evening. Did you see the ghost?"

"All I saw was a bunch of people running up and down the hall screaming, bats flying around my room, the duke strutting around acting like a duke, and a big ass snake getting dragged out of Danny Arneaux's bed."

Emma stopped scrubbing at Lily's hair. They exchanged a look and burst out laughing. It took a minute for the two of them to recover.

"Does the beastie really belong to Miss Witherspoon?" Emma asked as she snickered and picked up Lily's hairbrush.

"Which one? The snake or Danny Arneaux?" Lily asked, which set them off into another fit of laughter.

After the night's events, it felt good to laugh. Danny and his Regency coach hadn't spoken at all during dinner or the subsequent card games in the drawing room. But when they'd both disappeared from the drawing room and not come up the stairs, Lily knew something was up. If it hadn't been for the damned duke, she'd have caught his Cajun ass and Professor Prim and Proper in the middle of hot makeup sex in the garden.

"The actor gent's not a bad sort, according to the gossip below stairs at least." Emma braided Lily's hair and tied it off with a ribbon.

"He's charming as hell. Probably why the snake didn't bite him. Professional courtesy. But he did turn white as this ugly nightgown." Lily picked up the heavy cotton monstrosity Emma had dropped on the chair.

"Daresay he did. And as ugly as that gown is, it isn't covered in dog drool. You don't want to tell me how you ended up covered in dog drool from Mr. Arneaux's hounds, do you?"

"Not particularly." Lily pulled the slobber-stained gown off and shimmied into the clean one.

Emma took the dirty gown, refilled Lily's cup with hot chocolate, and waited.

Lily sighed. "I'd hoped to catch Danny in Samantha's bed. All I caught was those two furry monsters."

"What made you think Mr. Arneaux and Miss Higgins were doing the deed?"

"Servants talk, Emma. Except for you, dammit."

Emma grinned. "Servants stir up trouble too. Why do you care who Mr. Arneaux hops into bed with?"

"I don't," Lily snapped.

"He slept with you and didn't call?"

"Actually, he refused to sleep with me. And he didn't call."

Stupid! Why had she said that to Lachlan of all people?

"I see." Emma picked up the large black wool coat that had been lying on the foot of the bed since the night Lily had arrived in Scotland. "Shall I have one of the footmen deliver this to Lord Lachlan?"

Lily stared at the coat. She'd slept under it every night. She'd nearly put it on when she'd awakened to a winged rat fluttering around her room, but the bat had dive-bombed her head and prevented it. Then all hell had broken loose with the romance author screaming about a ghost in her room, Lily demanding someone rid her room of the bat, then Danny's little scene with the python crawling into his bed. She'd never dreamed life in a Scottish manor house would be so… something out of a teenage horror film without the murders and the obligatory tit shots.

As Lily took the coat and draped it over her arm, she didn't look Emma in the eye. "I'll take it to him tomorrow."

"I wouldn't count on that. The *servants' talk* says his lordship has gone off on another of his spells. Nobody can find him. Lord Lachlan asked Dougal to keep that poor wee dog in Himself's library. Hasn't been seen since."

"Nobody can find him? I saw him yesterday morning."

One of his spells? What did that even mean? Despite her proximity to the fire, Lily's body went cold.

"Aye. And that prissy sword person and Mr. Arneaux were shooting all afternoon. Lord Lachlan doesn't do well with gunfire. Not since he…. Anyway, Himself should have known better than to allow it. Now Lord Lachlan's gone off and God only knows where they'll find him this time." Emma nodded toward the tea table. "Finish your cocoa, miss. With luck, the ghost will leave us all alone for the rest of the night."

Lily hugged the coat to her and crossed to the window that looked out over the back gardens. Pitch black, until a bolt of lightning off in the distance lit up the sky. A soft rumble of thunder followed.

"You don't believe in ghosts, do you, Emma?" She turned back to look at the maid who stood in the open bedroom door.

"I don't not believe in them. I figure if people can be haunted, then so can places. And the family that's held Rosemount for hundreds of years has a great many reasons to be haunted. Don't we all?" Emma stepped into the corridor and closed the door.

Lily remained at the window and observed the storm in the distance. She remembered Lachlan's face when she'd hurled her confession about Arneaux at him. Not shocked. Not angry. No, she'd seen something wounded and sad in his eyes. She'd run into the house to avoid what he might say.

The only thing worse would have been if he hadn't said anything at all.

She'd spent every moment since on her quest to have Danny Arneaux kicked off the *A Matter of Honor* project before filming started. She'd plotted and schemed to catch him with his Regency coach. She'd told Teddy Rousseau to bait Arneaux during his lesson in the hope the actor would do something reckless or stupid or embarrassing. And all the while, the constant gunfire had tortured Lachlan to the point he'd disappeared. The duke wasn't the only one at fault. After their experience in the carriage, Lily knew her close-mouthed teacher had some issues with PTSD.

Lightning illuminated the fields behind the gardens. This time the thunder shook the house. Lily flounced onto the window seat. She buried her face in the fabric of the coat in her lap. Rain and evergreens—Lachlan's scent. And something else. She filled her lungs once more. Dog. The coat held the scent of Lachlan's little dog. The one with the ridiculous name. *Leonidas.* Lachlan had brought Leonidas to the manor house and left him with his brother. Why?

She jumped up and scanned the room, then spotted her ugly boots and wool stockings under the chair in front of the fire.

She took three steps to the chair and dropped to her knees. "Uuhnng!" Lily grabbed the boots and dragged them out.

She sat on the floor and tugged on the gray wool stockings under her nightgown. Once she had the boots on and tied, she went to the wardrobe and fished through the shawls and petticoats until she found the bag of modern conveniences she'd managed to save from Eleanor's luggage search. She didn't have a cell phone, but thanks to Raphael's concerns about power outages in the *wilds of Scotland,* he had tucked a military grade tac light into a little survival kit for her. God bless his rock hard former Marine ass.

Once she'd shrugged into Lachlan's coat, she picked up her leather satchel and dropped the flashlight into it. If she intended to go traipsing all over Scotland in search of her driving instructor, she'd be damned if she'd take one of the oil lamps or candlesticks Eleanor insisted they use. Lily peeked out her bedroom door. Nobody in sight. No noises either. Not even Arneaux's damned baying dogs. Or any flapping bats. The lamps placed on the tables under the portraits up and down the hall gave off enough light to make it to the top of the stairs.

It took a minute to get her bearings once she reached the first-floor landing. The library was at the back of the house. There was a terrace she could access and then stairs into the back gardens. And after that, she'd figure it out. She eased one of the library's double doors open, shimmied inside, and closed the door as quietly as possible behind her. Damn, the room seemed even bigger at night. A fire burned in the fireplace at the far end. In front of the fire, curled up on top of a mound of blankets, Leonidas raised his shaggy head and blinked at her. His tail beat against the blankets.

"Hey, buddy," Lily said softly. She knelt next to him and rubbed his head. "Where's your daddy? Do you think you can help me find him?" Leonidas licked her hand and wagged his tail again. "This is so a stupid movie idea. You don't look anything like Lassie or even Benji." She sighed. "I don't have a leash so we're going to have to trust each other, okay? You leave me alone out there, and I am going to be really pissed."

Thunder rumbled from the fields and rolled back toward the house. Lily got up, turned on her flashlight, and headed for the French doors that led onto the terrace. Leonidas trotted alongside her, tongue hanging out and tail wagging.

Once they got through the gardens and crossed the little footbridge over the ha-ha, Lily stopped and shone her flashlight across the fields and hills. She glanced down at the little black and white fluffball at her feet.

"Well, Leonidas, what do you say? Which way do we go? Where's Lachlan?"

The little guy took off like a shot, a blur of white that disappeared into the darkness. Great. Now she'd lost the man's dog. She ran in the direction he'd gone. A flash of lightning and a boom of thunder stopped her in her tracks. The storm had moved closer. She buttoned up the coat then glanced at her boots. Her boots might be ugly, but they and the itchy wool stockings did keep her feet and legs warm. Relatively speaking in a you-won't-freeze-to-death-in-the-first-hour sort of way. When she looked up, Leonidas sat in the middle of the path, head cocked as if to say, *You coming or what?*

"Lead on, Leo, but slow down. If I break my leg, Eleanor will insist they shoot me as part of the Regency experience."

The dog led her down a narrow little path she'd not taken in the few times she'd left the manor to escape all the dancing, card playing, and formal dinners Eleanor had subjected them to. She followed her four-legged guide down the hill for what seemed like hours. The sound of lapping water brought her up short. She panned her flashlight off to the left. They'd come to the lake. She remembered one of the footmen talking about it. Except he called it a *loch*.

Leonidas gave a little bark.

"I'm coming. I'd better not end up in the lake, little man. God only knows what kind of *loch monster* the duke keeps in there."

She kept on the path and held her flashlight so the beam hit the dog's white flag of a tail. He acted like he knew exactly where he was going. If it was to meet a lady friend or to find a bone he'd buried last year, Lily would find the most frou-frou dog sweater in Scotland and make the little flea bag wear it.

Why was she doing this? No one else seemed to be worried about Lachlan. She hardly knew him. Not to mention she was the last person in the world to deal with someone suffering some kind of breakdown. She'd been told often enough she had the empathy of Atilla the Hun. Some people just didn't. At least that was what she told herself. She'd met plenty of people just like her in the film business, and every single one of them had bigger and better careers than hers, which still didn't explain why she was— Lily stumbled over something and went down on her knees.

"Ow, dammit."

The first smattering of raindrops fell on her hands as she pushed herself upright. She'd also dropped the damned flashlight. Fortunately, it stayed lit, and she limped down a small embankment where the light shone in the darkness. She scooped up the flashlight, then swept the beam back and forth as she struggled back up the hill to the path.

"Leonidas?" Lily called as she spun in a circle in search of her canine guide. "Leonidas!"

Fabulous. He'd run off and left her. Typical male. She glanced back the way they'd come. More raindrops splattered her face. A few faint flickers of light showed her where the house was. Candlelight for the full Regency experience. All fun and games until one of them took a header down the stairs in the middle of the night. Or got lost wandering the grounds with a faithless dog.

"Dammit, Lachlan," she said as she stomped farther down the path. "Why couldn't you have *one of your spells* on a nice sunny day?"

She grimaced. *Cold, Lily. Really cold.*

"What the—"

If she hadn't looked up, she'd have run smack into a stone wall. As it was, she had to take a step back to use her flashlight to see what it was. Apparently, she'd wandered off the path and closer to the lake. That didn't explain the solid wall that rose into the night sky beyond the light of her flashlight. She took another step back.

A tower. A very old, very tall tower, and what looked like the ruins of a castle jutting out from each side of the tower. About the time Lily stepped into a sort of courtyard, Leonidas appeared out of nowhere. He sat in the middle of the courtyard and barked.

Lily bent down and patted her knee. "Come on, boy. Come here."

Of course, the dog got up and trotted through the tower doorway into God knew what. Lily sighed and followed him. He trotted up a crumbling staircase. Lily gathered the hem of her nightgown and tied it in a knot. She tucked the knot into one of the pockets of Lachlan's coat—which let a nice, chilly Scottish breeze whip up her legs and chap her butt.

Note to self, never go commando in Scotland.

The staircase came to a landing. Another rounded doorway stood across from the stairs. *Boom!* Lily jumped. Damned thunder. Lightning followed close behind and revealed the doorway that led to an empty room with several window arches on the far wall. Leonidas sat next to one of those windows, but he didn't look out, not even when the rain began to fall in noisy splashes into the opening. Lily stepped into the room and followed the dog's gaze to a dark corner. Breathing. Heavy breathing that rose above the arriving storm.

In fear of what she might find, she kept the flashlight

down by her side and edged closer to the corner. It illuminated the floor and her feet. A few more steps, and the light landed on what looked like a long slab of wood. It took a minute, but she recognized it as a very old table lying on its side. The top faced her. Movement from behind the table stopped her mid-step. Thunder shook the castle ruins, and Lily briefly wondered if the walls would hold, especially as the rumbles went on and on, louder and louder, accompanied by flashes of lightning that seemed to pause to take a bow before going dark only long enough to breathe between strikes.

Something moved behind the overturned table. Scrambled and scraped against the stone walls like a cornered rat. Lily took a deep breath, then another. She came around the end of the table and trailed the beam across the floor inch by inch into the corner. The light picked up his leather boots first, then the plaid of his kilt. She raised the flashlight higher.

"Lachlan." She kept her voice calm, despite the press of an animal cry against her throat. Her hand went numb around the flashlight. She nearly dropped it.

He sat with his back in the corner, knees drawn up under his chin. How the hell someone as big and tall as he managed to fold himself into such a tight, small figure, she didn't know. His face, paper white, stood out against the dark rocks of the stone wall behind him.

He gripped the big wooden stick he always carried so tightly his knuckles appeared the color of bones and ghostly thin. His eyes, filled with an eerie glow, stood wide open, but Lily would bet her Maserati he didn't see her or anything else. Whatever he stared at wasn't in this room.

Fear slammed through her. *You are not equipped to deal with this, Lily Randolph. No. Way. In. Hell.*

Something soft and furry brushed against the back of her

leg. *Leonidas*. Hiding behind her, the poor dog didn't know what to do either. Or maybe he did. He flattened himself on his belly and crawled toward his master but stopped before getting too close. Lily took her cue from him. She lowered herself to her knees and shuffled closer, then reached out and touched Lachlan's boot. When he didn't flinch or acknowledge her touch, she moved forward and slid her hand up to his bare knee.

"Lachlan."

Lightning flashed three times in quick succession, and the ensuing thunder struck hard enough it resonated throughout her body. Nature's sub-woofer turned all the way up and then some. Lachlan shook so violently Lily nearly lost her grip on his leg. He pressed his back into the wall as if he wanted to be part of it.

"Hell," she muttered.

Lily crawled next to him and put her palm in the middle of his chest. His clothes were soaked, and his skin was like ice. Still, he stared out the window and beyond. Pain pierced her heart. The man who walked these hills like a warrior out of a history book had been dragged back to some hell that had broken him, and she didn't know how to bring him back.

Leonidas crawled into her lap and rested his head on Lachlan's thigh. The heartbreak in the little dog's expression brought the sting of tears to her eyes, and her throat went suddenly raw. She worked her arm behind Lachlan's back and wrapped the other across his chest as far as she could reach. And she held on. Through each flinch, through every shiver, through the silence, save for the storm and his raspy breathing.

From time to time, she rubbed her hand up and down his arm in the hope that might warm him. At times he sat so still she'd lay her head on his chest to check his heartbeat. The fucking storm went on forever. How the crumbling ruin still stood against the howling winds and sideways rain, she had no clue. Lily tried to remember what it was like when she was a little girl and afraid of storms. She'd been afraid of a lot of things when she was a little girl. If anyone had comforted her, she didn't remember.

Movies. What did they do in the movies? She'd watched thousands of movies, whether she wanted to or not, to study the performances of rivals, to mimic emotions she had no idea how to portray. What did they do in the movies?

Another burst of light exploded into the room and stayed suspended like some megawatt flashlight held by an unseen hand. Lachlan gasped. He raised the stick he'd not let go of once.

"No." A shattered croak of a sound.

"Shhh." Lily covered his hand with hers and peeled his fingers back until the stick fell to the stone floor and rolled away. He grabbed her hand so tightly she nearly cried out. Somehow, she managed to drag their hands to his chest.

"It's okay. I'm here. It's okay." Yeah. As if her being there made anything better. There were half a dozen women back at Rosemount Manor much better qualified to do…whatever needed to be done.

Lachlan began to shake again. A scene from a movie flashed into her mind. She laid her head on his chest and began to hum. The name of the song escaped her. Some song Derek had their Alexa play over and over again when anyone in the house was upset or sad. It had the word *Hallelujah* in it. Other than that, she only remembered half the lyrics. Of all the songs she'd learned for films and auditions, for some reason, this was the one that came to mind. Maybe because the version Derek played had bagpipes at the beginning. Who knew? She kept humming the tune and singing the words she remembered.

Leonidas crawled into Lachlan's lap, his head rested

beneath Lily and Lachlan's hands. Lily continued to half sing and half hum the same song over and over again. Her voice vibrated against Lachlan's hard, muscled chest under his thin, damp shirt. She rubbed his back with her free hand. Maybe it was her imagination, but his spine seemed to relax as she rubbed. He'd held himself so stiff and tight she was afraid he'd snap in half.

She tried not to think about the why's of what she was doing. Hell, she didn't understand why she'd left the house let alone why she sat with her arms wrapped around a guy she'd known less than three weeks, a guy who was having a major PTSD episode in a crumbly castle in the middle of a thunderstorm. No one who knew her would believe it.

Screw them.

If she had to, she'd sing until her voice gave out. Something inside her told her this was where she was supposed to be. Even if her clothes clung to her like the leeches she'd read about in Samantha Higgins's handbook for Regency bootcamp. Her butt and legs stung like a thousand little needles attacked her. The muscles in her arms burned. That was when she noticed Lachlan had begun to shiver uncontrollably.

"Lachlan, honey, we need to get you somewhere warm. Wherever you've gone. Please come back."

Nothing.

She started to sing again, her voice little more than a harsh whisper. A weariness came over her, the kind when she'd been up for three days straight on a movie set because some obsessed director couldn't get the shot right. If she fell asleep, all three of them, counting Leonidas, would probably freeze to death. Bet she'd make the cover of *People* then. Her eyes closed. Her head dropped mid-note. The flashlight, still on, rolled out of her lap onto the floor.

"Lily?" His voice sounded like he'd been gargling with

rusty nails. At first, she thought she might be hallucinating. Lack of heat and access to Starbucks and electronics did that to a girl. "Lily?"

She lifted her head and looked up into those eerie amber eyes.

Chapter Six

Lachlan's vision pin-holed and very gradually opened, light filtering in like a candle at the end of a long tunnel—just like it always did after his mind went off the rails. The only aspect that changed from episode to episode was where he came out of it and after how long.

Not this time.

Lily?

He raised and lowered his eyelids a few times, not fast enough to be called a blink, but more trying to bring everything back into focus. Between that and some intermittent flashes of light, when he looked down, a woman's profile came into view. Was he dead at last? Were there such things as angels and heaven? If there were, he was in deep trouble.

Wait. He knew this profile. Also, the scent of gardenias and…wet dog?

Lily?

Couldn't be. She'd be the last person present during one of his *bad turns* as his father used to call them. She looked up at him as if he'd called her name. Maybe he did. His throat throbbed as if he'd screamed for hours. He reached into his scrambled brain to drag out something appropriate to say.

"Why—" His voice cracked, locked. He tried to draw breath.

Couldn't. Her gaze was fixed on him. He wanted to shrink away. He wanted… He didn't know what he wanted. She reached up and massaged his throat, her fingers gentle but firm.

"Let's get you up and out of here before we freeze to death," she said as she drew her arms from around him.

Cold. In a way he'd never been cold before, because he'd never been so warmed. She scooted back, braced her hand on the wall behind him, and rose in the economic grace of movement he'd only ever noticed in her. Leonidas danced around her feet. She extended her hand, and Lachlan tried to focus on her long, dainty fingers.

"Why are you here?" he asked in a level but barely-there whisper.

She tilted her head, bent down, and grabbed his hand. "Because you are. Can you get up? I don't think Leo and I can heft your big ass off this floor."

Thunder rolled in continuous waves of sound, punctuating her assertion. Lachlan flinched. He was home. In the Highlands. Rosemount. He took Lily's hand and slid his back up the cold, stone wall.

"Whoa there, cowboy." She planted her palms against his chest and pushed him back against the wall as he swayed forward. "Give yourself a minute. Stay right there." She bent to pick up a military grade torch and paused to give Leonidas's ears a scratch before she straightened.

Lachlan closed his eyes and flattened his hands against the stones that held him up. The ruins. He was in the ruins of Rosemount Castle, but not the tower. No one went into the tower. Except his brother. When Lachlan opened his eyes, a flash of lightning lit up the room. Lily stared at him as if he might do something—lash out, gibber like a madman, collapse into a heap.

"Ready?" She swallowed hard.

He watched her throat move, fascinated.

She put her arm around his waist and moved him into the middle of the room. "The rain has died down, but it could start back up. Let's get you home."

Lachlan let her guide him out of the room and down the narrow, worn stone stairs. Leonidas ran ahead of them, though he stopped and looked back from time to time. Lachlan's entire body ached, not in pains here and there, but in one long endless throbbing. He moved his feet step by step because she did as if she willed it with her slim arm around his back and her palm against his belly. They crossed the courtyard and moved onto the path around the loch. She turned left, and after a few steps, he realized where she led him.

"No." He stopped so quickly they both stumbled. "Not the house."

Lily still held him upright. The thunder rolled behind them. Lachlan twitched, a memory of a flinch. The noise was normal now, not amplified a thousand times by the miasma inside his head.

"Where then? We both need to get indoors. Leo is going to turn us in for animal cruelty if we keep him out in this shit much longer. Aren't you, boy?"

Lachlan looked down. His head spun a time or two. He still saw his dog's traitorous grin and tail wag at Lily's suggestion. "Home," he finally said. "Take me home."

"Where is— Never mind." She turned and moved them in the direction Leonidas took, past the ruins, and farther around the loch.

Lily put on her torch and kept it on the dog's furry arse as he led the way. She had pluck. He'd give her that. She'd come out in the middle of the night, found a madman, and now half-carried him somewhere she'd never been on the word of a mongrel dog.

"I'm fine from here," he said. "Thank you for…thank you, Miss Randolph." He stopped and tried to step out of her embrace.

She refused to let go. "Bullshit."

"Beg pardon?"

"Beg all you want. You're swaying like a frat boy on a three-day drinking bender. If I let go of you, you'll be face down in the dirt in ten seconds. I haven't gotten to the part in the Regency handbook that tells me how to tell a duke I left his brother out in a thunderstorm to die."

"Knox wouldn't care." He regretted the words the moment he said them.

"Relatives always care," Lily replied as she moved them down the path away from the manor. "Even if it's just about the cost of a funeral. How much farther?"

"Up the path and then across the sheep fields." He waited for her to complain or at least look back the way they'd come. She did neither. He wanted to argue, to send her away so he could lick his wounds alone. He also wanted her to keep on holding him. *Gealtaire*.

"Come on." Lily tugged him forward. "Leo's tired of waiting on us. He's the only one of us with any sense." She trained the torchlight on Leonidas and followed him.

As she dragged Lachlan along with her, he concentrated on putting one foot in front of the other. He knew what was coming. He'd been up for days. The arrival of guests at Rosemount always triggered his insomnia, his fear of people seeing him for what he was. After the last twenty-four hours, exhaustion waited for him like an insurgent sniper, ready to take a lucky shot.

"Nice torch," he said as he tried to shake the sleep that closed in on him from every side. "Military issue?"

"Torch?" Lily glanced up at him. "Oh. Right. Flashlight. A gift from a friend. Former marine."

"A good friend to have." A spurt of some hot, furious emotion shot through him.

"He and his husband are the only real friends I have."

Relief washed over him like a warm bath. He ignored her painful admission. She didn't see it as painful, and for that his heart broke a little for her.

"How did you keep it from Elle?"

"Raphael hid it in my luggage. Somehow, she missed it. She's smarter than your average Regency experience guest, but not smarter than a U.S. Marine." Lily shifted her arm higher around him. His weight settled onto her more and more as they walked.

"Clever one is Elle. Keeps my brother guessing. He can't stand her."

"Something your brother and I agree on. Please tell me that light up there is your house." The rain had started again, just a light drizzle, but the light show in the distance and the rumbles that echoed over the hills and fields weren't a good sign.

"Light?" He followed the path of the torch along the ground. A light flickered in his front window. Had he left it on before he'd fled the cottage and the walls that had closed in with the gunfire from the manor? "Yes. That's it. You can go back now. Ouch!" She'd struck him in the chest with the torch.

"If you shut up now you can save all that energy to climb this damned hill. You have to live in the middle of nowhere, up a hill, when your brother has a palace with a gazillion rooms and a cast of thousands working as servants?"

"A gazillion?"

"Shut up and climb." The rain came down harder, and the wind increased.

"Yes, miss." Lachlan bit his lip.

He concentrated on the pull of the muscles in his legs as he and Lily made their way up the little hill atop which his low, long thatch-roofed cottage stood. A laugh started in the middle of his chest and bubbled up to surface as an exaggerated cough. The look she shot him assured him Lily was not fooled.

They crested the hill just as nature let loose with renewed fury. The rain pounded against their backs as Lily struggled to open his front door. The smallest of cracks was all Leonidas needed. He was in the house in a single wiggle past the ancient oak slab door. Lily guided Lachlan in and let go of him long enough push the door closed and drop the bar lock he'd installed across it.

"Expecting an army of orcs or something? Wait a minute. Do *not* fall down."

Lachlan marveled at the way her mind worked. Reminded him of a child after too much sugar. She shuffled him over to the bed in the corner of his sitting room under the thick beamed ceiling. Lily had no trouble passing under the beams. Lachlan had to remind himself to duck because his entire being was focused on the beautiful, determined woman who'd hauled him from the ruins into the humble house he'd called home the last two years. He'd seen the photos of where she lived. His place was a hovel in comparison.

She threw back the quilts and comforter on his bed then pushed him down to sit on the sheet covered mattress. "Get out of those wet clothes. I don't suppose you have electric heat or anything like it in here."

"Electricity, yes. Heat, no. Use the fireplace." Lachlan toed off his boots then bent to peel off his socks. The lights went on, and he blinked at the sudden brightness.

When he looked up, Lily stood in front of the huge hearth, her bottom lip trapped beneath her teeth. Lachlan pulled his shirt over his head and lurched to his feet. "I'll get that."

"You'll get your ass back on that bed before you fall face first onto that ugly rug. I am perfectly capable of starting a fire." Hands on her hips, dressed in his winter coat and her "ugly" boots, she did present an imposing figure. Until he took in her chalky complexion, the circles under her eyes, and her rain-soaked hair that fell in her face.

He debated for a moment—half of him wanted to wrap her in a blanket and start a fire to keep her warm, and the other half wanted to do as she said because that was what she needed him to do. In the end, his body decided for him. He listed to one side and caught himself in time to land on the edge of the mattress. She gave a decisive nod, then turned to the wood box that sat on the hearth.

One by one, Lily extracted heavy logs and piled them onto the iron grate. Lachlan winced as he watched her struggle to lift the pieces of wood he'd chopped. She did a bonny job of stuffing the hearth with fuel, but when she found the long matches and attempted to light the fire, she met with a great deal of frustration—which resulted in some of the most creative foul language he'd heard since he'd left the military.

"Peat," he said quietly.

"What?"

"Peat and kindling. The box on the other side of the hearth." Lachlan rested his hand on Leonidas's back.

The dog had wasted no time joining him on the bed, and he watched Lily nearly as intently as Lachlan did. Someone was smitten. Maybe more than one someone. He shook his head. Thunder crashed nearby, and as the seconds ticked by to the flash of lightning to follow, his vision narrowed, his muscles twitched, and the long dark tunnel to his memories exploded open.

A feminine squeal of delight snatched him back into the light. Lily danced in place and clapped her hands. "I did it. It's burning." She bent toward the healthy blaze she'd started and rubbed her hands together.

"Never doubted you."

"You're full of it, buddy," she said as she turned and backed her lovely arse toward the source of heat. "I thought I told you to strip. Don't be shy on my account. I've seen a man in his underwear before."

"Not wearing any."

Her expression of half shock and half…interest was one he'd not expected from her. It didn't last long.

"Where do you keep your clothes?" She peered down the narrow corridor to the left of the fireplace.

"First door on the left."

She disappeared into the dark of the hallway. Lachlan scrubbed his hands over his face. He needed to sleep. Lily's presence in his house warred with the aftermath of his flashback. Like the shocks after an earthquake, he couldn't guarantee either the duration or the form over the next few hours. He didn't want her to see him like that.

Lily took so long he nearly went after her. The moment he pushed against the mattress to try and rise, she marched up the hall, arms loaded with clothes. She still had her torch in her hand. Once in the sitting room, she shook her head, switched the heavy light off, and placed it on Lachlan's desk.

"The damned Regency police have me so confused I forget to even try to turn on electric lights." She tossed him a pair of joggers, a t-shirt, and the thick flannel dressing gown

Knox had given him for Christmas last year. "Put those on." She waved her hand at his bed shoved against the sitting room wall. "Is there a reason your bed is in—"

"Economy. I am a Scot after all. Sleeping in here means I only have to keep one fire stoked and burning. And I don't have many visitors."

"What's in here?" She pushed open the door to the right of the fireplace and disappeared inside. "Kitchen. Very small kitchen."

Lachlan listened to the noises coming from behind the door as he slid his joggers on under his kilt then unwound and removed the wet plaid. He tossed it over a ladderback chair next to the bed. By the time he'd struggled into the t-shirt, she emerged from the kitchen dressed in one of his flannel shirts and another pair of his joggers. Both were entirely too big for her, which made her look incredibly sexy. He draped the dressing gown across his lap.

"I put the kettle on. I think we could use some tea and then a nap. Put that robe on. You'll catch pneumonia. Besides, it'll cover up all that." She waved her hand up and down in his direction.

"That?"

"That shirt and sweatpants don't leave much to the imagination."

He gave himself a slow inspection. "Pardon?"

"You'll get no pardon from me, Lord Hot Body. It's a sin to be built like that. There's the kettle." She hurried into the kitchen like she had something cooking and it was burning.

Lord Hot Body?

A few minutes later, Lily backed out of the kitchen and returned with a mug in each hand. The rich bergamot scent reached him as she handed him one of the mugs. Lachlan wrapped his hands around the heavy stoneware and allowed the heat to seep into his fingers. She sat on the old leather ottoman in front of the fire and took little sips from her mug. They drank their tea in silence.

Leonidas burrowed under the covers at the foot of the bed and settled for the night. Eventually, Lachlan finished his tea and sat the mug on the ladderback chair. She was right. Tea was exactly what he needed. And she needed to go back to the house. Or rather he needed her to go back. She was there under the illusion his *spell* was over. He knew better.

It took two tries, but he staggered to his feet and headed toward his desk.

"What are you doing? You need to get in that bed and get some rest." Lily put her mug on the mantel and met him halfway.

"My cell phone." He pointed at the desk. "Abercrombie can send someone to fetch you back to the house."

"First, I am not a stick. Nobody fetches me. Second, if I were Abercrombie, I would kill anyone who called me this early in the morning in the midst of a storm and asked me to do anything. Third, if Sergeant Witherspoon of the Regency Brigade finds out I was anywhere near a cell phone, she will make me do embroidery or watercolor painting for weeks."

He blinked several times. Didn't help. His brain had turned to mush as he watched her talk, so confident, bright, and fierce. "What?"

She grabbed his arm. "Come on." She dragged him to the bed and pushed him onto it. "Get in and skootch over."

While she went to the light switch, he did as she told him. Then to his utter amazement, she padded across the assortment of rugs on his floor and crawled into bed with him. She turned on her side and faced the fire.

"Good night, Lachlan. Try to get some rest." She snuggled under the covers.

"What? Why?" He lay on his back, arms at his sides, and tried not to brush against her.

"Jeez. You're like a two-year-old. Why? Why?" She turned over and patted his chest. He rolled onto his side and gazed into her delicate face. "You've had a rough night. And if it is okay with you, I'd rather not go out in this storm. Besides, you might need someone here in case…well, in case whatever dragged you into the hell in your mind comes after you again."

She didn't look away. He *couldn't* look away. So much of the time, her eyes revealed nothing but that hard-bitten cynicism she wore like a cloak. Not now. He found himself drawn into those twin pools of soft, dark brown that sparkled with flecks of gold. She knew. Somehow, Lily Randolph knew more about the things that haunted him and drove him into the night than any woman should know. Even now the voices and visions in his head beat at him with fists of guilt and doubt. It hurt to breathe. It hurt to be. Of all the hurts, the worst was that she knew. Shouldn't matter. It did.

"It's okay," she said softly as she pressed her palm to his chest. "Sleep. You look like hell."

Lily rolled back onto her side and left him staring at the incandescent black silk of her hair. He raised a shaky hand to touch—*No!* Lachlan sat up and started to crawl over her.

She turned her head and glared at him. "What the fuck do you think you're doing?"

"I'll sleep in my room." He tried to move.

She blocked him with a knee pressed to his groin. "Your room? The room with no bed, no curtains on the windows, and no fire in the fireplace? The room that's colder than my mother's heart? I don't think so. You might as well crawl back to that horror movie set your brother calls a castle." She pushed him over onto his back and sat up. She was bloody gorgeous when she was angry. Frightening too.

"I have no interest in jumping your bones, asshole." She

poked him in the chest. "I thought you might want some company in case of nightmares or something. Even if it's my company, it's better than nothing. I'm sorry I'm not a nurse or some pretty Highland lass or lad, depending on how you swing."

"I—" He'd spoken more in the last fortnight or so than he had in the past two years—for the most part to this woman. He hadn't the foggiest why, especially as she rendered him speechless most of the time.

"As soon as this storm lets up, and I see an inch of daylight, I'm out of here. So, roll your ass over and *try* to sleep. Act like I'm not here, and I'll do the same. Good. Fucking. Night." She flounced back onto her side and pulled the covers over her head.

Lachlan eased onto his side of the bed and moved over until his back made contact against the wall. The storm had strengthened while they'd argued. The thunder shook his little cottage. Leonidas wriggled up to rest against his chest. Each time Lachlan flinched, the little dog burrowed closer to him. He listened closely for any sign Lily had fallen asleep. Not a chance. In fact, if the pattern of her breaths gave any indication, she didn't sleep because she was mad as the devil to be sure. He searched for something to say.

"I dinnae like men." Aye, that probably wasn't the best thing to say.

"What?"

"Pretty Highland lass or lad. I dinnae like men. Not like that."

"That makes two of us right now." She punched her pillow. "Between my latest ex, Danny Arneaux, and you, I'm ready to swear off men forever. Why aren't you asleep?"

The trouble with starting a conversation with her was he hadn't done conversations in years, and he didn't talk about his *spells*. Talking didn't help. Not so far. He gently moved

Leonidas to the side and then rolled over to face the wall. Then rolled back. *Dammit!*

"I didnae want to hurt you," he blurted.

"Too late."

"Physically."

She turned over to face him. "Why would you?"

He twisted onto his side, his back again to the wall, and swallowed against the sandpaper in his throat. "Nightmares."

She blinked. Her face appeared ethereal and fey in the light from the fireplace. "Nightmares?"

"I…lash out. Knock Leonidas off the bed. Blacked Knox's eye once."

"Your brother needs a good black eye. And you wouldn't be the first man to knock me out of bed." She smiled as she said it, but in a sad way that said there was more to the story.

"I cannae promise you—"

"You won't. If you start flailing around, I'll punch you in the nuts."

"Bloody hell." He resisted the urge to cover his groin.

"That's what I did to the last guy who knocked me out of bed. Worked fine."

"You're a right one, Lily Randolph," he murmured.

"And you're a braw man, Lachlan Innes. Nae doubt it."

"You have a verra good Scot's brogue."

"And I didn't need a Regency coach like some people I know."

"Want to talk about it?" he asked.

The sudden blankness of her stare said she had no doubt what, or rather who, he meant. "Nae," she replied. "Want to talk about your nightmares?"

"Nae."

"Then can we finally go to sleep, for a few hours at least?" Lily yawned to drive home her point.

"Ye'r sure?" His brogue always came out when he was tired. Or stressed. Or—

"Here." She moved closer and rested her head on his shoulder, trapping his left arm beneath her head. Then she grasped his right hand in a surprisingly strong grip and placed their hands on his chest. "You can't move without my knowing it, and if you do, I'll bail out of the bed and wait for you to wake up. Okay?"

She was warm and soft, and smelled faintly of gardenias and rain. She was so tiny, despite her height and those long, glorious legs. Her heartbeat against his ribs had his entire body on alert. Leonidas scooted down between her feet and his calf.

"And don't worry if Mr. Happy gets excited. I can always punch him too." She sighed and yawned again as she settled in next to him.

Mr. Happy? Between that image and the nightmares swimming in the back of his mind, he'd not sleep a wink. At least he didn't have to worry about injuring her. His fight against her allure proved futile. Her presence in his bed was better than any toddy. Despite the storm that aimed its fury directly at his cottage, he flinched less and less. The visions of roadside bombs and the screams of the dying receded.

His eyes closed and refused to reopen. The muscle spasms born of the combatant tension the day and evening had brought on subsided until only the faint memory of the ache remained. In the middle of all this was Lily Randolph—sharp-tongued, foul-mouthed, bossy, unafraid, and...kind. And it *was* simply kindness. He'd be a fool to read anything else into her behavior. The verra last thing he needed and the verra last thing she wanted. The verra last....

No! Not that way! Fire! So much fire! Move! Move! Machine gun fire. It wouldn't stop. It never stopped. And the screaming. The shouting. Where were they? Where were his men? A blinding boom and the searing pain of shrapnel. He was falling. Falling. Get up. Get up, dammit! Go toward the screaming. The screaming!

"Fuck!"

Lachlan bolted into a squatting position on the corner of the bed. He wedged his back against the walls and tried to focus on something, anything to let him know where he was. He couldn't see, dammit. His vision was all black smoke. He smelled burnt flesh and the acrid scents of a firefight at close range. A dog barked softly. Rain. Somewhere it was raining. Not a storm, but a steady fall of rain against…a roof?

The bed creaked under the weight of someone climbing onto the mattress. The bed. His bed. He swiped at his eyes. His entire body shook. Cold. As if ice had settled into his bones. A hand rested on his bicep. He jerked away. Someone was speaking to him, softly but insistently.

"Shhh. It's me, Lachlan. You're home. Come back. You're safe. Here. Here." Gentle arms wrapped around him.

He wanted to see. The voice. He knew that voice. He needed to find that voice. A light pierced the miasma of darkness. A face—ivory skin, big brown eyes, delicate features, plump raspberry-colored lips. Soft palms caressed his cheeks and jawline then circled his shoulders once more.

"Look at me, Lachlan. Look at me."

He concentrated on the lilt of the voice, the way she said his name with the smallest touch of a Highland accent. Lachlan blinked. The noises faded. The smoke cleared. The scent of gardenias chased away everything else.

"Lily?" he rasped.

"Got it in one. Good boy. Come back up, Leo. He's back, I think."

Her face came into focus. Not right. Her bottom lip. A spot of blood and a tear at the corner. He gripped her upper arms and pushed her back. "What did I do? What did I do? Tell me!"

The darkness curled in at the edge of his vision until all he saw was blood.

Chapter Seven

Lily had to get a handle on this situation, and quick. She'd lived with Derek and Raphael long enough to know the nightmares after a PTSD episode had the potential to send an explosive situation nuclear. She set her face in as calm and unconcerned expression as her acting skills allowed under the circumstances.

"You didn't do anything. I bit my lip when I bailed out of bed. That's all. The worst thing you've done tonight is snore like a bear and steal the covers."

His fingers dug into her flesh, but she didn't think now was the moment to mention it. Not if his glassy eyes and his labored breathing were any indication. No, he didn't need the truth. He needed plausible. Lily did plausible on a daily basis.

"Are you sure?" he demanded. "What happened?"

"Before or after you jumped onto the corner of the bed and screamed *Fuck!* at the top of your lungs? Leo and I slept through anything else. Didn't we, Leo?"

She glanced at the little dog who lay on the bed with his head between his paws gazing at Lachlan with deeply concerned devotion. The dog needed to be in the movies. She'd lied about them sleeping. The physical manifestation of Lachlan's night-mare had kept them awake—though she'd been slow to react to his flailing fist. Only one, maybe two knuckles caught her before she rolled onto the floor. No need for him to know.

He loosened his grip on her arms, rubbed them absently, and did a slow, jerky scan of the room. Lachlan leaned forward to rest on his knees. He let go of Lily and rubbed his palms against his thighs. "Shouldn't have stayed."

"Do all Scots chew a point like a dog with a bone or just you?" She crawled up to sit beside him, her back propped against the wall.

He rocked back, raised his knees, and propped his tightly clenched fists on them. "Are all Sassenachs as stubborn as you, or is it just you?"

He leaned his head against the wall and closed his eyes. Lily frowned. Even in the dim light of the fireplace his skin was washed paper white. The gray light of dawn made a weak attempt to peek into the room from the window next to the front door. His black wool curtains did a damned good job. They kept out the light and the cold. They kept out pretty much everything.

"Feel better?" she asked as she wiggled her fingers at the dog.

The little fuzzball crawled forward on his belly. He accepted pets from Lily but wedged himself into the tight space between Lachlan's raised knees and his belly.

"No," Lachlan said.

"Want some tea?"

"No."

"Breakfast?"

"No."

"Want me to leave?"

He settled his butt on the mattress and stretched his legs out in front of him. Lily waited. Nothing. His breathing gradually slowed, but he still didn't say a word. She grabbed the quilt and blankets and pulled them over her legs, then back up over his. Leonidas grumbled in his sleep, then settled with a sigh.

She turned toward Lachlan and rested her head against his arm. "Go back to sleep. I'll wake you if you get too rowdy."

He slid his hand under hers. Though his palm was rough, his touch was gentle. He brushed his thumb against her little finger from time to time. Erotic as hell, but much more. Lachlan craved connection. She'd bet her entire wardrobe of *Jimmy Choo's* on it. But he was afraid. Of what? Who the hell knew? *He* probably didn't even know. Welcome to Lily Randolph's life. Connection was scary as hell, and it hurt even worse.

Lily moved her head around to try and find a soft spot on his arm. No luck. The man's rock-hard muscles did not give. He did, however, give off heat like an old-fashioned furnace. So, despite the fading fire and the drafty cottage, between him and the covers, she was nice and toasty.

She sighed. This entire misadventure wasn't her. She didn't rescue deeply wounded men. She didn't ache to understand and soothe the pain they hid from the world. Not even for Raphael. Derek took care of him. Lachlan, though, had no one, apparently, and of all the people involved in this misbegotten boot camp, he was the only one who didn't have an agenda where Lily was concerned. She owed him. That was it. No other reason.

A soft snore startled her from her reverie. Lachlan had fallen asleep sitting up. Really asleep. Honestly, she could leave now, and he'd be fine. He was safe, and he had the dog.

This early, she could sneak into the house, and no one would know she hadn't spent the night in her room.

He wrapped his fingers around her hand.

Fine. She'd close her eyes for a minute. Maybe two. If the nightmares came back, she'd know. She'd learned the pattern of his breathing and the rhythm of his heartbeat. If they changed, she'd wake him. One thing she'd accomplished as a child on movie sets was the ability to sleep lightly and wake up in an instant. No problem.

THIS REGENCY SHIT WAS FOR THE BIRDS. IT WAS COLD AS HELL in her room, and Lily decided she'd stay in bed until the whole boot camp thing ended. She opened her eyes and tugged the covers closer around her. Hot and distinctly canine smelling breath wafted against the back of her neck. If Danny Arneaux's mutts were in her room—

Lily sat up so quickly Leonidas barked in response. *Leonidas.* "Lachlan?" She checked out the rest of the room. Nobody. "Lachlan?"

She kicked off the covers and climbed out of bed. The fire had died down. Once she added a few of the logs from the rack by the fireplace and a couple of the blocks of peat, the fire licked its way back to life. That was when she noticed her boots on the hearth. Her nightgown was draped over the ladderback chair, which now sat in front of the fireplace. Lachlan's coat hung over an old leather armchair. Her stockings festooned a lamp behind the old chair. She'd left all of that in the kitchen.

Kitchen.

She stuck her head in the doorway, but the little room was empty. Despite the rugs scattered across the stone floor, the cold seeped through and hurried her steps as she went down the hall and looked into the bedroom and the bathroom.

He was gone.

She glanced at the clock. It was after ten. A peek out the curtains showed a sunny sky. A good thing and a bad thing. If Lachlan was out in the sun, he was likely fine. Though her having illusions about sneaking back into the house? Not happening. She might as well get dressed. It wasn't as if she'd never had to sneak around and lie about her whereabouts.

It only took a few minutes for her to get out of Lachlan's clothes and back into her lovely Regency nightwear. Much as she hated it, sneaking back into the house *and* being caught in his clothes was too much even for her. Once she was dressed, however, Lily didn't want to leave. She sat down on the edge of the bed and stroked Leonidas's head.

"He's okay, isn't he, Leo?"

The dog gave a couple of enthusiastic tail wags in response.

She studied the cottage. All the opulence of Rosemount Manor, and Lachlan chose to live here. She shook her head. The last thing she needed was to get involved in Lachlan Innes's life. Time to do something with her hair and get on with her own life. This film was too damned important for her to get distracted, no matter how sexy the distraction. Besides, she still had to figure out a way to get Wentworth to dump Arneaux from the project.

"There has to be a hairbrush around here somewhere." Lily spied her flashlight on Lachlan's desk. If he'd left his cell phone, she was in serious trouble. Some temptations were easy for her to resist. Asshole men and cell phones were not on that list. He had a laptop somewhere from the cords draped over his desk chair. She picked up her flashlight. That was when she spotted the white post-it next to it under a....

"Oh."

The Regency-style hand fan made of the most unusual feathers she'd ever seen was gorgeous. An artist of great skill had worked actual bird feathers in deep shades of brown, cream, and mahogany into exquisitely carved sticks of some dark wood. Tiny bits of gold stones—some type of quartz, decorated the sticks. Lily had never seen anything so incredibly beautiful.

She picked up the post-it.

THANKS.

L

HER EYES STUNG. SHE BLINKED FURIOUSLY. SHE WAVED THE post-it back and forth at her side to the point it flew out of her fingers toward the fire.

"Shit!" She scrambled around on the bricks of the hearth until she recaptured the little scrap of paper.

Leonidas barked once and hopped off the bed to go to the door. Lily stood and listened. A light tap at the door elicited another soft bark from the dog. Lachlan wouldn't knock to come into his own home.

She started across the rug-covered floor. She tripped over her boot laces, cursed under her breath, and sidled up to the window. With her little finger, she lifted a corner of the dark curtains. *What the—*

"Emma." She snatched open the door, then dragged the maid inside before she slammed it shut. "What the hell are you doing here?"

Dressed in full Regency maid regalia, the red-haired woman threw back her cloak and revealed a heavy sort of carpet bag, then handed it to Lily. "I told Miss Witherspoon you had an early breakfast and went for a walk. It'll be easier to sell the lie if you didnae show up in your nightgown and Lord Lachlan's coat."

Lily grabbed the bag and rifled through it. "Whatever they are paying you, Emma, it isn't enough."

The bag contained one of those plain wool Regency dresses, a petticoat, the corset thing, clean wool stockings, and a big heavy shawl. She was so happy to see the clothes she refused to complain about the ugly dress. And screw modesty. She shucked her coat and nightgown and let Emma help her wrestle her way into the Regency get-up. When she sat down to put on the stockings and lace up her boots, Emma gathered the nightgown and last night's stockings and shoved them into the bag.

"How did you know I was here?" She tried to sound nonchalant.

"I'm a verra good guesser."

Lily finished tying her boots then looked up. "Does anyone else know?"

"Nae. And if we move our arses, they won't."

Lily kissed Leonidas, who had climbed back into bed, on the snout. "Be good."

She tucked the flashlight into Emma's bag and the maid took it from her, then hit it beneath her cloak again. The post-it, Lily crammed into the bodice of her dress between the corset thing and her skin. The fan, however, she held in her hand as she and Emma exited the cottage and closed the door behind them. They strode up the path that led to the lake. Everything looked very different in the light of day. The water appeared glass smooth, and the sounds of water birds and little waves lapping the shore settled her jangled nerves.

"Still don't want to tell me how you found me?" Lily believed Emma when she said no one else knew where she was. She really did. But....

"Urquhart."

"Urquhart? He knows?" Lily wouldn't have pegged the old horse master as a gossip.

"Nae. He came to beg a bit of breakfast from Cook. He and the lads were talking, and he mentioned he'd seen Lord Lachlan at the mews with his birds. Said he looked right as rain. When I got to your room and saw the empty bed, I knew why."

"If you wanted to win at Confuse the Sassenach, congratulations. Could you explain all of that and use small words? I didn't get a lot of sleep last night."

Emma shot her a sideways glance and a smirk.

"*Not* because of that."

"Well, that's a damned shame."

"Tell me about it." They shared a grin. "Now explain."

They trekked around the bend of the lake, and the castle ruins came into view.

"Lord Lachlan does nae smile, Miss Randolph. Ever. The closest he comes is with his birds. But when he goes off on one of his spells, even the birds cannae help. He stays away from them for days after. That lad, Tommy Burke, looks after them. His lordship says he does nae want to hurt them. But today he's at the mews, working and flying his birds. 'Tis no accident, now 'tis it? You fretted about him last night 'til you went out in the storm and found him. Tell me I'm wrong."

"Is it true the ruins are haunted?" Lily had no intention of discussing the details of last night with Emma, or anyone else for that matter.

She stopped and gazed up at the windows in the tower that overlooked the lake. She avoided the courtyard and the empty rooms of the building that jutted out from the tower. Where Lachlan chose to hide was his secret to keep. She wouldn't betray him by drawing attention to the ruins.

"Aye, so they say," Emma said as she stepped back from the tower and crossed herself.

"By the same ghost who showed up at that little freak show in the house last night? The one that chased the maids and scared that dowdy little author?"

"Nae, not her. The Innes Witch, the ghost from last night, never comes to this side of the loch. The first duke was locked in the room at the top of the tower while his ma drowned his wife as a witch. On certain nights you can see him in the window screaming her name."

"Jesus. Does this family have any happy stories?" She remembered Lachlan huddled in the corner of that stone room trying to hide from the ghosts of his memories behind a broken table.

"Time will tell, miss. Time will tell." They came to the bridge across the ha-ha. "I'll take this bag along to the laundry."

"And I think I'll stroll around the gardens for a while. Make sure somebody sees me before I have to report to Miss Witherspoon."

"If ye want a longer walk, the mews are on the top of the hill behind the stables."

"I'll take that under consideration. Thanks, Emma. You're a peach."

"Thank ye, Miss Randolph, for looking after our lad." Emma strode off, her long Amazon-like strides taking her to the house before Lily could even think of a response.

Lily stood and watched the opinionated maid disappear beneath the terrace.

She would never say it in a million years, but Lily found the formal gardens at the back of Rosemount Manor to be magical, especially when she had them all to herself. Even now in March, when many of the flowers weren't in bloom, the ordered greenery and perfectly situated statues took her to a place where time stood still. The view across the fields dotted with sheep and the forest beyond put her in the mind of the character she'd been cast to play—not the ugly dresses, antique furniture, and expensive dining room table settings. To Lily, this garden was where a woman who waited for a husband she hardly knew to come home from war might stand and wonder....

A vision of Lachlan screaming himself awake and horrified he might have hurt her came to mind. Lily touched her finger to the still tender spot on her lip. Her response would have been very different had any other man split her lip, even accidentally. It had taken her years to learn to stand up for herself. It was second nature now—and screw anyone, man or woman, who made her react otherwise. There was safety in being a four-star bitch. However, she'd entered this wounded man's world, his nightmares, of her own free will. If he'd injured her, it would have been her fault, not his, even though nothing was ever her fault. Not anymore. Never again.

She flattened her palms on the top of the beautiful marble fence rail and leaned over to inhale the icy air. The bite to her lungs cleared her head. Time to get back to work. This film, this role, had to be her entire focus right now. She didn't have time for anything or anyone else. Lily turned and started up the gravel path between two beds of dormant roses.

"Hey, Lily," Danny Arneaux said as he ambled down the path, his hands clasped behind his back. He looked ridiculous in his kilt, romance hero white flowy shirt, and boots. "I want to talk to you."

"About?" She tried to brush past him.

"Dr. Higgins." He caught Lily's hand and dragged it through his crooked arm.

He really expected her to stroll through the gardens with him like some wimpy Regency chick? "Your problem, Arneaux, not mine."

She tried to drag her feet with little success. He steered them into the beginning of the maze, and when they came to one of the stone benches, he waved his free hand to indicate she should sit. What she wanted to do was slap his face and walk back to the house. But as she'd already slapped him once since they'd arrived in Scotland, she decided to pace herself. He'd piss her off again at some point. That much was certain.

She sat, and Danny dropped down next to her. "Actually, you're the problem. Not mine, but hers."

"Hers?"

He rolled his eyes. "Dammit, Lily, don't play innocent with me. With everyone else, yes, but not with me. I've known you too long."

"You haven't known me at all, but that's your loss, not mine." Lily didn't know why it still galled her after all these years. He wasn't even her type. Not anymore, at least.

"You and Teddy Rousseau are doing everything you can to undermine Dr. Higgins's position, and I want it to stop. You're pissed at me, come after me. Leave her alone. She's worked hard to get where she is, and she deserves a chance."

"You really don't find it insulting that Wentworth hired a second-string Regency consultant as your coach? That's what she is, you know. She's never done this before, at least not as the top dog. Did she tell you that?"

"Well then, she fits in perfectly with the two of us, doesn't she?" His green eyes practically crackled sparks. "A couple of second-string actors with a second-string Regency coach. We're getting what we deserve. She's not. She knows her stuff. Have you read that handbook Eleanor gave us? Samantha wrote that. Not her boss, who your friend, Teddy, thinks is the Regency shit."

"I've flipped through it." She'd read the entire thing once

and had started it a second time, but the Cajun pain-in-the-ass didn't need to know that.

"Try reading it. You might learn something. It's about time both of us started learning this acting gig instead of getting by on our looks and our reputations. Trust me, that boat has sailed for both of us, and the gators are closing in."

Ouch! That stung. Granted, it stung less when he included himself. Who'da thunk it?

"Don't talk to me about gators when I'm still wiping your dogs' slobber out of my hair. I almost drowned when those two attacked me."

"Ah, yes, during the savage beastie battle of bats and ghosts."

Actually, most of the slobber happened afterward, when she'd entered Samantha's room trying to catch her and Danny together, but Lily wasn't going to admit that.

"Don't forget the snake." She smiled despite herself. The sight of him lying in that bed frozen with fear while that big-assed snake had him trapped had made her night.

"I'm trying to, but His Grace won't let me." He offered her a tentative grin.

"Good for him. I didn't think he had a sense of humor."

"He doesn't about most things, especially not about his brother." Danny stared at her intently. "The duke asked me to speak to you."

Lily's heart slowed to a slushy standstill. She pulled her shawl around her shoulders and cocked her chin up a notch. "To speak to me or to warn me?"

"A little of both. Don't slap the hell out of the messenger. I know Eleanor hired Lachlan to teach you how to drive and all that, but…look, Lily, the guy's a mess. The duke worries about him, and the last thing the poor guy needs is someone like you—"

"Someone like me?" It was on now. Arneaux was earning his next slap and then some.

"You're a tough nut, Lily. It's not your fault. Your mom raised you that way, but Lachlan Innes isn't in a good place right now, and someone as together as you is the last woman he needs hooking up with him for some fun."

"He's teaching me to drive a carriage, not the first ten positions in the *Kama Sutra*." She jumped to her feet. "You *and* the duke can kiss my ass. I may be my mother's daughter, but I don't do backwoods aristocrats from Bumfuck, Scotland. Tell your buddy, *His Grace*, his little brother is safe from the Hollywood whore." She headed up the path as fast as she could go and swallowed hard with each step. She'd be damned if she let Danny Arneaux see her cry.

"Lily, wait."

His steps crunched the graveled path behind her as he ran to catch her.

"Wait up, dammit." He grabbed her arm.

Lily turned and punched him in the stomach as hard as she could. He grabbed his gut and gasped for breath. "Never piss off a woman who lives with a body builder, you swamp-water gator fucking piece of shit."

He started laughing, coughed, and laughed some more. "That was good," he said, his voice tight and thin. "You're much better at cussin' than you were when I met you."

"I've had lots of practice since then. Do me a favor. Don't speak to me for the rest of this boot camp thing." She dropped into a perfect curtsy. "Good day, sir." Her British accent was spot on.

"Lily, I'm sorry." He hurried to catch up and walked with her toward the house, matching his strides to hers. "I didn't mean it like that, and I'm sure the duke doesn't either. I just… I agreed to speak to you because I like the duke, and I like his brother. They don't really communicate, but Knox is used to taking care of his brother. It's hard when someone you care about is in trouble, and you can't figure out how to help them. I know from experience."

She stopped, folded her arms across her breasts, and waited. Even an asshole had his moments, apparently.

"The duke is scared, and I understand that. He doesn't want Lachlan to end up...like my cousin. So, take it easy on Lachlan, okay. You are kind of hard to resist, and he could end up getting hurt. You and I are used to it. He's not." He shrugged and started up the steps to the terrace.

"Arneaux," she called.

He stopped and looked over his shoulder at her.

"What happened to your cousin?"

"He blew his brains out." This time, when Danny walked away, he didn't look back.

A chill shot through Lily. She turned her gaze toward Rosemount's stables and beyond.

Lachlan?

Chapter Eight

Lachlan flung his arm up and out to release the golden eagle he'd been working with all morning. The bird soared toward the low hung clouds and emitted a piercing scream as it wheeled and rode the wind currents left over from the storm. Lachlan closed his eyes and tuned in to the sound of the tiny bells attached to the eagle's jesses. Behind him a gentle chorus of bells sounded from the other birds tethered to the five occupied perches outside the mews.

"He's a right one is The Bruce, ain't he, my lord?" Stopping beside him, Tommy raised his hand to his brow to shield his eyes as he followed the big bird in flight.

"Aye, Tommy. He's in fine form. Is he back on his feed?" Lachlan continued to follow the eagle's dance across the sky.

"He is. Had over four hundred grams for his breakfast."

They stood and watched the magnificent winged predator dip and dive and glide for the sheer joy of doing so. After a while, with a tap to Lachlan's shoulder, Tommy jerked his head back toward the enclosed mews area. In addition to indoor flights, perches, and nest boxes for each of the birds, the building housed a kitchen and avian infirmary area. Part of Tommy's job was to prepare the rodent and rabbit content of the birds' carefully measured meals.

Elle had asked Lachlan to do some falconry demonstrations for the Regency boot camp and to instruct Danny Arneaux in the basics of the art. Lachlan had wanted to refuse, but the actor had impressed Urquhart, which was no mean feat. After meeting Arneaux, Lachlan decided the man was a decent sort, until Lily…. Aye, she and Danny Arneaux had history between them. Unfinished history.

He whistled for The Bruce. No matter how many times it happened, Lachlan still marveled at the way the bird dropped from the sky and alighted on his heavily gloved arm. Many would see the bird's obedience as a product of training or simply a response to the fact Lachlan and Tommy provided The Bruce with food. In the beginning that was true, but now, after several years together, the eagle responded as a matter of trust and faith—which every day took hours upon hours of hard work and understanding to build.

For the last two years, Lachlan had tried to learn from his birds—about joy, freedom, and trust. He'd tried. Apparently, birds of prey were smarter than former soldiers. Except for last night. He headed to the outdoor perch and secured The Bruce's jesses to it. The hefty bird stepped onto the metal half-circle padded with jute and ruffled his feathers until he settled in place.

Last night.

He'd crept out of bed and left Lily asleep a few hours ago. She deserved her sleep. He didn't want to wake her because if he did, she might want to talk. Lachlan wasn't ready for that. He'd slipped out of the cottage, gone for a swim in the loch, then come to the mews to think. To think about Lily Randolph and why she'd come looking for him, why she'd stayed, and why he knew to his bones she'd never tell anyone what she'd witnessed last night. His memory was a little blurry, but no one had to tell him what she'd seen and heard. His episodes all played out in the same crippling, humiliating way.

Lily had made things better. Easier. A light at the end of a tunnel that usually took days to find. She trusted he wouldn't hurt her. He trusted her to…well, he wasn't really sure what she'd done. Or how.

Lachlan untied the jesses of the regal female eagle owl and offered his gloved hand. She stepped onto the glove and pecked at the leather before she settled down. He stroked a finger of his free hand down her breast. She snapped at his finger. He smiled. Morgana was an owl who knew her own mind. Rather like Lily Randolph.

He sent the bird into the air. Morgana flew low over the open fields that seemed to go on forever before they reached the hills and rocky tors in the distance. She circled a particular area. Probably spotted some poor unfortunate creature who'd best scramble for cover if it hoped to live. A shadow crossed his mind. Death from above, death from all around him—loud, fiery, punctuated by screams.

Lachlan blinked several times before he shut his eyes tight. A delicate face with gold flecked eyes and raspberry lips loomed in his memory.

"Shhh. It's me, Lachlan. You're home. Come back. You're safe. Here. Here."

Safe. He'd returned to Rosemount because it was one of the only places in the world he'd ever considered himself safe. Not that danger had bothered him all that much. He'd sought it out, courted it even. To him, growing up in a family as volatile and chaotic as his, there was a certain kind of security in not knowing what the hell was coming next— until life showed him how horrific the silence that followed chaos sounded and felt. He'd gone for danger, and Knox had gone for respectability and a buttoned-up life. What were his nightmares like?

Last night, for the very first time in two years Lachlan had managed several hours of sleep without nightmares, without any dreams at all save for the sound of a sweet voice that assured him he was safe. He was home. *Home.* In the arms of a deadly sexy Sassenach actress with a mouth like a sailor and legs that made fools like him weak at the knees.

He whistled for the owl. She paused in her hunt and circled back toward him. He had to signal her twice more before she finally came to land on his glove without her prize. Whatever she'd hunted had escaped to live another day. Just has he had. He rubbed his chest with his free hand. Morgana struck at his knuckle.

"That was amazing." The voice from his dreams, breathless enough to stir his cock and send a shudder of lust through his body, came from behind him.

He turned to see Lily striding up the hill toward him, her long dark hair whipped back by the wind. She wore a hunter green wool dress with a black and blue plaid wrapped around her shoulders like a shawl.

"Why didn't you tell me you were a falconer?" She stopped beside him and squatted down to gaze at Morgana with rapt admiration.

"Didnae ask." He grasped her fingers before she touched Morgana. "She bites."

"If I was as beautiful as her, I'd bite too." Lily straightened and pushed her hair out of her face. "I can't believe you get to work with all these birds, and you didn't say anything about it. Do you have any idea how—"

"You are," he said, his voice so gruff and scratchy he hardly recognized it.

"I am? I am what?" She moseyed over to the next perch where The Bruce sat preening himself.

"Beautiful."

She looked over her shoulder at him. For a minute, her expression was completely unreadable. Then she sort of half smiled. "Thank you." She stepped closer to him. "How are you?"

"Good. I'm good. You?" He reached out and tucked a loose strand of hair behind her ear. "Your lip—"

"Is fine." Her face flushed bright pink, which took the hard edge from her beauty and gave her an ethereal air.

Lachlan refrained from shaking his head. He followed her to the next perch where the Harris hawk sat and clicked its beak.

"Tell me about your birds. Do they all fly?" She stood with her arms behind her back and leaned toward the Harris.

Lachlan stared at her. Such a delicate creature. She'd dragged him back from hell by the sheer belief she could. He suspected she accomplished a great deal that way. It took an incredible kind of strength to do that.

"Lachlan?"

"Do you want to fly him?"

He tugged off his leather gauntlet then took her hand. He fitted the glove over her fingers and tugged it high onto her upper arm. He led her closer to the Harris hawk and helped her position her arm so the bird could step onto her hand.

"His name is Culloden," Lachlan said softly into her ear. The scent of her shampoo and the gardenia perfume she always wore settled into his nerves and relaxed the shoulders he didn't realize he'd tensed.

"Hello, Culloden," she whispered as she rose to her full height and turned toward the open fields. "Do you have any idea how gorgeous you are?" She gazed back at Lachlan, her face flushed pink once more. "What do I do?"

He stood right behind her, his chest against her back and shoulders. He covered her free hand and folded it to her waist. With his other hand, he guided her arm back in line just behind her shoulder. "Relax," he murmured. "Let me guide you. We'll flex your arm up and forward, and he'll do the rest." Lily and Lachlan moved as one, and Culloden flung himself into the air. Lachlan took a short step to stand beside her.

"I did it," she gasped. "Look, Lachlan. Isn't he magnificent?" With her hands clasped tightly in front of her, she gazed skyward with such rap attention Lachlan was helpless to look away.

From her. From the light of unfettered joy and awe in her expression. His heart lifted as if this moment had reached into his chest and torn away the cobwebs and creeping vines of guilt, anger, and despair so thick he'd never even considered a life without them. He drew in the Highland air, so clean the scent stung like the cut of a razor, and filled his lungs to bursting, holding it for a moment, then two, as he studied the unpracticed beauty of Lily Randolph as he suspected few men had ever seen her.

Suddenly, he understood why she, of all people, had been able to pull him out of the firestorm of his memories. His birds had taught him one very important lesson. With true beauty came true strength, the kind of strength against which even the most skilled predators held no sway.

"Will he come back?" Lily asked as she shielded her eyes with a raised hand against the sun that glinted from around the clouds.

"How could he not?" Lachlan murmured.

"What?" Lily turned her head toward him. "What did you say?"

"Nothing." Lachlan let loose a long, sharp whistle. He stepped behind Lily and raised her arm. "Position your hand."

She complied at once. With his free hand, he fumbled in

the pouch at his waist and drew out some bait to place along the line of her gloved forefinger.

"Do I want to know what that is?" she asked, her voice low and rather breathless.

"No. Steady."

"Why is it the only time you speak clearly is when you're barking one-word orders?"

Lachlan whistled again as the Harris hawk appeared out of the clouds. Lily's huff of frustration at his refusal to answer her question brushed her body against his. Sparks of electricity sizzled in his veins.

"He's coming back," Lily cried, her head thrown slightly back to follow Culloden's return.

"Steady," Lachlan said. "Steady."

The hawk dropped out of the sky to land lightly on Lily's gloved hand. Lachlan grabbed the jesses and drew them between her thumb and forefinger. Culloden immediately plucked up the bait and swallowed it in two gulps.

Lachlan pushed her fingers together. "Grip the jesses. Let's him know you're in charge."

"I am?"

"Aye."

She tossed him one of her half-grin half-frowns that meant she wanted him to talk more. She had no idea how much more he'd spoken with her than with anyone else since his return. Nor did she know when he didn't speak, it was her fault. She either rendered him speechless or made it more fun not to speak.

Fun?

"Set him down here." Lachlan indicated the half-circle padded perch from where she'd picked up Culloden. "He's heavy."

"He's perfect." She bent to the perch, and the hawk stepped quickly onto the jute padding. The jesses slipped through her fingers and dangled so the bells jingled slightly.

"Are they so you know where the birds are?" She indicated the bells.

He nodded.

"How many birds do you have?" She strolled down the line of perches, stopping to speak softly to each bird.

"Twenty-six."

"Where?" She came back to stand in front of him before she splayed her palm lightly on his chest.

He swept his arm toward the buildings of the mews. Accepting his unspoken invitation, she hurried ahead of him, then opened the first door she saw. Lachlan followed her into the kitchen where Tommy stood at the cutting board butchering a—

"Oh my God." She spun to face Lachlan. "Is that a—"

"Yes, it is." He grabbed her elbow and steered her through a doorway then down a narrow, crooked corridor into the infirmary.

"Sorry, miss," Tommy called from the kitchen.

"No problem," Lily called back. She swiped her hand across her mouth. Then she slowly turned in a circle to take in the metal tables, machinery, and glass-front cabinets. "This is like a hospital. Are you a veterinarian?"

"No," Lachlan replied. "Licensed falconer and raptor rehabilitator."

"Don't let him fool ye, miss. Most of these birds come in injured. His lordship makes them fly again." Tommy came in from the kitchen. He gave his hands one last wipe with a dishcloth, placed it on a counter, then stuck out his hand. "Tommy Burke, Miss Randolph. 'Tis an honor to meet ye it is."

Lachlan rolled his eyes. Lily shot him a glare and stepped forward to take the silly lad's hand.

"How sweet." She shook his hand. "Very nice to meet you, Tommy. Do you help with the birds?"

"Aye, miss. As much as his lordship allows. He fair dotes on his birds, he does."

Lachlan made plans to strangle the boy later—especially when Lily glanced up at Lachlan with an odd expression that made his stomach hurt.

She spotted the large oxygen cage mounted on the wall at the far end of the infirmary. "Oh, who are these two little ones?" Lily hurried to the glass front then looked back at Lachlan.

"Those two are orphans, Miss Randolph." Tommy joined her in front of the glass-enclosed cage. Two owls, still sporting the downy feathers of young birds, sat huddled together on a long, wide wooden perch covered in thick Astroturf. "Some wanker steward on an estate in Northumberland chopped down half its home wood and killed their mother. Their gamekeeper sent them here. Himself here has quite the reputation for—"

"Isn't it past time you're off to school?" It was all Lachlan could do not to squirm in his boots.

"Aye," Tommy said with a grin. "The two littluns haven't had their breakfast." He tugged the front of his hair and beat feet back into the kitchen.

"Glad I don't work for you," Lily observed, hands on her hips.

Uh-oh!

With a slam of the outer door and a whistled off key tune, Tommy had left Lachlan alone with Lily. And she was less than impressed with his people skills from the tilt of her chin and the fire in her eyes. There was a reason he spent most of his time with his birds and his refugee dog. He hadn't the foggiest what to say next, so he moved to the counter and organized what he needed to weigh and mix up to feed the two young owlets. All the while, Lily moved about the room murmuring little snippets of recognition of some of the supplies and equipment. Lachlan had never been more aware of anyone in his life. Well, at least not anyone who wasn't trying to kill him.

"Okay, you win," she finally said as she came to stand entirely too close to him.

"Win?" Dammit his voice cracked. Again.

"The silent treatment. You win. Now, what are you doing?" She brushed against him as she leaned in to observe what he did.

He wanted to tell her he wasn't ignoring her. Hell, he couldn't ignore her at this point, not even when she was across the estate from him. He gave his brain a shove into gear.

"We need to feed the owlets."

He handed her a glass dish full of small bites of organ meats mixed with various supplements and vitamins. Once he'd gathered a couple of sets of stainless-steel feeding forceps and another dish of food, he moved to the front of the oxygen cage. He glanced back. She stood in the middle of the floor and clasped the glass bowl as if it held some sort of treasure.

"I can feed one of them?" It wasn't really a question. By the time the last word left her mouth she had put her bowl on the counter next to the cage, grabbed up a set of forceps, and popped the latch on the cage door.

"Not if one of them takes a finger." Lachlan pushed the door closed. He took down two feeding perches from the shelf overhead and placed one on each side of the cage. He opened a drawer and took out a shorter, less bulky, coarse leather glove. "Stand back a bit."

"Do they not teach Scots words like 'please' or 'thank you'?"

"I...." He concentrated on lifting the protesting owlet out of the cage and putting it on the feeding perch. "That is...."

"I got your note," Lily said softly. "And the fan. I love it. Thank you."

He settled the second owlet on its perch and removed his glove. Once he'd trapped a piece of meat in the forceps, he offered it to the bird. "Tommy cuts the meat up but make certain it isn't too big for the bird's beak." He waited for the baby to gulp the food down completely. "Give him enough time between bites. They don't have sense enough to stop."

"Like Arneaux eating cranachan. If they keep serving it at dinner, he'll eat his way out of the lead in this film."

"Mrs. Gordon's cranachan is legendary."

Lily snorted and offered her owlet a bite. "So is Arneaux's gluttony." She jumped a bit when the bird's beak snatched the meat off the forceps. Just as quickly, her face lit up with a brilliant girlish smile. Lachlan sensed his own face stretch and his mouth turn up slightly. He picked up the next piece of meat and fed his owlet. Lily watched him intently and copied what he did. Except she kept up a constant stream of encouragement as she fed the hungry young owl.

"Such a good boy. Take your time. Eat it all up." Her movements, graceful and meticulous despite her nervousness, reminded Lachlan of her arms around him last night, her hands on his face as she soothed away his nightmares.

They finished the feeding, and Lachlan put on the short glove to lift both owlets back into the cage. He cleaned up the bowls and forceps then put them into the autoclave. Wordlessly, he led Lily into the building that housed the large cages for each of the twenty-six birds. Fortunately, each was labeled with carefully printed signs in sturdy metal holders to identify the individual birds. Some cages were empty, of course, as there were birds outside on perches. The facility boasted four long, tall flight cages as well.

At the far end of the building a flight that stretched the entire width of the facility contained two golden eagles—male and female. In addition to trees, perches, and feeding stations, a small pond occupied one corner of the flight. Lachlan was about to introduce the birds to her when Lily gasped.

"He only has one wing. What happened?"

"Some bastard shot him. He sat out on the moors for weeks. 'Tis a wonder he survived."

The female chose that moment to fly to the feeding station, snatch up one of the trout Lachlan had caught that morning, and return to the platform where her mate sat and waited. She offered him the fish and waited while he ate his fill.

"She stayed with him the entire time. Fed him. Looked after him," he said.

"She can fly."

"She can. She's still wild, too wild for me to handle. I've tried to set her free, but she wilnae leave him." Lachlan walked to the wire door that led out of the flight area. "Eagles mate for life."

Lily followed him as he headed slowly toward the birds still attached to their outdoor perches. "Miss Witherspoon has a falconry demonstration scheduled for next week. Can you teach me how to fly the birds? I'd love to see Arneaux's face when I—"

Lachlan spun on his heel, hands fisted at his sides. "I'll not have ye use my birds to get back at yer ex, *Miss Randolph*."

Where the devil had that come from? Emotions he'd not had to deal with in ages bubbled up and refused to be tamped down. It took him a minute to discover the noise in his ears was his heart pounding like a blacksmith's hammer.

Lily's face went white. Then the lovely rose undertone of her skin flushed, got brighter, and turned nearly red. "Well, excuse the *bloody hell* out of me." She snatched the heavy glove he'd tucked in the waist of his kilt and slapped it against his chest so hard it stung. She produced a perfect English accent at will, and when she was angry, no less. He watched her storm across the mews yard and start down the hill.

Shite!

He strode after her. "Lily, wait."

"Wait?" She turned, then pounded back up the hill in a heartbeat. "For what? For you to decide to spend a little more of your limited vocabulary insulting me? Am I supposed to feel privileged that you talk to me, even if you spout typical male bullshit?"

"I...you cannae...." As usual when it came to her, his brain shut down.

"I cannae? I cannae what, hmm, Lachlan? I dragged your sorry ass halfway across Scotland during a damned thunderstorm in the middle of the night, but, by all means, don't do me any favors that might interfere with your relationship with another muscle-bound monument to testosterone and male ego."

"I dinnae have a relationship with Arneaux. Ye do." Why was it when his brain finally connected with his mouth it spat out codswallop like that?

"I hate to break it to you, but you can't believe everything you read on the internet. Danny Arneaux and I have never—"

"Ye dinnae have to be lovers to have a relationship, Lily." He swallowed hard. "Whatever happened between ye two isn't over. Not for ye at least."

"Bullshit," she muttered.

"Why?" Lachlan asked.

"Why what?" Lily stopped and folded her arms across her chest, though she didn't turn around.

"Why do you spend so much time on someone you say

you hate?" He flexed his hands. In his left, the grain of the leather glove she'd slammed into his chest dug into his palm.

"Why do you spend so much time blaming yourself for what happened in Afghanistan?"

Every cell in his body stilled. The world stopped around him as if he'd stepped into a room on another planet. Her words filtered into his brain one at a time. While he slowly put them together, nothing stirred, not the wind, not a cloud in the sky, especially not Lily Randolph.

"Did he—" The words stuck in his throat. The rage, however, simmered like a lamb stew on a fireside hob.

She spun toward him. "A man doesn't have to rape a woman to hurt her. He doesn't even have to screw her. Sometimes it's about what didn't happen, what could have happened, or what she could have done and didn't."

He stared at her and flexed his hands to keep from wrapping his arms around her. As fragile as she was now, she'd break if he did, and she wasn't the sort of woman who wanted to break.

"Whatever happened between Danny and me has nothing to do with the way I feel about him now."

Lily blinked a few times and, right before his eyes, became the woman he'd met that first night—tough, driven, and as mission oriented as any hardened grunt he'd ever trained. Take no prisoners. Show no mercy. A bone-deep ache set up behind his ribs.

"And?" he urged.

"Wentworth never should have cast Arneaux in this film, let alone in the lead role. This film is the most important thing in my life. I won't let him screw it up. The last time he interfered in my life I lost everything. I won't let anyone do that to me again. Not him. Not anybody."

"I see."

"No, you don't. And it's okay if you don't want to teach me—"

"I'll teach ye. Falconry. If ye like. Less dangerous than the phaeton."

She laughed. The low, sultry sound went straight to his cock. "I don't know about that. Your big brother seems to think I'm dangerous to you no matter what."

"Pardon?" What the hell did Knox have to do with anything?

"His new best friend, Arneaux, warned me to stay away from you. Apparently, *His Grace*, your brother, asked him to tell me to stay away from you." In a sudden change of attitude, she pushed up on her toes and kissed the corner of his mouth, slowly and with sweet, hot tenderness. "Is that what you want?"

His heart jumped.

I'm going to kill my sodding brother.

First, he was going to kiss Lily Randolph until she told him to stop.

Chapter Nine

❧

LILY BARELY HAD TIME TO NOD CONSENT TO THE UNASKED question in his eyes, when, Lachlan dragged her into his arms and sealed his mouth to hers. She fisted her hands in his long, thick hair and held on for dear life. His palms were rough and his hands strong but so tender as he cupped her face and held her still while he plundered her mouth with the sweetness of a lover and the searing power of an invading army.

Dear God, the man could kiss.

She met his tongue, stroke for stroke. She pulled back only enough to nip his lower lip, the one she'd studied and craved all night. He growled in response, deep in his chest so it vibrated against her breasts and propelled her even closer. She wanted to crawl inside Lachlan Innes and live there forever. On some level she was aware of the wind biting at her skin as it gusted across the hillside, but everywhere her body touched his, she burned.

She gasped for air, and he sucked her upper lip between his teeth so he could torture the sensitive flesh with the tip of his tongue. A sharp whimper of pleasure bubbled up from her throat. Lachlan trailed his lips along her jawline to press to the spot where the sound still vibrated against her heated flesh. He glided his hands down her arms and around her waist, resting one on her hip. The warmth of his fingers as he slid them beneath her shawl and pressed them against her back made her sigh.

He sank slowly to his knees and brought her with him. She kissed and nipped a trail from the corner of his mouth to the sharp edge of his jaw, the soft spot on the underside of his chin, then down the front of his throat and back up the side to a spot behind his ear. He tasted of salt, fresh air, and rain. He moved beneath her fingers like a sun-warmed lion as if he needed her touch, wanted it. She bit his ear lobe, and a long, deep shudder went through him. Lily laughed softly.

"Ye'r killing me, lass. Killing me." He groaned and lay back until his back rested against the hillside with Lily sprawled on top of him.

With her elbows braced on his chest, she caressed the lines of his face with her fingertips. Lachlan closed his eyes and tilted his head back to allow Lily access to his throat. She alternated touches with butterfly soft kisses.

A sudden thought flitted across her mind. She stopped in the act of bringing her lips to his. "Are you kissing me to get even with His Grace?"

"Who?" He blinked at her, his eyes fiery with desire.

She smiled against his lips. "That is such a good answer."

She did kiss him then and tangled her tongue lazily with his. He curved one of his hands over the swell of her ass. Lily squirmed against him and found what she was looking for—an impressive, thick line pushing up from his kilt. She slid her hand down and caressed him through his kilt. So, the stories were true. Nothing between that stellar erection and her except the plaid fabric wrapped and belted at his waist.

"Is this your walking stick, Lord Lachlan, or are you just happy to see me?" she asked in her best Mae West.

He held her gaze, his eyes luminous pale gold pools Lily wanted nothing more than to bathe in, to wash away so many of the hurts she kept behind the locked and barred door of denial in her heart.

"First of all, my walking *stick* is called a staff. Second, I am always happy to see ye, Lily. Last night. I didnae think… you…." He turned his head.

She brushed a kiss across his chin and gently used two fingers to tilt his face back toward her.

"And I'm happy when your Scot's brogue kicks in. Very sexy." Not to mention it only happened when he was flustered and sincere. A combination Lily found more than sexy, more than…anything.

"My father hated it."

"Your father was an *arse*. I see where your brother gets it."

Lily went completely still. The change in Lachlan came over him in less than the blink of an eye. His expression turned to stone. His eyes darkened, flat and unreadable.

"Knox had no right."

"Shhh." She kissed him and stroked her hand up his cock. "It doesn't matter. I don't take orders from His Grace or Danny Arneaux or any man. Now, where were we? Oh!"

Suddenly, she was on her back in the grass with six feet of ripped Scot on top of her. She wrapped her hand around the back of his head and drew him down for a kiss. He teased her with short, silken tastes of his lips. His quick dots to the corners of her mouth, her nose, her cheeks, and her eyelids frustrated and excited her. When he finally gave her the kiss she wanted, she couldn't help the soft sigh that escaped her as she slid her tongue along his.

They groaned in tandem as she wrapped her legs around his hips. His lips were cool, his tongue sleek and hot. Her shawl had fallen free under her shoulders, but she barely noticed. Lachlan's hard sculpted body offered warmth, a shield against the wind, and something she'd only had a faint memory of for years. Security. Comfort. The possibility of peace.

A scent of lavender floated on the breeze.

"Lachlan," she whispered when he kissed the point of her collarbone exposed by the neckline of her dress.

Baaaa!

"What the devil!" Lachlan pushed up on his hands.

It took a minute, but Lily opened her eyes and reached up only to encounter something soft, wooly, and... chewing?

She raised her head and looked around. Sheep. Dozens of them.

"Here," Lachlan commanded as he rolled off her. "Leave off you nosy bugger." He shoved a large black sheep away.

Lily glanced at Lachlan expectantly.

"Stuck his cold nose up my kilt." He pulled her into a seated position and wrapped his arms around her.

Lily snorted before helplessly shaking as loud, raucous laughter erupted from her. She couldn't stop. She turned and collapsed against his chest.

"'Tis nae funny," Lachlan declared as he continued to try and shoo the sheep away from them.

"Yes," she gasped. "It is. You were goosed by a sheep. I thought you were having a seizure."

"Try a sheep's nose on *your* bare *arse*."

"Bare? Let me see." Lily squirmed around and tried to lift his kilt.

"Nae!" He clamped his hand over hers.

"Oh, I see. You'll let a sheep see it, but you won't let me."

"He didnae ask." He held her hand in place and the heat seeped through his kilt into her palm. She flexed her fingers, and the ripple of his muscles sent a shot of fire between her legs.

"Did the mean sheep frighten you?" She used her index finger to draw a circle against the wool stretched tightly over his ass.

"How'd ye like a cold nose on yer bare *arse?*" His deep voice rumbled in his chest. His lips, so often drawn in a hard, determined line, creased up at the sides.

"Depends on the nose," she murmured. The sheep continued to mill around them. There was something intimate and sweet about lying in the grass in the middle of a herd of sheep. The soft brush of their fleece. Their musty, wild scent. The music of their voices as they bleated amongst themselves.

Then there was Lachlan—his amber gaze intent, and his mouth still drawn in that ghost of a smile. He warmed her body with his heat and honed frame. He warmed everything else with the way he treated her—as Lily, just Lily. She never realized how much she longed for that until she met him.

"Regency ladies didn't wear drawers," Lachlan said, his fingers suddenly tangled in the folds of her skirts.

"What?" Lily heard what he said. Her every nerve began to sing like canaries at the brush of the wool fabric up her legs.

"Elle told me Regency ladies didn't wear panties." He half closed his eyes.

She grabbed his wrist. "And *why* were you discussing ladies' underwear with Eleanor Witherspoon?" Lily pushed him flat on his back then rolled on top and straddled his hips.

"Don't remember." He used both hands to pull her skirts up inch by torturous inch.

"Bullshit." She leaned down and kissed him hard. "What do you think you are doing, sir?"

"Besides trying to see how authentic ye are?" He gave an odd little whistle. "Giving the ram a clear shot at your lovely *arse*."

Lily shrieked and rolled away. Lachlan held her and wrapped himself around her as they tumbled over and over down to the bottom of the hill. The sheep scattered, bleating at the top of their lungs. The air, filled with the scent of grass, wool, and Lachlan, swirled around them. All the while, his rich, dark laughter resonated through her bones. They reached the bottom of the hill, and he still chuckled as he cradled her against his chest.

The sheep immediately reassembled around them. Lily tried to push them away, but she was laughing so hard she couldn't.

The sharp barks of at least two dogs sounded from just beyond the top of the hill as a gruff male voice called out in the distance, *"Trobhad a-steach fodha! Trobhad a-steach fodha!"* The dogs and the calls came closer.

Lachlan leapt to his feet in a single graceful move. He reached back and offered her his hand. Lily, however, sat where she was. The view was too good to pass up. His kilt was caught at his waist in the back, which gave her a perfect view of the finest male ass she'd ever seen. She reached up, the need to discover how hard and deep those muscles went nearly a mania. He grabbed her hand and pulled her to her feet with ease. He positioned her behind him with one arm just as an elderly man in a tweed jacket, sweater, kilt, and boots came over the top of the hill. He wore a tweed cap with a sort of feather and pin combination on one side of it and carried a tall staff similar to Lachlan's. Two black and white dogs raced down the hill ahead of the man and circled the sheep. The old man shouted a few more commands, and the dogs gathered the sheep and headed them down the clearing between one hill and the next.

The man reached the bottom of the hill as Lily cupped Lachlan's bare ass. He jumped nearly a foot but didn't say a word.

"Lord Lachlan," the white-haired gentleman said as he tugged the bill of his cap.

"Young Graeme," Lachlan replied solemnly with a nod.

Lily reached around him with her free hand. "Hello. I'm Lily. I'm visiting Rosemount Manor." The shepherd shook her hand. "What are your dogs' names?" she asked as she peered around Lachlan, her hand never leaving his butt cheek.

The old man pointed with his staff. "Thas Sky and tother is her boy, Fleet."

"They're lovely and very smart."

"Oh, aye, miss. They're the best in the Highlands. *Latha math, mo thighearna.* Miss." He touched the bill of his cap once more, whistled to the dogs who already had the sheep well up ahead of him, and continued on his way.

Lily dared not move until the shepherd, the sheep, and the dogs disappeared around the bend. As the last sheep and dog trotted out of sight, Lachlan glanced at her hand on his ass. She raised an eyebrow and squeezed.

"Better than a sheep's cold snout?" she asked.

"Much. But if Young Graeme saw it, every soul in twenty miles will know it by supper."

"Would you care?"

"No. You?"

She gave him one last caress and adjusted his kilt before she clasped his bicep in her hands. "Walk me back as far as the little bridge?"

He brushed the grass from her shoulders and out of her hair. "Aye." They walked for a while in silence. Somehow simply having him beside her, clasping his arm made a simple walk calming.

"*Latha math?*" she asked, not quite mangling the pronunciation.

"Good day."

"*Mo thighearna?*"

He sighed, at least as much as a man like him could. It came out as a short huff. "My lord."

"Ah. You don't like it."

"It's unnecessary."

"To you, maybe. He's an old man, even if you do call him *Young* Graeme. Old men need their traditions."

"If you say so."

She hid a smile as they continued down the way the sheep had taken until they came to a set of rock steps cut into the far hillside. After she'd stepped up on the first step, she turned to face Lachlan and sifted through his hair, scattering the leaves and twigs he'd acquired on their trip down the hill. He held her gaze, though the laughing, rounded edged man he'd been had faded the closer they got to the manor.

"He *is* Young Graeme," he suddenly said.

"He's sixty if he's a day."

"Sixty-five. His father is Auld Graeme. He's eighty-three and tends the flocks on the far side of the estate."

"Will that be you at eighty-three? Wandering the hills of Rosemount with a couple of dogs and some sheep? Tending your birds?"

"Aye."

"Sounds wonderful."

He gave her a look of patent disbelief.

"There are far worse ways to spend a life." She leaned in to kiss his cheek. To do more would have her in his arms with her legs wrapped around him in a heartbeat. The time wasn't right. It might not ever be, but now…no. Lily started up the steps.

"Come tomorrow."

She turned back. His immovable expression and those uncertain eyes struck at her heart.

"For falconry lessons."

"And phaeton driving?"

He shook his head, then released his little huff of a sigh—the one she'd begun to find kind of cute. "Yes."

"Deal. See you tomorrow." She continued up the steps.

"Knox had no right to think you're dangerous to me, let alone send some actor as his messenger boy."

Lily froze but didn't face him. "It doesn't matter, Lachlan." A sudden sting of tears blurred her vision. Men didn't defend Lily Randolph. They didn't. Except...this man. She took a deep breath and kept going.

"It does to me."

She sensed his gaze on her even after she continued across the lawn toward the house.

THE LAUGHTER COMING FROM THE DRAWING ROOM UP AHEAD was her first clue. Lily had spent her entire adult life and most of her childhood in Hollywood, the most fake and vicious place on earth. When the hair on the back of her neck stood up at the sound of laughter, she'd bet her best Louis Vuitton bag the object of that laughter was her. She flattened herself against the silk wallpaper and edged as close to the open drawing room doors as she could without revealing herself to the Regency hen party.

"I don't know what surprises me more," Samantha said in her snooty British accent. "That she's been engaged five times or that she actually found five men brave enough to even consider taking her on."

"What a wicked thing to say," Bella Stepford, the costume

mistress said. "Wicked, but true. Five engagements and not a single wedding. I find that sad."

"For whom?" This question came from Eleanor. "Lily Randolph or the five who got away?"

"She is a handful," the mousy little author said. "She'd make a great Regency heroine, but I'd have to write a real alpha male to deal with her. I understand even Mr. Arneaux refused to date her. Isn't that right, Samantha?"

What the fuck? Lily knew Danny Arneaux was an asshole, but he had no right to discuss her with that bitch of a Regency coach. And she had no right to tell everyone at this so-called boot camp. Her throat burned and she swallowed hard. She shouldn't let them get to her. Who gave a fuck what this bunch of nobodies thought? They'd all started to act like friends, but they were just like everyone else, jealous and spiteful women.

She'd done what she had to do to survive. What did these bitches know about that? Lily would rather be feared than loved anyway. She swiped at her eyes and swallowed again. Lachlan's words floated back in memory.

"Knox had no right to think you're dangerous to me, let alone send some actor as his messenger boy."

"It doesn't matter, Lachlan."

"It does to me."

SEVERAL HOURS LATER, AS LILY SAT IN THE DRAWING ROOM and learned the supposedly feminine art of embroidery, the memory of his gaze stirred prickles of electricity up and down her skin in waves. The sensation did a real number on her concentration. She had to find something to distract herself.

Lily lifted her head and began to study the room. She didn't normally go for the overdone antique look. She liked clean lines and modern furniture. Definitely in short supply at Rosemount Manor. This room was beautiful, but intimidating.

The carpets stretched from wall to wall over dark hardwood floors were obviously expensive, old, and done in patterns of blue, gold, and black. The furniture was all heavy with mahogany wood and blue silk damask upholstery. The tables all had intricately carved legs and tops polished to a high sheen. The accent pieces, like the sideboards and the small chests that Samantha kept calling commodes, had incredible detail work. Everywhere sat expensive items of porcelain and crystal. Lily didn't know much about art, but she recognized names like Turner and Landseer on some of the paintings.

Bella Stepford, the film's costume mistress, cleared her throat. Loudly. She'd caught Lily surveying the room instead of her stitch work. The woman taught as if everyone in the room intended to go into professional embroidery as their life's work. All Lily wanted to do was appear realistic in the scenes where this task was required. She took in the expressions of the other ladies present.

Dr. Samantha Higgins, supposed Regency expert, held her embroidery hoop as if it was a fish she just caught and wanted to throw back.

Good.

The little author gal looked like the perfect Regency spinster. She sat in a chair by the fire in a drab gray dress and those ugly boots they were all forced to wear. She had some weird Martha Washington white hat on her head, but Miss Anna Chase was totally into the embroidery and seemingly intended to graduate top of the embroidery class. Her little flowers actually looked like flowers.

"How about you, Miss Randolph?" Bella peered over Lily's shoulder. "You don't appear to have made a great deal of progress." The woman's snotty English accent grated on Lily's nerves. It reminded her of Lachlan's brother, aka The Duke.

Lily tilted her head back and smiled sweetly at the fifty-something woman who looked closer to grandmahood than she should. "I'm not a hearts and flowers kind of girl, I mean, lady."

"That much is clear." The older woman patted her on the shoulder and strode to a sideboard across the room.

"Ouch." Eleanor leaned toward Lily across the tea table. "That was a bit harsh of her."

"Not really." Lily held up her embroidery hoop. Stitches went in every direction. Strings of brightly colored thread hung from the fabric like streamers.

"Oh!" Eleanor recoiled as if poor embroidery was contagious. "That's…um…very colorful?"

"Thank you, Miss Randolph," Dr. Higgins said from her spot on the settee. "I suddenly feel quite accomplished." She gave Lily a half-assed smile and went back to her needlework.

"Bitch," Lily muttered.

"Come on, Lily," Eleanor said quietly. "Samantha is really a great person once you get to know her."

"She turned Arneaux's two slobbering hounds loose on me in the middle of the flying bat, shrieking ghost, hissing snake part of this vacation from hell."

"You mean to tell me you didn't enjoy catching Danny in bed with my snake?" Eleanor turned a sideways glance at Samantha who was listening to some instruction from their embroidery teacher.

"I plead the fifth." Lily had to smile despite the fact she was pissed at Eleanor for taking her phone. Make that *phones*.

"More tea, miss?" Like a ghost, the maid, Tildie, stood at

Lily's elbow, teapot poised over the delicate bone china teacup on the table in front of her.

"Yes, please," Lily said and ducked her head to avoid Eleanor's pointed stare. A plate of picture-perfect strawberry tarts appeared next to Lily's cup.

"Mrs. Gordon sent these up for you." Tildie curtsied then left the room as quickly and quietly as she'd entered.

Every eye in the Duke of Turra's drawing room turned on her. She didn't have to look at the other women to verify it. She'd be damned if she'd give them the satisfaction.

All through lunch and the entire afternoon, the servants had given Lily special treatment. She'd enjoyed it until she realized every soul at bootcamp stared at her like she'd sprouted horns whenever a servant did something extra for her, bowed or curtsied to her, or murmured her name with something other than fear or dread. Granted, she'd been a bitch since she'd arrived, so having servants dislike her wasn't unexpected. She didn't want to be here. Or at least she hadn't before.... She'd been a little better lately, but not enough to earn preferential treatment.

The silence stretched out like a Hollywood red carpet, except for Bella's inane chatter as she sorted through a stack of materials on the table where she'd deposited all her embroidery supplies.

Lily studiously glanced around the slightly oppressive room and tried to imagine Lachlan growing up in this house. Couldn't picture it. Or maybe when she pictured it, she saw how far apart their worlds really were. A log settled in one of the fireplaces and sent a thud and a hissing sound into the quiet. When she finally looked at her companions they'd gone back to their needlework.

Thank God.

"Very well, Miss Randolph," Miss Stepford said as she plucked the embroidery hoop from Lily's limp fingers. "Let's try something other than flowers, shall we?" She shoved a new embroidery frame already loaded with fabric into Lily's hands and dumped a handful of embroidery threads in her lap. With a militant slam, the woman put a yellowed piece of paper onto the tea table next to Lily's plate of tarts.

Lily leaned over and looked at the paper. "What is it?"

"The Innes family coat of arms. It's a simple pattern any schoolgirl might do. Try it." The old drill sergeant of a designer marched to the far end of the drawing room, then lowered herself into a large high-backed chair in front of the third fireplace in the room. After she gave each of them a prison warden sharp stare, she picked up her own embroidery and went to work.

"I think you upset her," Samantha said without looking up from her work.

"Upset is what little old ladies get when their cakes fall," the normally quiet author said. "Miss Randolph pissed her off."

Lily snickered. So did Miss Chase. Eleanor bit her lip, which didn't hide the smile she fought. Samantha simply shook her head.

"Oh, lighten up, Miss Prim and Proper," Lily muttered. "If Regency women sat around doing embroidery all damned day it's no wonder they drank so much."

She scratched the back of her neck where her wool dress itched like a bad case of poison ivy. The strawberry tarts called her name, so she grabbed one and bit it in half. Eleanor tossed one of Rosemount's beautiful linen napkins at her.

"I'm pretty sure Regency women did more than just sit and embroider samplers and drink tea," Miss Chase said, though she didn't look up from her needlework. "They gossiped."

"Undoubtedly," Samantha said, and looked right at Lily.

"But we all know where gossip can lead, don't we, *Miss* Randolph?"

Lily paused only a second then took a sip of tea from the cup she'd raised just before Samantha's dig at her. She took a second sip then returned the cup to the saucer as delicately as she could.

"I don't know, *Samantha*. Is it gossip if it's true?"

The Regency coach blinked a few times, then smiled. "Should have let Mr. Arneaux's dogs eat you," she muttered, but not quietly at all.

"Probably." Lily began to organize her embroidery threads.

"What *did* Regency ladies gossip about, Dr. Higgins?" Eleanor apparently thought it was her job to keep the peace in addition to running the entire "Regency experience." She was also in charge of giving Lily dirty looks.

Samantha, however, glanced up with that *I-know-all-things-Regency* smugness. The click as someone opened one of the doors behind Lily wiped that expression off better than a Clorox wipe. The professor did a double take and tried to put her embroidery down on the settee beside her.

"The duke," she said as she listed to one side and got to her feet.

Eleanor snorted. "I doubt they'd gossip much about our duke. Oh…shi-shoot." She shot out of her seat.

What the fu—

Lily turned in her chair so fast she heard vertebrae crack. The Duke of Turra, aka Lachlan's Asshole Brother, stepped into the drawing room and closed the door behind him. He stood, hands behind his back and surveyed the room.

"Good afternoon, ladies." He inclined his head.

That was when Lily realized every other woman in the room had risen and given him a nice curtsy. Well, Eleanor's curtsy was half-assed, but Lily was beginning to think

Eleanor either wanted to push the duke into a fountain or screw him. Or both. He did have…a look. He was at least as tall as his brother. Like Lachlan, the duke's hair was a dark brown, nearly black. His eyes, however, were blue, at least in the natural light and candlelight of the drawing room. He wore a kilt of the same pattern and color as Lachlan's but with a blue cable knit cashmere sweater—Ralph Lauren, unless Lily missed her mark—which she never did when it came to fashion. His tall, polished black boots shone like mirrors.

The entire time she'd inventoried him, she hadn't moved out of her seat. He had taken several steps into the room and now stood where it was obvious his unreadable stare landed squarely on her.

Great. Well, hell.

She pushed out of the chair and tossed her embroidery frame onto the really pretty side table next to her. She fisted one side of her wool skirts and executed a deep curtsy.

"Good afternoon, Your Grace."

"Miss Randolph. Are you enjoying your stay at Rosemount Manor? Please, sit, ladies. It wasn't my intention to disturb you."

Jesus, every one of them dropped back into their seats like they had hooks in their asses, and someone had reeled them in. Lily, on the other hand, took her time. Once she finally quit fiddling with her skirts and picked up her embroidery again, he'd taken one hand from behind his back and extended it toward her. In it? Her satchel. The one she'd left at Lachlan's cottage last night. How did he—

Fuck.

"I believe this is yours?"

Lily took it from his outstretched hand. "Thank you, Your Grace."

"Certainly." The duke gave her a hint of a bow. "One of

the footmen found it in the gardens this morning under a bench. You must have left it there last night."

He was a damned good liar.

Someone had found the satchel all right, but not in the garden. Considering Lachlan would never have given it to his brother to return to her, she didn't know how the duke got it, but the scenarios going through her head pissed her off. Big time—especially as Anna the author, Samantha the Regency coach, Eleanor the boss lady, and Miss Picky the costume designer, all stared at her and the duke as if they expected one of them to turn into a frog or the ghost of a witch.

"Miss Randolph, I wonder if it might—"

The French doors at the back side of the drawing room, the ones that led to the back terrace, slammed open so hard everyone in the room jumped.

"Knox. Leave off." Lachlan stood on the terrace, just outside the doors, his chiseled jaw tense, and his eyes flat and hard.

"Lachlan?" The duke looked shocked. Rattled even.

"Yer study. Now."

Lachlan strode down the terrace out of sight. He never looked at Lily. Not even once. No, he only had eyes for his brother. If Lily knew Lachlan, and she was beginning to, the shit was about to hit the fan for His Grace.

Chapter Ten

LACHLAN FOUGHT TO STEADY HIS BREATHING. *FOUGHT*. A violent way to tame a perfectly natural act, but necessary because if he gave in to the next most natural act, he'd pound Knox into a bloody pulp right there on the terrace. Grief, sorrow, fear, confusion—he'd allowed those emotions free rein of his body and his mind every day since…that last day in Afghanistan. But not rage. Never rage. He'd parceled his rage out like the most caustic of poisons because the destruction of his anger burned him and everything and everyone it touched.

Right now, he wanted to touch his older brother. With fists.

Against his better judgement, he'd tried to excuse Knox's sending Arneaux to warn Lily to leave him alone. He'd chalked it up to a misguided attempt to act the protective older brother. Not that Lachlan really believed that of the high and mighty Duke of Turra, but he'd tried. Lachlan had had enough conflict in Afghanistan to last a lifetime. The last thing he wanted was a war with his brother.

Then the arrogant bastard had sent McGinty to invade Lachlan's privacy and to check on whether Lily had spent the night with him. There could be no other reason for the obedient steward to enter the gamekeeper's cottage when Lachlan wasn't there. The old Scot's mission was to provide Knox with information about Lachlan's sex life. The longer he contemplated the duke's interference, the higher Lachlan's rage burned. It was time to beard the lion in his den. Otherwise, Lachlan would not be answerable for his actions.

He shoved the French doors at the far end of the terrace open and strode into Knox's study, hands stretched against his kilt to keep him from punching the current Duke of Turra dead in the face. The previous duke's formal portrait above the monster of a stone fireplace didn't help—especially when the two men seated in the tall-backed leather club chairs on either side of the hearth stared at him as if he'd lost his mind. Again.

"Yer Grace," McGinty said as he lumbered to his feet.

"Knox?" Danny Arneaux unfolded his long frame from the chair and wiped his hands down the front of his new kilt.

"Gentlemen, if you will give us a minute," Knox said as he came around Lachlan and headed for the open tantalus in the corner.

"Stay," Lachlan said with a sharp gesture of his hand. "Ye two are in the thick of this."

The actor and the estate steward tried their best not to look at each other and failed miserably. If the guilt written on their faces was a book, it'd be *War and feckin' Peace*.

"Drink?" Suddenly, Knox was in front of him with a heavy crystal glass of whisky in each hand.

Lachlan slapped the offered glass away. It landed on the carpet with a muffled thud, and the contents soaked into the red, black, and yellow hand-woven pattern. Knox stared at the mess as if by doing so he could command the glass to scoop up the spilled whisky and hop up on the table next to McGinty's chair.

"This is Turkey carpet and over four hundred years old," he observed before he took a sip of the glass in his other hand.

"Fuck the carpet." Lachlan folded his arms across his chest. Anything to keep from doing what he'd wanted to do for the last hour.

"Perhaps a better choice than—"

Lachlan blinked, and the next thing he knew he had a handful of Knox's jumper clutched in his hand, and he'd pinned Knox to the gold silk wallpaper under a Landseer painting of the ruins of Rosemount Castle.

"Enough, lad," McGinty growled as he tried to wrench Lachlan away from the duke.

"I'm nae a lad anymore, McGinty. Ye'll find that out yersel' the next time ye step foot in my home."

"He did so under my orders," Knox said, his voice steady as a rock despite his situation. "And the gamekeeper's cottage belongs to the estate."

"I knew that. McGinty doesn't take a shite without yer permission." Lachlan didn't mean what he said, but he could only control so much.

"Try to keep the gloves above the belt," Danny Arneaux stated as he came to stand at Lachlan's other side. He reached up and pried Lachlan's fingers free of Knox's sweater. "How about you two go to neutral corners and take a minute before you both say things you'll regret."

"Screw you, Arneaux. Didn't take His Grace long to turn you into one of his lap dogs." Lachlan swiped the back of his hand across his mouth.

"You're not my type," the actor said with an annoying

grin. "I don't screw anybody with the same thing under his kilt as me."

McGinty chuckled.

Lachlan glanced at the big man and shook his head. "Didn't mean it," he mumbled.

The steward nodded. "I know ye didn't."

"And if the gamekeeper's cottage isnae mine, Yer Grace, I'll go now and clean it out. Urquhart's sister has an apartment to let over the pub." Lachlan turned and started for the French doors.

"Lachlan, wait, dammit." Knox crossed the room and grabbed his arm.

Lachlan glanced down at his brother's hand then up into his hard, unreadable face. Whatever Lachlan's expression, it made his brother let go and take a step back.

"I was concerned. You disappeared. Mrs. Wallace recognized the signs. The storm...I didn't think—the gunfire...." Knox speaking in incomplete sentences was a new experience.

Lachlan could tell the duke didn't care for it much.

"The gunfire was on me," Arneaux said. "I—"

Lachlan silenced him with a raised hand. "Does nae explain him ordering ye to tell Miss Randolph to stay away from me. Does nae explain him sending McGinty into my home to check up on me like I'm some vicar's virgin daughter."

"Good one," Arneaux muttered.

"McGinty went to the cottage to see if you'd come home." Now it was Knox who stood, fists clenched, as he clearly fought his temper, a gift both of them had received from their horse's arse of a father. "I didn't know if you were dead or alive. No one could find you, dammit."

"Bullshit. Ye'll nae say another word against Miss Randolph, Knox Innes. Ye'll treat her with the respect ye would any guest in yer home. She's a lady. Understood? Everyone else at Rosemount needs to understand that too." Lachlan glanced at Danny Arneaux who raised his hands in surrender and grinned.

Lachlan tried to take a deep breath. His lungs didn't cooperate. The portrait of his father loomed at him. The walls moved closer together. There had to be entire trees in the fireplace. The heat suddenly seared his skin like the heat of the desert or the scorch in the aftermath of a fired rocket launcher. He hated this room. Always had. He took a step back toward the French doors. He had to leave. Now. An image of Lily as she took her satchel back from Knox came to mind. He'd watched from the terrace as she'd stared the almighty Duke of Turra down and dared him to say a wrong word. Lachlan's lungs relaxed. Knox stood there. He knew what was happening. His gaze of pity and condescension....

Fucker.

Lachlan crossed the four-hundred-year-old Turkey carpet in two strides, cocked his fist back, and nailed his brother dead in the jaw. Knox stumbled backward onto his desk and sent papers and expensive antique metal objects flying. Lachlan pushed his way past McGinty and Arneaux who, once they stopped gawking, ran to help His Grace.

Once Lachlan reached the French doors he turned and saw Knox shake off the steward and actor's assistance. His brother took a step toward him. The normally cool and collected duke shook with anger. A nice red mark bloomed on his jaw. It'd be a bruise by morning. Lachlan stepped toward him. McGinty moved to stand in the middle of the space between them, arms folded across his broad chest.

"Ye couldnae find me so ye sent McGinty to track me down?" he shouted. "Lily Randolph found me. She came out in the storm to find a man she hardly knew and dragged him home. A stranger, Knox. So, take yer concern and shove it up yer ducal arse."

He didn't wait for a response. Another minute in the study and he'd lose his mind, what little he had left. He flung open the doors and careened down the terrace steps into the back gardens. By the time he reached the bridge over the ha-ha, he was ready to break into a run. An odd sensation stopped him. He stood, one foot on the bridge, and looked back toward the house. Knox loomed in the open doors. That wasn't what stopped Lachlan. Down the terrace, Lily, her hair around her face, gazed at him. From this distance, he couldn't read her expression. Maybe he didn't want to, but he drew her into his lungs and let her presence filter into his blood because he'd be damned if she didn't steady him better than six pints of stout or a few hours of hot….

Now he really needed to leave—before eagle-eyed Lily spotted exactly how glad he was to see her. *Glad.* When was the last time he was glad? Well, other than the minute his fist connected with Knox's jaw. He glanced back toward the study doors as someone blundered through the gardens toward him. Knox looking for round two?

"You missed your calling, Innes," Danny Arneaux announced as he fought his way through the boxwood hedges. "Should have been a boxer. Damn. I've got limbs up my ass." He reached behind and began to pull twigs and leaves from under his kilt.

"If Abercrombie sees what ye did to those hedges he'll send the head gardener after ye with some clippers, and he won't be going for yer hair."

"At least not the hair on my head. Abercrombie's a damned tattletale. Come on." Danny stepped onto the bridge.

"Where?" Lachlan asked even as he followed the actor across and headed up the path toward the ruins.

"You got beer at your place?"

"Aye."

"Real beer. Not this Regency stuff?" They walked side by side down the path, around the ruins and up the hill toward the fields.

"Tennent's Lager. Regency beer not good?"

"Tastes like ass. And not in a good way."

"Not touching that."

"Smart man. Did you enjoy hitting your brother?"

Lachlan slowed his steps but didn't stop. The sun hung low over the hills at the edge of the sheep fields. Not quite sunset, but close.

"A bit."

"Hmm. How about the duke. Did you enjoy hitting him?"

"They're one and the same."

"I don't think so. Not for you two."

"He's yer friend?"

"Haven't known him that long, but sort of. Knox is, at least. The jury is still out on His Grace."

"Figured that out, did ye?"

"What?"

"Knox is only human when he's Knox. The duke is a bloody robot."

"Who'd you coldcock?"

Danny waited while Lachlan unlocked the cottage and ushered him inside. Leonidas launched himself off the bed with an explosion of sharp barks as he danced around the two of them. Lachlan indicated one of the old horsehair armchairs in front of the fireplace. Arneaux promptly slumped into it and propped his booted feet on the fender. Lachlan stepped into the kitchen and fetched a couple of bottles of Tennent's from the fridge. Once the two of them sat slouched in the chairs with their feet up and their beers open, he waited for the actor to pose his question again.

"Cold beer?" Danny took a long pull on his bottle and exhaled his satisfaction.

"Habit. There's hot and then there's Afghanistan hot."

"Ah. Is Knox too much like your father? Is that the problem?" Arneaux's attention tended to turn on a dime. Lachlan had learned that much about the man at least.

"Nay. He's nothing like our father, thank God. My brother is a Sassenach duke through and through. Stiff upper lip and stick up his arse."

Arneaux choked on his beer. "So that's whose jaw you tried to break? The Sassenach duke?"

Lachlan shrugged. Not because he didn't want to answer, but because he honestly didn't know. He'd never considered if he dealt or even felt differently when it came to the boy he grew up with and the duke his brother became. Oceans of water under that bridge. He did want to know one thing, however. And with Danny Arneaux full of Tennent's Lager and enjoying the heat from the fire blowing up his kilt, Lachlan picked his moment.

"What is it between you and Lily?"

Nothing like throwing a grenade into an attempt at male bonding. Whatever the bloody hell that was. Leonidas climbed into the chair with him and settled half on Lachlan's leg and half on the chair arm. Lachlan rested his hand on the little dog's back.

Danny slid even lower into his chair. The beer bottle dangled from his fingers. "Short story. Sad story. Bad ending." He stared into the flames that licked at the wood and peat in the hearth.

"That's it?" For Lily to hate the man the way she did there had to be more to it than that.

"I see Captain Regency hasn't confiscated your computer." Danny nodded toward Lachlan's desk. "Everything about Lily's life is out there for the world to see."

"Captain Regency?"

"Miss Eleanor Witherspoon. When she took Lily's last cell phone, I thought at least one of them was going to be bitch slapped to Aberdeen and back."

"Nothing on the internet about you and her. I looked."

Danny looked at him askance. "Checking up on her?"

"I didn't really know who she was when I met her."

"Trust me, you could read every word written about her since she first stepped on a sound stage at ten years old, and you still wouldn't know the first thing about her. Not really. Lily Randolph has issues."

"Don't we all," Lachlan muttered.

"Not like her. At least, I hope not." Danny studied him for a moment. He finished off his beer and put the empty bottle next to his chair. "But that's not my story to tell. I don't talk about people behind their backs, especially women." He sat up and clasped his hands between his knees. "I never meant to lead her on, and I never slept with her. Anything else, you'll have to ask her."

Lachlan had learned how to gauge a man. When you trained young men to kill, you damned well better be able to read them. Danny Arneaux told the truth, as much as he could and as he saw it. Truth wasn't always a straight road. Sometimes it wasn't a road at all, just a rocky path with more twists than a Karen Rose thriller.

"Why didn't you sleep with her?"

"Ask her. Got another cold one before I have to go back to the land of Mr. Darcy and warm, nasty beer?"

"Did Regency boot camp turn you into a gentleman?"

Lachlan gathered Leonidas under his arm and went back into the kitchen. He returned with two more bottles of beer. He and Arneaux sat in silence for a while as they drank their beers and warmed themselves by the fire.

"So," Danny said after a while. "What's going on between *you* and Lily?"

Lachlan looked at him. "What's going on between you and Dr. Higgins?"

❧

LILY HAD READ DR. HIGGINS'S REGENCY MANUAL FROM COVER to cover. There was not a single word in it about how to sit through a six-course dinner and not remark on the large multi-colored bruise on a duke's jaw. Eleanor had somehow persuaded the man to dress in period clothes for meals at least. The contrast of his jacked-up jaw against the white of his perfectly tied cravat made the bruise stand out even better. And better was the word. Lachlan had punched his brother in the face after the arrogant assed duke had tried to warn and humiliate Lily with the return of the satchel she'd left in Lachlan's cottage.

Everyone in the drawing room knew it because they'd all scrambled out the terrace doors and sneaked as close as they dared to the study to hear what happened. They hadn't been able to make out much of what was said, but the crack of a fist against flesh was unmistakable—especially after that mousy little romance writer, who'd lurked closest to the doors, had made her mic-dropping completely-out-of-character remark.

"Somebody just knocked the shit out of the duke."

At that, they'd decided to make a haul-ass retreat to the drawing room, where they laughed for at least ten minutes at the writer, her remark, and the idea of anyone hitting their duke. Lily took another forkful of peas to fill her mouth so she wouldn't start laughing again. None of the women at the table looked at each other for the very same reason. Lily was strangely warmed by the thought. She'd never really had female friends. Her mother tended to see other women as rivals, and Lily's experience with other women validated her mother's opinion. Lily's last personal assistant was a case in point.

"More potatoes, miss?" the footman at her elbow asked.

"No, thank you. Perhaps His Grace might care for some. Soft foods are better when one is nursing a jaw injury."

Lily smiled sweetly at the footman, who appeared to have turned to stone. To her right, Teddy Rousseau choked on his wine, spluttering drops all over the antique Irish linen table-cloth. Eleanor Witherspoon stuffed a huge, buttered roll into her mouth. Danny Arneaux sat head down with a hand over his mouth. The other dinner guests broke into a chorus of coughing that made one of Lily's mother's pot parties look like amateur hour.

Through the entire collective attempt at polite reactions to her huge thrown shade, Lily deliberately ignored the duke. Now, however, she had no choice. Every head had turned toward the head of the table where the duke waited for Lily to notice him. Once she did, he slowly raised his wine glass to her in silent salute, his face, as always, fixed in cold seren-ity. Lily lifted her glass and saluted him in response before she took a long draught of the expensive, rich red.

As if by some agreed on signal, the dinner went back to normal. Chatter on Regency approved topics—the weather, sheep, books, fashion. *Shoot me now.* The chatter did give Lily the opportunity to observe her fellow inmates in Regency bootcamp. More to the point, it gave her the chance to watch Danny Arneaux watch Samantha Higgins. Which he did. A lot. Especially when the teacher wasn't looking. He wanted Miss Regency Police. Bad. Had they slept together yet? Hmm. Hard to tell.

"Care to enlighten me, Miss Randolph?" Teddy said.

"Enlighten you about what, Teddy?"

"Why Lord Lachlan felt the need to strike his brother?"

"You'll have to ask him. Or you could always ask His Grace. If you do, let me know." She stood with the other ladies as they prepared to leave the table. "I want to watch."

In a matter of minutes, the ladies were right back where they'd spent most of the day. Sitting in the drawing room drinking tea and talking smack about men.

"I have figured something out," Lily announced as she took the cup of tea Eleanor handed her. "I know why Victorian women wore those ugly, damned bustles."

"Why is that?" the costume mistress asked.

"Because Regency women spent so much time sitting around, their asses spread, and they had to have something to cover up that wide load."

Complete. Silence.

Followed by spluttered tea and screams of laughter. Even Samantha had to laugh. Then they all had to reach for the silk damask napkins to put themselves and the expensive furniture in order before the men joined them.

"When you suggested the duke eat some potatoes, I thought Mr. McGinty would choke on his tongue," Miss Chase said.

"I almost felt sorry for His Grace," Eleanor said. "Almost."

"I felt sorry for the footman," Lily confessed. "He had that deer-in-the-headlights look. I didn't think he was ever going to move."

Soon the conversation moved on to tamer things than teasing a duke. Lily's heart did a little tilt. They all seemed to have so much in common. At the beginning of this little adventure, she didn't give a damn about any of them or about what they thought of her. Lately, she kind of wished to be part Yof the group. Probably just a result of being out of contact with Derek and Raphael and her other friends, few though they might be.

If she decided to be completely honest with herself, with she seldom did, Lily wanted someone to talk to about Lachlan. About how he made her feel. About how scary it was to know he'd gone after his brother for her. She had no idea what was going on between them, and having someone to talk it over with might leave her less confused.

"What's it to be tonight, ladies?" Mr. Sylvan Goode, their Regency dance master asked as he and the other gentlemen entered the room. "Whist or piquet?"

Lily rolled her eyes. The other ladies got up and began to organize pairs for card games. Lily backed toward one of the sets of carved double doors that led out of the drawing room. Weariness dropped over her like a wet blanket. An odd itch started at the back of her neck and wandered around her body. The low neck of her lavender silk gown irritated the hell out of her. She wanted the safety of her room and the comfort of her bed.

"Going somewhere, Lily?"

She spun to face Danny Arneaux. How the hell did he sneak around like a cat after a canary? The man was six and a half feet tall, dammit.

"I am so not in the mood for your shit," she said out the side of her mouth.

"I owe you an apology," Danny whispered in her ear. "I might even grovel."

"I'm listening." A thousand thoughts went through her mind, but at the very front stood Lachlan Innes—which scared the living hell out of her.

"Let's go for a little walk in the greenhouse," Danny said.

Lily hesitated, then nodded. He used a hand on her elbow to guide her to those doors she'd been headed for. With a quick lift of the latch, he had them both in the hallway before anyone even noticed they were gone. He offered her his arm. She didn't take it. They walked down the worn Persian rugs over polished wood floors, down a set of stairs, and finally ended up in the huge glass house that ran the length of one wing of the manor.

Danny held the door, and Lily stepped into the warmest room she'd so far encountered in Scotland. It was like stepping into a lush garden set in Hollywood, except this room was permanent, and had been for hundreds of years. She lengthened her strides and led them deeper into the incredible garden of exotic colors, scents, and shapes. Lily actually liked this part of Rosemount Manor the best. Perhaps because it reminded her of California. Or perhaps because it existed as an incongruous, stubborn creation too determined to be to realize what a miracle it was.

"This isn't a greenhouse, Arneaux. It's called an orangery or a conservatory."

Lily sat on one of those dramatic fainting couches, situated across from a floor-to-ceiling cage full of brightly colored finches. Their little sounds offered a soothing background noise and blended with the various fountains scattered throughout the room. The couch was done in a deep green velvet but was kind of hard despite its soft appearance.

He dropped onto the low stone wall built around a group of flowering camellias. "Looks like my grandmere's greenhouse. A little bigger maybe."

"You mentioned an apology. Get on with it. I have embroidery to do."

"Fine. I owe you an apology. I should never have said anything to you about Lachlan. It's none of my business. The duke shouldn't have asked me to do it, but I should have been man enough to tell him no."

Damn. He was serious. Lily almost felt bad for him.

"Apparently, Lachlan is the only man in Scotland with guts enough to tell His Grace no." Lily fiddled with her silk skirts.

She needed a minute to process Danny Arneaux apologizing to her. She wanted to trust him, but she'd trusted him before, and it had ended in humiliation and the loss of the only parent she'd ever known.

"I'll accept your apology," she finally said as she caught Danny's gaze and held it. "But we both know you don't think I'm good enough for the duke's brother. Just because you won't say anything about it to me doesn't mean you won't run your mouth to Lachlan the way you apparently already have to the duke."

"Haven't said anything to either of them."

"No? How about your Regency coach? Or was that little ladies' hen party about my love life I overheard a figment of my imagination?"

"Shit. I'm sorry, Lily. I was pissed at the time. But I did tell Lachlan I never slept with you." He tugged at his cravat then scratched his ankle.

For a man who spent his life in jeans and loafers with no socks, those stockings had to be killing him. Not to mention the knee breeches. At least she hoped so.

"That is hardly a ringing endorsement," she said. "Typical male—I don't want her, but you can have her."

"Jesus, Lily." He jumped to his feet and ran his hands through his hair. "The guy has been through enough. If I thought you gave a damn about him, I'd have kept my mouth shut completely. He doesn't need his first relationship after what he went through in Afghanistan to be with someone who is guaranteed to break his heart. I know you think we're all heartless bastards, but one or two of us do have feelings, you know."

"What the hell makes you think I'd break his heart?"

So much for his apology. He was just like all the rest. A selfish asshole.

"If you'd been raised by anyone other than your mother, I might not think you'd hurt him."

There it was—pity. His expression said it. His voice oozed with it. Her skin flushed, then went cold. It always did when someone mentioned her mother.

"My mother did the best she could. She raised me to become an Oscar winning actress, in case you forgot."

"How can I forget? You never let me forget it because she never let you forget it." He paced back and forth in front of her. "She did anything she could to keep you in the business, including pimping you out to me for a damned role in a movie. Was I the first guy she tried that with or the last?"

"Fuck you." Lily jumped to her feet and tried to go back up the little path through the orangery.

"We already had that discussion." He stepped in front of her. "And we're going to finish this discussion for good."

"There's nothing to discuss. You led me on, pretended to be interested in me, then dumped me. I was the biggest joke in Hollywood for weeks."

"I thought you needed a friend," he all but shouted. "Your mother was a damned shark. She made Joan Crawford look like Mother Teresa, and we all knew it."

"You disappeared without a word."

"I sent you a letter, dammit."

"You left me to deal with the fallout," she shot back, but in the back of her mind she wondered *letter?* as she added, "And the next time she told me to sleep with someone for a part, he expected it because you didn't say a damned word to deny I'd slept with you. I had to make the decision to go through with it or to fire my mother. All by myself. It would have been nice to have had one person in my damned corner for all of that."

Stupid. Stupid. Stupid.

Lily didn't want him to feel sorry for her. She didn't want him to feel anything at all. She wanted him off this film.

"It doesn't matter anymore," she continued. "If Wentworth has any sense, he'll cut you and find someone capable of an Oscar worthy performance to play Captain Rothgate. But you go find your Regency coach and give it your best shot. I'm done with you." She turned and dashed toward the main house.

Danny chased after her. "You got an Oscar for playing a sad, compassionate lonely, abused little girl. Wasn't much of a stretch, was it, Lily?"

She rounded on him so quickly he almost ran into her. He skidded to a stop and grabbed her arms to keep from bowling her over.

"What do you want from me?" she demanded.

"You've had all the compassion beaten out of you, Lily. It's a shame because you'll need it to play Rothgate's wife. But you'll really need it if you stand a snowball's chance in hell of any kind of decent relationship with Lachlan Innes. Because that's something you damned sure can't fake." He brushed past her and headed for the French doors into the manor.

"Why a letter?" she called after him. She never got a letter that her mother didn't read first—which told her all she needed to know about his letter's fate. "Why not an email or a text?"

He stopped, his hand on the double door latches. He turned and leaned against the doors. "My mom. She always said the important stuff deserved a letter. Something about someone going to all that trouble made you want to read it. The mystery of the sealed envelope, or something like that. Emails and texts can be deleted and ignored. With a letter, there's a better chance someone will read it before they tear it up." He shrugged. "Decide what you really want, Lily, if you can. You deserve to be happy, just like anyone else. Just figure out what or who is going to do it for you. 'Cause I sure as hell don't have any idea what it's going to take."

He was out the doors and down the hall before she knew it. One day she'd persuade him to teach her how to slip in and out of a room like a damned ghost.

Ghost.

Lachlan wasn't the only one fighting ghosts. Lily had her own to deal with, and Danny Arneaux was one of them. She hoped maybe Lachlan had dealt with one of his when he socked his brother in the jaw. For her. She needed to find out.

Chapter Eleven

THIS WAS A HUGE MISTAKE. LILY HADN'T MADE A MISTAKE LIKE this since…well, she didn't have an exact date, but her last such error in judgement had Danny Arneaux's name written all over it—which should have had a don't-do-this-warning with a capital D on it for her.

Why the hell did Regency evening gowns have forty damned yards of fabric in them? Lily stopped in the middle of the pebbled path and wrapped even more of her skirts around her free hand. Free, because she held her flashlight in the other hand, from which wrist still dangled her ridiculous little silk purse. Her reticule or *ridicule*, as Lily called it. Not quite midnight and her Cinderella ass had a helluva time between the dress that tried to trip her and the evening slippers that kept her feet in a constant state of pain and about to slip right out from under her any minute. She should have taken the time to change clothes or at least to put on some real shoes.

If you'd gone back to your room, you never would have left it.

That wasn't completely true. She would have left her room eventually. Just not tonight, and she definitely would not be wandering around the estate in the middle of the night in fricking winter. At least it wasn't raining. Not yet, anyway. She didn't even have a shawl to wrap around her shoulders, bared by the off the shoulder neckline of the light lavender gown Emma had strapped her into before dinner. Lily had no idea where she'd left her shawl—the dining room, the drawing room, the conservatory? She'd held onto the little purse for a reason. The shawl, however, hadn't even merited an afterthought. Until now.

Great!

Now she'd have to worry someone would find the shawl and come to her room to return it. She'd burn that bridge when she came to it. Nobody would believe she'd gone down to the library to find a book to read. Lily had cultivated her image as a carefree fashionista with no other interests than shopping, lattes, and the state of her nails to the point everyone believed it. Sometimes even she believed it. Life hummed along with a lot less trouble that way.

Speaking of trouble.

The wind blew the faint but familiar scent of lavender and heather around her. She'd reached the ruins and the tower, and the wind followed her along the path by the loch. Lily wrapped her arms around herself and walked a little faster. A weird tingle danced along the back of her neck. Intermittent crunches echoed on the path behind her. She stopped. Took a deep breath. Then turned to look back the way she'd come. A light flickered in the window at the top of the tower. *What the hell?* A feminine sigh sounded in the darkness just past the point where Lily could see. Then soft laughter, laughter she'd previously heard along the corridors of Rosemount Manor, floated across the loch toward the far shore.

"Screw this," Lily muttered as she started back toward the

manor. The wind practically slapped her in the face. "O...kaay."

She hesitated and glanced back over her shoulder toward Lachlan's cottage, then took a deep breath, turned, and began to power walk toward his home. Getting across the fields was bad enough. To climb the hill, she had to fight her dress and still try to keep hold of her flashlight. Her shoes had become two dew-soaked lumps of satin tied to her legs by ribbons that had started to cut off her circulation. The last several yards, she used her hands to pull herself up a knee-high rock wall around Lachlan's little front yard, or garden as the Brits called it.

Whatever her original reason for traipsing across the estate in the bitter cold, right now, all Lily wanted was to get someplace warm. She pushed the little gate open and marched up the path. The sound of Leonidas's sharp little barks made her smile. No sneaking up on that little guy. The door opened, and a furry missile scurried out to slam into her legs.

"Hello, Leo." She scooped him into her arms where he began to lick every bit of her makeup from her face.

"Lily?" Lachlan stood in the doorway, head bent to avoid hitting the top of the frame. "Are ye daft, woman? It's freezing. Get in the house." He strode out with a heavy wool blanket in his hands, wrapped it around her, then practically carried her and the dog into the cottage. He shoved her into a chair in front of the fireplace. Leonidas settled in the chair beside her, his head rested on her thigh. "Why are ye here?"

"You ask me that every time you see me. Is this the start of a philosophical discussion or do you really not want to see me?" She put her hands on the arms of the chair and started to get up.

"Sit." He knelt on the braided rug and began to rummage under her dress and petticoats.

"I am not a dog, Lord Hardass."

"The dog isn't larking about in the middle of a Highland winter dressed for a fancy ball." He ran his hands up her leg and untied the ribbons around her calf, then did the same to the other leg. She sighed in relief. Her legs prickled at the return of circulation.

The slippers he peeled off her feet were nearly black with dirt and damp. He placed them on the hearth then took her left foot in his hand and rubbed it between his big, calloused hands. Those rough spots on his palms wreaked havoc with her delicate silk stockings, but dear God they were heaven on her icy feet. She closed her eyes and settled back into the chair. The heat from the fireplace seeped into her bones, and the scent of oak and peat flowed over her.

That wasn't the only scent. *Lachlan.* Evergreens, rain, and sandalwood soap.

His hair was damp. He was shirtless with a pair of black sweatpants riding low on his hips. Barefoot. It seemed he'd just gotten out of the shower. His body radiated a sauna-like heat. His breath was sweet and sharp like mint chocolate chip ice cream?

"Pardon?" He stopped rubbing her feet and glanced up at her.

Damn! She'd said that out loud. If that wasn't bad enough, her feet started to get cold, and the fabulous sensation his hands created on her skin began to dissipate. She wiggled her toes. He took the hint.

"I hope you had more than mint chocolate chip ice cream for dinner." Holy guacamole he was a magician. A few more minutes of this, and she'd be asleep, or wrapped tightly around him.

"Had some beef jerky too," he muttered as he rested his hands on her knees under her dress. "These stockings have to come off."

"Okay." Her voice caught, and her heart kicked into overdrive.

Their eyes met, held. He took a deep breath, then tossed the front skirt of her dress into her lap so quickly that Lily jumped. He studied the tied garters for a minute, flicked a look up at her again, and went to work untying the ribbons that held up her stockings. He rolled each stocking slowly down her leg and tugged it off her foot. The flashlight and little purse slid to the floor.

Lily watched the firelight play on his body as, still on his knees, he shook out the stockings and hung them over the back of the chair opposite the one she occupied. When he twisted away from her, she cut off a gasp. His back, a work of art with beautifully defined muscles, was marred by several horrific scars that slashed across his ribs and splattered across one shoulder in a deep, puckered starburst pattern. Unable to stop herself, she reached out and covered the one on his shoulder with her palm.

Lachlan stilled. His skin hummed with a fevered heat and energy. Inch by inch, he relaxed into her touch. He didn't look at her but continued to smooth out her stockings as if he had to arrange them just so in order for them to dry. She waited.

"Shrapnel," he finally said. "From a roadside bomb."

She drew her fingertips slowly down and across to the deep furrows across his ribcage.

"Machine gun fire. Strafed me while I was trapped face down on a street in Kabul." He turned. She dropped her hand as he moved on his knees and stopped directly in front of her. He placed his hands on her bare knees. "Why did you come?"

Lily picked up his right hand and traced her forefinger across his bruised knuckles. He flinched when she touched a spot where the skin was torn. "You hit your brother. Because of me."

"Hit him because of him. He's an *arse*."

She tilted her head to one side.

"He had no right to say anything about ye." Lachlan leaned closer, his eyes locked with hers. "Not to Arneaux, not to anyone."

"It doesn't matter."

Her heart clenched, then started to pound against her ribs. He dropped his gaze to her lips. His chest rose and fell in one powerful breath.

"Aye. It does."

He reached out and sifted his hands through her ridiculous hairdo. Antique hairpins and combs tumbled into her lap like rain. She watched his mouth, the memory of their first kiss lured her like every temptation she'd ever fought. And lost.

"Lily?" he whispered, so close to her the dampness of his skin brushed against her cheek. A request? A prayer? A plea?

She closed her eyes and offered the only amen she knew. "Aye."

His lips touched hers. Gently at first. An exploration of suffusing warmth and a softness that surprised her. A mouth often drawn tight and hard was suddenly cloud soft and shivery sweet. She gasped, and he put his arms around her and begged entrance with tiny flicks and caresses of his tongue. He sank into her and she into him. Lily slid her palms up his chest and around his neck. His hair, so thick, long, and silky proved the perfect distraction for her hands. She wanted to touch him everywhere, but dear God, when a man kissed like Lachlan Innes, any distraction had to be a sin.

Her body went limp as she slid from the chair to her knees and molded herself to him. Lachlan leaned back and cradled her against him as he pressed his palms to her cheeks and angled her head to plunder her mouth more fully. Lily couldn't breathe, and she didn't care. She existed inside the flame that was this man, and still, she wanted more. So much so that when he drew back enough to trail kisses down her throat, she whimpered at the loss—until he skimmed his teeth up the side of her neck and nipped at her earlobe. Continuous shivers raced through her. He scorched a trail of kisses and tiny bites down to the spot where her neck slid into her collarbone. How did he know? Every touch there made her jump and her nerves fire.

He skated his hands into the neckline of her gown and slid it down to reveal her breasts pushed up by the abbreviated stays Emma had strapped her into a few hours ago. Lachlan shoved the plain cotton fabric away and ran his thumb across her nipple. Lily moaned as he lowered his head and ran his tongue around the taut bunch of nerves. He drew her breast into his mouth, licking and teasing as he sucked. Lily held his head to her and reveled in the sensations rioting through her. He freed her other breast and stroked the underside with his forefinger. Every touch reached the point between her legs that already ached in anticipation.

He released her breast, pressed one last tender kiss to her nipple, and sighed as he rested his forehead against her collarbone. "We cannae do this."

"Why?" she asked in a tone just shy of a wail.

He mumbled something against the top of her breast. She stroked his hair and bit her lip in frustration. "What?"

"I…havnae been with a woman in a long time."

"Could have fooled me."

He huffed a short laugh and raised his head. He kissed her. Hard.

"I dinnae have any protection dammit."

Something warm and sweet settled around her heart.

She'd never tell him of the men who'd hadn't even given protection a thought let alone forced themselves to stop in consideration of it. Lachlan wanted her, unless that thick baseball bat that had suddenly appeared in his sweatpants was a figment of her imagination.

Lily brushed an open-mouthed kiss across his lips. She flicked her tongue out to trace the outline of his mouth, then delved inside to lick the roof and insides of his cheeks. His chest rose and fell. She broke the kiss, leaned to the side, and fished around the puddle of silk skirts pooled around her on the fireside rug. Once she found the little silk purse, she paused to nip at the glorious muscles along his ribcage.

Lachlan growled and wrapped his arms around her like an iron band, and Lily was pathetic enough to soak in the hypnotic glow the arms of a man like Lachlan produced before she held the reticule up between them. His brow furrowed in confusion. Lily opened the bag and showed him the contents—three gold, foil-wrapped condoms.

"The ever-efficient Miss Witherspoon put a box in every bedchamber. She said if modern house parties were anything like Regency house parties, she wanted us to be prepared. I tucked a few in here before I came down to dinner. Just in case."

"Ye came here to seduce me." His face became completely unreadable.

"May I remind you, you kissed me. After you had your hands up my skirt undressing me?" Her stomach sank. She dropped the little purse to the floor. "But if you've changed your mind…."

He grabbed the bag and tossed it onto the bed in the corner of the sitting room. "I haven't changed my mind about taking ye to bed since the moment I met ye."

For the first time in her life, Lily didn't know what to say.

He got to his feet and dragged her up with him. "Don't ye

dare apologize or say something flip. Ye are a gloriously sexy woman, Lily Randolph. Any man would have to be half dead not to want ye."

"I don't want just any man," she said softly. She meant it. She'd never wanted any man the way she wanted Lachlan, and not just in bed.

"Tell me what ye want, Lily. I'll move heaven and earth to be sure ye have it." He brushed her hair, which had come completely loose from her coiffure, away from her face.

"You. All I want is you." In her bed. That was all she meant. Anything else was…. Oh!

Lachlan swept her into his arms and crossed the room to the bed. He lowered her to the floor, allowing her body to slide down his. He hissed slightly when her hip brushed against his cock. It only took a second for him to go to the door, lock it, and turn out the electric lights. The room was small enough the light from the large fireplace bathed everything in a golden glow.

Suddenly, he stood in front of her. He brushed his hands across her bare shoulders and down her arms. The faint scrape of his calloused palms raised goose bumps everywhere he touched. She shivered. Her nipples tightened. He saw it happen and covered her breasts with his hands, then he touched his forehead to hers.

"Are ye—"

She cut him off with a kiss. Lily rose on her toes and cupped his face in her hands. She sucked his bottom lip into her mouth and teased it with her tongue. A little fissure of delight danced through her as she slid her mouth across the abrasive temptation of his stubbled cheek—the stubble there despite him probably having shaved that morning. The soft spot directly under his chin proved irresistible. With her hands on either side of her face, she tilted his head down to kiss his eyelids, eyebrows, nose, and the corner of his mouth.

"Take me to bed, Lachlan."

"Aye." His deep voice broke, rough and harsh.

He pulled her against his chest and reached around to undo the back of her dress. She pressed a kiss to the puckered scar just below his collarbone, then rubbed her palms up his ribcage and slid them around to cover his nipples. When her nails scraped across his pecs, he growled so deeply in his chest the vibrations shot through her palms, down her arms, and across her breasts.

"Damn," he muttered as he dealt with fasteners and tapes and— "Pins. There are bloody pins in this dress."

Lily laughed. "Welcome to the Regency."

"No wonder the men fought duels. Women's dresses were booby-trapped."

He finally loosened the bodice of the dress enough to slide it to her waist. Once he did, he knelt to tug the yards and yards of the ball gown over her hips and down to her feet. He gazed up at her. She was naked except for the half corset thing, her stays, positioned so her bare breasts were held up like some pagan offering. He reached behind her to untie the laces.

"Leave it," she murmured as he pressed his lips to the inside of her thigh. "Please."

"Why?"

"It's the one part of Regency dress I like. Makes my boobs look…sexier."

She hoped like hell her full body blush didn't show in the light from the fire. Instinctually, she lifted her hands to cover herself. Lachlan captured her wrists and rose slowly to stand, brushing his body against hers. He kissed her palms and placed them on his shoulders. Determination shone in his eyes and showed in the clench of his jaw. He had the stays unlaced in seconds, pulled them away and tossed them to the floor.

"There is nothing on earth with the power to make yer breasts more gloriously erotic than they are, Lily Randolph. I'll murder the man who says otherwise."

Never had a man looked at her as Lachlan did in that moment—fierce, certain, passionate, primitive, and sexy enough to have her body throbbing to screw him into a coma. He lowered his head and drew his tongue across the top of one breast. Lily shivered, a full body shiver that echoed through every nerve before it settled on the wet and ready entrance to her core.

He drew one nipple between his lips and sucked hard. Lily gasped and clasped her hands to the sides of his head. Suddenly, he lifted her and laid her across the thick quilts on top of his bed. His worship of her breasts took her breath away—soft caresses with his roughened fingertips, and long, deep velvety kisses before he moved up her body to possess her mouth again. He'd shed his sweatpants, and Lily wrapped her legs around him. Then he dragged his cock across her labia and made just enough contact with her clitoris to send her into spasms of anticipation.

"Lachlan!"

Propped on his elbows, he brushed the hair from her face, already damp with sweat. "Are ye certain?" he murmured, his tone even despite the swift movement of his chest against her breasts. "We can stop right now and—"

She grabbed a handful of his long, sleek hair with one hand. With the other, she patted around on the bed, found the little bag, and opened it. "Ye stop now, and I'll murder ye in yer sleep, Lachlan Innes."

He laughed—whether at her or her attempt at a Scot's accent, she neither knew nor cared. His laugh was dark, deep, sexy as hell, and it pressed his rock-hard abs against her belly and his groin against hers. She whipped one of the condoms out of the little silk bag and attempted to tear it open with her teeth. Dammit! Her hand shook, and the muscles in her jaw weren't strong enough.

Lachlan bent to take the foil wrapper between his teeth while Lily held it. She plucked the condom free and tried to sit up and reach for his cock at the same time. He rose on his hands and watched, his eyes hot and heavy-lidded as she rolled the condom down his cock before she squeezed and got in a few purposeful strokes. He arched his back and groaned.

"No more," he gasped. "I've been dreaming of this since I saw you standing in the moonlight in the gardens that first night."

Lily lifted her hips in invitation, and he fit himself to her entrance before he plunged inside in one swift, powerful stroke. They gasped in tandem and arched into each other to the point their hipbones clashed.

Lily planted her feet on either side of his thighs and ground her hips against him. He withdrew halfway, and her body protested the loss of his thick length. After a few strokes, they caught a glorious rhythm that hit Lily's every erogenous zone with an erotic accuracy she'd never dreamed possible. She dug her nails into the magnificent taut muscles of his back. He hissed and leaned into her embrace. He brought her to the very edge over and over, only to stop mid-stroke before she fell, and she had to search her mind for words to beg him to let her come before her heart exploded out of her chest.

"Lachlan," she gasped.

She squeezed her eyes shut, and the scent of sex, of him, the clean quilts, and even the rain washed over her. Searing heat soaked into her skin everywhere their bodies joined, and her nerves fired with sensations so sharp they stung. On a soft moan, she opened her eyes, and there he was, this beautiful man, his face awash with a restrained joy, but his gaze fixed on her face as if she knew the answer to some vital question. She didn't have the power to look away. A little smile teased at one side of his mouth.

"There you are," he murmured. "My Lily." He quickened his strokes. Lily threw her legs around him. "Stay with me, Lily. Stay with me."

The orgasm roared through her like flames in a brush fire. She didn't care if she burned to ashes, she wanted it to go on forever. She held on even when her muscles turned to jelly. Lachlan's gaze never left hers until he finally threw back his head and shouted her name. Even then his body continued to thrust into hers over and over until, as if by some mutual hand, they collapsed into each other, bodies slick and sated, going from hot as hell to shivery cold. Lachlan managed to drag one of the quilts over them. He raised his head just enough to kiss her so softly and gently tears sprang to her eyes.

She'd been having sex since she was sixteen years old. She'd fucked, screwed, and everything in between, but she'd never made love. Until now.

This was bad, really bad. And she wanted to do it again as soon as possible. She would. As soon as she awakened from the addictive lure of this man's arms, the soul-deep comfort of his chest beneath her cheek, and from the hypnotic pleasure of his hand in her hair and his lips against her forehead. How the hell could a woman even think of crawling out of his bed? Or out of his life?

❧

Lily was half asleep, but she knew the difference between Lachlan's kisses and Leonidas's expression of affection. She raised her hand and scratched the little dog behind his ear, which was enough to distract him from cleaning her face. She eased her way out of Lachlan's arms and sat up to squint at the clock on the mantel. Nearly five in the morning. They'd slept for several hours. Well, sort of.

They'd used the second of her condoms after Lachlan had shocked her out of a sound sleep with his tongue between her legs, coaxing a mind-shattering orgasm out of her before she was even fully awake. The third condom came in handy after Lily returned the favor, but not before Lachlan, propped on his elbows, watched her lick and suck his cock to the point he grabbed her with a growl and shoved the condom on just before he lowered her onto his erection, so slowly they both moaned until they were hoarse.

Even now, Lachlan lay sprawled across the bed on his stomach with one arm stretched across the spot where she'd lain. Unable to resist, Lily leaned over to kiss the starburst scar on his shoulder. He stirred a bit, then settled. Leonidas burrowed under the covers to rest on Lachlan's feet.

Lily padded around the room and gathered the various pieces of her clothing. Somehow, she managed to wiggle into all of it but the stays and the stockings. The tie at the neck of the back of her silk gown gave her some trouble, but she tightened it enough to hold the dress up. Emma might have to cut the knot out and have the costume people put a new ribbon on it. Her evening slippers were dry, but stiff and not too clean. She slid them on and half-assed tied the ribbons around her ankles. The sun had not come up, but Lily didn't want to chance getting caught sneaking into the house even in the gray light of dawn.

With her stockings, little silk purse, and flashlight in one hand, and several yards of dress skirts and her stays in the other, she watched Lachlan sleep as long as she dared, then finally slipped out the door. She made it out the gate and up the narrow lane before she looked back at the little cottage. Smoke still wafted from the chimney. She hurried around the loch. A heavy mist floated on top of the water like whipped cream on an ice cream sundae. The wind blew cold off the water, but hardly disturbed the mist at all. That odd scent—heather, lavender, and fresh earth swirled around her.

"Hello?"

Lily rolled her eyes. She was talking to the wind now? She broke into a sort of half-run half-power walk. For some odd reason, she glanced up at the tower as she skirted the ruins toward the path to the ha-ha. A light shone in the top tower window. Weird. Worse, there were lights on in the bottom floor of the tower as well. Lachlan had told her his brother kept a private office in the tower, a place to escape the activity in the main house since all the "tourists" had arrived.

"Shit," she muttered as she tip-toed past the tower.

The last thing she needed was for Duke High and Mighty to catch her sneaking back to the house after a night of crazy, wonderful sex with his brother. The brother who had punched him to defend her. A flutter of feminine laughter sounded behind her. *Oh, hell's bells!* Lily couldn't decide which might be worse—turning around to see the supposed Innes Witch behind her or turning around to see the Duke of Innes giving her the death glare for screwing his baby brother.

The creak of a door opening settled it for her. She ducked around the corner of a crumbled wall next to the tower.

"Fine. Have it your way," a familiar female voice declared. "I'll be damned if I ask you again, *Your Grace.*"

A door slam and footsteps on the pebbled path had Lily slinking deeper into the darkness, but not so far that she didn't see Eleanor Witherspoon stomp past dressed in Regency nightclothes. Thin. Muslin. Nightclothes. She also carried that damned velvet bag with all the confiscated cell phones in it.

What was Eleanor doing with the duke, in his tower, in

the middle of the night? That eerie laughter sounded somewhere behind her. Lily peeked around the wall then scurried across to the lawn that led to the bridge into the back gardens. She reached the first row of hedges and made the mistake of looking back. Standing in the middle of the path, in the full light from the open door of his tower, the Duke of Innes acknowledged her with a nod.

Lily looked past him at the figure standing behind him. A woman in simple medieval looking clothes with her head bowed.

"Good morning, Miss Randolph," the duke said in his snotty British accent.

The woman behind him raised her head. She looked exactly like Eleanor. But Eleanor had already gone back to the house.

Lily took a faltering step backwards. "Who the hell—" She dropped the clothes, purse, and flashlight, whirled, and ran like hell for the main house.

Chapter Twelve

As he came out of the delicious fog left over from several hours of truly deep sleep, Lachlan admitted the hyper-awareness that came with PTSD offered a singular advantage. Someone was in his house, someone distinctly *not* Lily. Someone who used the fire poker like a cudgel to try and beat the flames into existence. He didn't want to roll over. Not yet. The bed was warm and smelled of Lily and sex. Beneath the flannel sheets and heavy quilts, a sort of kingdom of comfort existed, in his mind at least. He didn't want to leave.

Horace cologne.

Damn!

Lachlan rolled over so quickly, Leonidas yipped and scrambled out from under the covers to stand at the edge of the mattress in search of the intruder. A fierce protector until the little traitor saw Knox seated in the worn horsehair chair in front of the hearth. Leonidas had distinguished tastes in friends. Anyone who had ever scratched his ears, rubbed his belly, or fed him even a morsel of food was a friend. Knox dangled a piece of bacon from his fingertips.

Leonidas leapt from the bed and had the bacon in his mouth in a heartbeat.

"How'd ye get in?" Lachlan asked as he sat up and swung his legs over the side of his bed.

"Your door was unlocked." Knox nodded toward Lachlan's desk. "Mrs. Gordon sent breakfast." A large silver cloche sat on the corner of the desk.

"Thanks. Bye."

Lachlan bent over to fish around the floor and find his sweatpants. Once he did, he flung back the covers, then stood to drag them on over his naked arse before he shuffled to the chair in front of his computer, the chair that faced away from his brother's stony scrutiny. He lifted the cloche and scooped some eggs onto an oatcake. Once he added several strips of bacon, he slapped another oatcake on top and began to eat.

"You've put on some weight," Knox observed. "And you look like you've been sleeping better."

Lachlan grunted in response and took another bite of his food. He noticed the thermos next to the cloche. A quick blind search of the desk's surface turned up a chipped and stained teacup. He opened the thermos, but before he could pour the steaming Earl Grey into the teacup, a clean mug appeared from over his shoulder. He took the mug and filled it from the thermos.

"Why are ye here?" he asked, still unwilling to face his brother.

"Mrs. Gordon asked me to deliver your breakfast."

"Pull my other leg. It's got bells on it." Lachlan took a sip of his tea and another bite of his makeshift sandwich.

Knox actually laughed. Briefly, but he did laugh. Lachlan finally spun his chair around to face the fireplace. Then he wished he hadn't. Seated in the chair with one booted foot propped on his knee, Knox, dressed like every English lord who walked the halls of Parliament, held Lily's carefully folded stays and stockings.

Lachlan snatched the articles from his brother's hand, tugged open the bottom desk drawer, dropped Lily's clothes inside, then slammed it shut.

"If ye'r done digging around my home for other people's possessions, ye can go back to intimidating the villagers and shagging the help."

"That was our father, not me."

"How the devil would ye know? Ye left before the old bastard really got going." He swallowed hard. He didn't want to do this. Not now. "I was here the entire time. For the tarts, the whores, the drugs, the bloody phone calls to come and fetch him from the pub or from the police station after some husband beat him bloody." Lachlan couldn't breathe. Where the hell had that come from? He jumped up and nearly knocked the desk chair over. "Let yersel' out." He started toward the corridor to the bedrooms.

Knox stood and grabbed Lachlan's arm. "Wait."

"For what, Knox?" Lachlan stared at his brother, tried to see some hint of feeling in the man's face. Nothing. "It doesn't matter. I'm fine." He glanced down at his brother's hand on his arm.

"It does matter." Knox let go of him. "I'm well aware of… what I left you with and why you ran away to the Army as soon as you could."

Lachlan's nerves fired all at once. His skin threatened to crawl off down the corridor and leave him a naked corpse of meat and blood. He didn't want to talk about this, not with Knox. Not with the glow of his night with Lily still coursing through his veins.

Knox reached out to him. Lachlan raised his hands to fend him off.

"I need ye to leave, Knox. I need to…get to the mews. Yer

Miss Witherspoon expects me to put on a show for her little camp next week."

"You don't have to. Miss Witherspoon is not *my* anything, but I'll tell her to leave you be."

"Like ye told Lily to leave me be? It's a little late to play the concerned older brother. I survived Afghanistan. I can survive an American actress."

It was all he could do not to clench his fists. He wanted to hit someone, and Knox was the perfect target. Even if His Grace's chin still wore the marks of his last attempt to set their relationship straight.

"She's been engaged at least half a dozen times, Lachlan." Knox's pitying gaze twisted Lachlan's stomach.

He was suddenly so damned tired. "Fuck ye, Knox. Get out. Don't break into my house again. Nobody's here to watch ye pretend to be concerned about yer dicked in the nob brother."

The windows across the front of the cottage rattled in protest against a sudden gust of wind. A quick scent of lavender and heather brushed across Lachlan's face. He met his brother's gaze, stunned. The duke actually looked startled. Like something out of a childhood memory, the two of them slowly perused the room, muscles tense in expectation. As quickly as the scent arrived, it was gone.

Knox bent down and scratched Leonidas's ears, then strode to the cottage door, opened it, and stepped through, his head bent beneath the low-slung door jamb.

"I didn't break in. The door was unlocked. You might want to tell the young lady to lock it behind herself. Then tell her not to drop her underwear on the path outside the tower. Next time, someone less discreet might find it."

"Showing up in my house and rubbing my nose in it is not discreet. It's ye being an arrogant shite, and ye know it."

Knox stepped out into the little front garden of the

cottage and strode to the gate. Lachlan stood in the doorway, unable to think of what to say. His brother had scrambled the hell out of his brain.

"I am sorry, Lachlan," Knox said, and something very like sadness flitted across his face. "I truly am. For everything."

"Over and done, Yer Grace. No worries." Lachlan braced his hands in the doorway. He watched his brother start up the path toward the tower. "Knox," he called.

Knox looked over his shoulder, his face stony except for a raised eyebrow. Something he knew Lachlan always found funny.

"Is she back?" It was almost worth it to see the unshake-able duke go half a shade pale.

"She?"

"This is me, brother. Ye were in that room. Ye smelled her on the breeze, same as I. The Innes Witch—"

"Is a story they told us to keep us from wandering the fields at night. The most dangerous women in our lives are the living ones dressed in costume eating breakfast in my formal dining room this morning."

A fierce rush of wind howled across the fields and sawed between them.

"Bullshite. You don't believe that any more than I do." Lachlan rubbed his hands up and down his bare arms against the sudden cold. "I didn't see her, but I lived through the same childhood you did. Denying it doesn't make it a fairy tale."

"Yes, but I'm the one who was beaten and punished and sent away for believing in ghosts. You denied the existence of the Innes Witch for years. Now you believe?"

"I don't know. Ye'r the only one who saw her, who spoke to her."

"Ask yer girlfriend. She saw something that made her

drop her clothes and run for Rosemount like the devil was after her."

In a few quick strides, Knox was out of sight and out of earshot.

"Bloody hell," Lachlan muttered.

He ran both hands through his hair, stepped back into his cottage, and slammed the door. Leonidas stood on the desk chair and helped himself to the remains of Lachlan's breakfast.

Lachlan shook his head. "Don't tell Mrs. Gordon."

He sat on the bed and dragged Lily's pillow across his chest. He buried his face in the soft folds of the simple cotton pillowcase and feather pillow. Gardenias. With a lung-filling sigh, he fell back across the bed, the pillow still clutched to his chest.

"She's been engaged at least half a dozen times, Lachlan."

What did it matter? He wasn't involved with Lily with an eye toward marriage or anything else long term. A roadside bomb in Fallujah had ended all of that as far as he was concerned. The fact the Innes Witch only appeared when a love affair was doomed had absolutely nothing to do with the cold chills that ran through his body or the crippling tension that wrapped around his chest like a vise.

Damn Knox. Lachlan already had questions about Lily slithering around in his head. Questions he'd decided he didn't need to know the answers for in order to continue whatever was going on between Lily and him. He didn't want to know. Cowardly? Maybe. Self-preserving? Hell yes. All of which made him little better than his brother when it came to judging Lily.

He should never have slept with her—and he'd sell his soul to sleep with her again. He covered his face with her pillow and screamed into it so loudly and so long Leonidas jumped on the bed to check on him. Lachlan sat up and scratched his furry companion on the butt with one hand while he scrubbed his own face with the other. A quick glance at the mantel clock told him he needed to get a quick shower and get on with his day in a hurry. He had a phaeton driving lesson with Lily in less than an hour. All he had to do was decide when to return her underwear. Then ask her why at least six men hadn't been able to steal her heart.

"What the bloody hell am I doing?" he asked as he got up and stumbled down the corridor to his bathroom.

Falling in love, you fool.

"YOU SHOULDN'T HAVE GIVEN THEM THEIR HEADS." LACHLAN gripped the back of the phaeton bench for dear life.

The carriage fairly flew down the narrow country lane between the village and Rosemount Manor. One turn taken too quickly, and they'd all end up in a ditch or worse. The faint rumble of thunder behind them caused his heart to stutter for a few beats. Then Lily laughed and glanced at him, her eyes bright and her face alight with sheer joy. Her bonnet had fallen back and to the side, held on by the ribbon tied under one side of her jaw. Her tiny, gloved hands held the reins and guided the team as if she'd been doing it for years.

Just the sight of her having such fun eased the tension in his chest. Other parts of his body tightened, but he'd ignore those. For now. Rain splattered at their backs and soon surrounded them in a gentle downpour. They raced through the iron gates at the entrance to the estate. The rattle of wheels on the cobblestone drive competed with the increased patter of rain. Lily reached over and squeezed Lachlan's leg.

"Isn't this amazing?"

"More amazing with two hands on the reins." He picked

up her hand and tangled it in the leather strips that were the only thing between the two of them and broken necks. "Try to slow them down."

"What do you mean, try?" She sat up, all indignant affronted woman, and worked to bring the team back under control.

"It's raining and they're headed for home." He tried not to sound smug. *Tried* being the operative word.

Something about Lily made him lighter, more amused by simple things. Alive. They raced through a rainstorm in a two-hundred-year-old carriage with a team in the traces on the verge of running away with them. For two years he'd avoided risk like the plague. Quiet, dull, and uneventful had become his daily routine. Yet today, he risked his life to see Lily smile.

She pulled back on the reins in increments, just as he'd taught her. "You might have told me," she groused between gritted teeth. She tossed him a glare.

He offered her his most bland expression. "I did."

He propped one foot on his knee and stretched his arms across the back of the driver's bench. With luck, she wouldn't notice the white-knuckle grip he used to keep himself from flying off the seat next to her.

She managed to slow the horses from a full gallop to a fast canter as they took the turn toward the front of Rose-mount Manor. Two women in Regency dress, complete with face-hiding bonnets, ran toward the house. Lachlan saw the huge puddle they'd have to skirt to get around the fountain and reach the double doors that Abercrombie, Knox's snooty butler, held open for them. Maybe Lily didn't see it.

The phaeton headed right for the puddle. It was hard to tell, but Lachlan suspected the two women clumsily running in their long dresses were Elle and Dr. Higgins. When he realized Lily had steered the phaeton in line with the puddle, he didn't suspect. He knew. He leaned forward and dropped his propped foot to the carriage floor.

"Lily, do you really—"

Splash!

Shriek!!

"What the hell!" Samantha shouted.

Lachlan turned on the bench to see the two women snatch off their drowned bonnets and make some very un-Regency-like gestures toward the phaeton that now headed for the stables at a speed just below breakneck. He'd never actually seen that much water shoot quite that high before today. The last thing he saw as they rounded the house toward the stable gate was the two ladies slogging toward Abercrombie who, completely out of character, stood in the doors with his mouth hanging open.

"Oh my God, did you see their faces?" Lily bounced on the seat as she reined in the horses and steered them into the stable yard.

"Through the wall of water you tossed up? Not bloody likely."

Lachlan found himself torn between admiration for her driving skill and horror at what she'd done. The line between harmless prank and deliberate cruelty was a thin one.

Once the phaeton came to a halt, Urquhart's lads swarmed out of the main stable block and set to unhitching the horses and rolling the carriage into the carriage house where they would check it for damage and wipe it down. Lachlan jumped down from the bench, then turned to help Lily. She propped her hands on his shoulders, a smile on her face, though uncertainty shone in her eyes. He grabbed her around the waist and allowed her body to brush against his as he lowered her to the ground.

"Was that necessary?" he whispered in her ear.

"Definitely," she replied.

"Why?"

The rain was really coming down now. Lily's hair was flattened to her head. Lachlan untied the ribbon that held on her bedraggled bonnet and handed her the ruined item. She gazed up at him. The deluge had erased her makeup and her pale skin appeared translucent. Her lips, tinged blue, still called to him more alluringly than any drug. He resisted the temptation and waited.

"I don't know," she finally said. She shivered despite the wool shawl around her shoulders.

"Come on." He led her into the main stable block.

Whilst a few of the lads tended to the horses they'd unhitched from the phaeton, most of the others sat on cane-back chairs and barrels around an old wooden table. Presently, the table held what looked like the remains of lunch and a haphazard game of cards. The minute Urquhart's crew saw Lachlan and Lily, they leapt to their feet and doffed their caps.

"As you were," Lachlan said as he led Lily by the elbow to a set of stairs on one side of the stables.

Once they climbed the stairs and entered Urquhart's office, Lachlan pushed her into the rocking chair in front of the huge, old wood-burning stove. He sat down on the ottoman in front of the chair and proceeded to remove Lily's boots. He got up and propped her feet on the ottoman, which he dragged closer to the stove.

"Do you have a foot fetish, Lord Lachlan?" Lily asked as she wiggled her stockinged toes and sighed.

"What?" Lachlan stood in the open doorway of the office.

"You are constantly removing my shoes."

He snorted. "You're constantly getting your feet wet."

He turned to bellow down the stairs only to find one of the young men who'd been seated at the table below now standing in the doorway with a loaded tray in his hands.

"Thought the lady might like a cup of tea," he mumbled, his face now bright red.

"How sweet," Lily said as she leaned forward in the chair to peer around Lachlan. "I'd love a cup of tea. Ooh, and scones."

The lad ducked his head and brought the tray to the low-slung tea table in front of the rocking chair. Lily allowed him to prepare her tea and made a great fuss about how perfect it was and how well he'd prepared the tray. Lachlan leaned against the door jam, arms folded across his chest, one ankle crossed over the other.

He watched her draw out the shy young man, who was more comfortable with horses than people unless Lachlan missed his mark. She asked about his family, the horses, the people in the village. Lachlan found it nearly impossible to reconcile the gentle, concerned woman who asked a clumsy lad to make her another cup of tea with the blood-in-her-eye woman who'd nearly drowned two ladies and spewed such hatred at a man whose only sin was he *hadn't* slept with her. Which one was the real Lily, and did he really want to know?

"That'll do, lad," Lachlan finally said.

The boy tugged at the front of his hair and scurried past him and down the stairs, his boots raising a racket as he went. Once the noise faded to nothing, Lachlan strolled over to the worn oak low stool across the tea table from Lily and sat. At first, she tried to ignore him. He for damned certain had no chance to ignore her.

She slathered a scone with some of Mrs. Gordon's home-made strawberry jam, topped it with a hefty dollop of clotted cream, and turned eating the bloody thing into an erotic dream. The little noises of pleasure she made, and the way she flicked the tip of her tongue out to capture smears of cream and jam from the corners of her mouth.… One more minute of that and he'd have her on the floor in front of

Urquhart's stove. Naked. He needed to do something to distract them both from the desire that pulsed between them with each passing moment.

"How many times have you been engaged?" He'd needed to do something but probably not that.

She put down what was left of the scone. Her face, which had been soft and light, went hard and cold. "Depends on who you've been talking to—Danny Arneaux or your brother."

"What is that supposed to mean?" Lachlan's temper started to rise, and he had no idea why. He'd asked.

"Why did you bother to ask me? Arneaux thinks he knows everything about me, and I am sure the duke can Google with the best of them. Or maybe he and Eleanor discuss it when she visits him in his tower in the middle of the night."

What the hell? Knox? And Elle? He did *not* want to get into that at all. Not whilst the woman who'd rocked his world last night now looked as if she wanted to murder him and leave his body in a bog somewhere.

"Arneaux didn't mention it."

"So, it was your brother. Great." She rocked out of the chair and began to pace the wooden floor in her stockinged feet. "Did he give you names and dates or just a number?"

"A number." Something about the way she wrapped her arms around herself and the stiff way she held her body made it impossible for him to do anything but tell her the truth. "Six."

She stopped and flopped back into the rocking chair. "I guess I should be grateful he got it right. Apparently, Arneaux keeps track of the number of proposals. He assumes I accepted them all."

"How do you—"

"Because his girlfriend has told everyone at this little boot camp, that's how."

"Girlfriend?" he asked as meekly as he knew how. Nearly eight years at war gave him a fair knowledge of when something was about to explode.

"Little Miss Higgins. I heard her talking about me when I managed to sneak into the drawing room without them noticing. Generally, when I walk into a room, everyone shuts up."

"That's hardly fair." A space behind his ribcage caught and ached.

"Life is frequently unfair, honey." Lily shrugged. "Or at least that was what my mother always said. Usually when she was about to sell off something of mine because she'd spent all my money."

"I'm sorry. Forget I asked." He clasped his hands between his knees and dropped his head. "Bit pissed because I woke up to Knox sitting in my parlor, holding your underwear." He turned his head to look at her.

"Oh God." Lily covered her face with her hands.

Lachlan gave a dark laugh from deep in his chest. She looked up and glared at him.

"It isn't funny. I went back after breakfast and couldn't find them. I'd hoped a wild animal had dragged them off."

"Knox? A wild animal? Hardly." Lachlan snorted. "The only thing my brother has ever been wild about is architecture. Had to give it up to become the duke."

"That's…sad." She caught his gaze, held it. "I mean it. Acting is all I ever wanted to do. I don't think I could give it up for anything."

"Feeling sorry for His Grace?" Lachlan tried to smile, make it a joke, but it wasn't. Not completely. Until Lily pointed it out, he'd never considered how much Knox gave up to come back to Scotland and become the Duke of Turra.

She shook her head. Once she'd pulled the knitted tea cozy from the old, Brown Betty teapot, she refilled her teacup and poured one for him. When she lifted it and put it into his outstretched hands, she slid her palms around his fingers and held them there for a moment.

"Thank you for last night," she said softly.

He shook his head and bent to kiss her fingertips. "No. Thank you."

She leaned back and left the cup of tea in his hands. He took a sip, propped his arms on his knees, and let the cup warm his fingers, which had suddenly gone cold. Lily took a couple of gulping swallows of her own tea.

"Six times," she said, still holding her teacup tightly in her hands. "I've been engaged exactly six times."

"Lily, you don't—"

"I was barely seventeen the first time. I did it to try and get out from under my mother's thumb. She paid him to break the engagement."

He glanced up at her in time to see the very real pain of that memory in her eyes. As quickly as the heartbreak of that loss appeared, it vanished—replaced by the haughty carefree face she put on so easily. He suddenly found it hard to breathe.

"The other five were on me." She shrugged. "Bad choices. Some by me, some by them. I've been stupid enough to believe men in the business picked me because they loved me or were at least interested in me. I wasn't working regularly. I acted like I was famous, but it was all bullshit. Either they bought it or maybe they thought half-assed famous was better than a nobody."

"There is nothing half-assed about you, Lily Randolph." He'd probably said that more forcefully than he meant to because she widened her eyes and looked a little nervous. "Sorry."

"Don't be. Ever." She put her teacup on the table and stretched her feet out toward the stove. "Part of your charm is you didn't know who I was the first time you looked at me with lust in your heart." Lily fluttered her eyelashes at him and gave him a cheeky, sultry smile.

Lachlan forced himself to remain serious, channeling his brother's disapproving ducal scowl. "It was dark."

"It wasn't so dark I couldn't see the lump in your kilt, Lord Well-Hung." She winked.

He couldn't help it. Lachlan coughed, then laughed so hard he had to grab his teacup and suck down half the contents. When he caught his breath, he said, "Lust in my *heart?*"

She snorted. "You're a man. That's where you keep your lust."

"Is it?" Lachlan thought he'd left his heart in Afghanistan. Now? He didn't know where it was.

He met Lily's gaze. She stretched like a cat and settled into the rocking chair.

"Why did you—" she said in unison with his, "Have you ever—"

The both broke off, then he said, "Ladies first."

"Have you ever been engaged?" Lily studied him carefully. He felt like one of his mother's butterfly specimens.

"Why did you splash Elle and Dr. Higgins?" he countered.

They started at each other. Below them, horses and men moved about. The sounds they made rose faintly, similar to white noise. The stove hissed and popped at random intervals. Lachlan's heartbeat thudded in his ears. Loudly. The noise nearly deafened him. He wanted an answer to his question. More importantly, he didn't want to answer hers. Somehow, the words were lined up on the tip of his tongue like a supply convoy. Words he'd not spoken to anyone.

The rockers on the old chair began to pick up speed as

she rocked. The creaked rhythm matched the beat of his heart.

"They're doing all they can to keep Arneaux in this film. They've looked down their noses at me from day one." She gifted him with a frighteningly insincere smile. "Oh, and most of all, it's because I am a hard-hearted, five-star bitch. That's why I splashed them. And I'd do it again."

Her serene *I-dare-you* face and matter-of-fact tone didn't fool him. Her fierce grip on the arms of the chair and the violent pace at which she rocked told him more than any words.

Damn.

"I was engaged once. Briefly." That word convoy changed gears swiftly and lost its brakes. "She died in Afghanistan. Roadside bomb."

Chapter Thirteen

❧

AFTER LACHLAN'S LITTLE ANNOUNCEMENT, HE'D NOT SAID more than a few perfunctory words to her. He'd escorted her back to the front doors of the main house and disappeared with a squeeze of her hand and a miserable half-smile.

Lily prided herself on managing to survive the rest of the day without an attempt to murder any of her fellow Regency *campers*. She had spent most of that time convincing herself the almost addictive need to be with Rosemount's gamekeeper had everything to do with the great sex and nothing to do with their last conversation. Not that it had been much of a conversation.

They'd both proven themselves cowards. She'd not even tried to sneak out of the house despite a stroll through the gallery after dinner with the other "ladies," which had allowed her to see a light on at the front of Lachlan's cottage.

This morning, he'd sent her word that he'd canceled her driving and falconry lessons due to the weather, which was why she spent mind-numbing hours confined to the humongous manor house with people she either couldn't stand, or who couldn't stand her or who wanted to suck up to her for God only knew what reason.

The only bright spot was the servants. They deferred to Lily at every turn. They anticipated her needs, made certain she received the best of everything, and generally treated her like a queen. So much so that when Lily and the other ladies sat around the parlor doing needlework, the romance writer remarked on it.

"You must be a very generous tipper, Miss Randolph," Anna said. "The servants dote on you."

Lily shrugged in response, uncomfortable with the conversation and attention.

"She's right." Eleanor put her embroidery hoop in her lap and stared at Lily so pointedly, Lily had no choice but to stare back. "They've been catering to you at every meal. The cook is sending up your favorite treats with every pot of tea we order."

"I haven't seen any of you back away from them." Lily glanced at Samantha Higgins who had just taken a bite of a strawberry tart.

"I've seen battalions of footmen up and down the stairs with buckets of hot water for her bath," Miss Stepford observed, head down as she continued to work on her sampler.

"I'm pretty sure even Regency ladies bathed." Lily was ready to smack someone at that point.

"Not twice a day." Samantha reached for another tart and arched her eyebrows at everyone in the room.

Of course, they all nodded in agreement and looked at Lily as if they expected an answer.

So, she gave them one. "Robbie, could you be a dear and fetch my blue shawl? It's draped across the blanket chest in my room."

"Yes, miss." The young man in the kilted uniform bowed and scurried off to do her bidding.

Lily smiled sweetly at them and went back to stabbing her embroidery. If she imagined she was stabbing the other women in the room, they didn't need to know it. Although from the looks they shot her, they knew.

Then after another agonizing dinner and hours of card-playing, she'd lain awake in her bed and relived every moment of making love with Lachlan.

When she woke up the next morning she asked for breakfast in her room. She didn't have the patience to deal with the ladies' snide remarks and Arneaux's weird glances her way. She had no doubt the duke had told him about her spending the night at Lachlan's and losing her stays and stockings on the way home.

She snapped off a bite of the toast she'd just buttered. "I feel like I'm fifteen and locked in a convent school," Lily muttered. "Cue Joan Crawford and a wire coat hanger."

She reached for a piece of bacon and saw a note tucked under one of the plates on the tray Emma had placed across her lap before she went into the dressing room to check on Lily's clothes for the day. She dropped the bacon and snatched up the note.

COME TO THE FALCONRY DEMONSTRATION?
Lachlan

LILY JUMPED OUT OF BED SO FAST SHE NEARLY DUMPED THE breakfast tray in the floor. She caught it and sat it on the side of the bed.

"Emma," she yelled. "Emma, I need. Whoa!" Lily nearly ran the poor maid over as she came out of the dressing room.

Emma glanced at the note in Lily's hand and grinned before she dumped the petticoats and wool stockings she was carrying into Lily's arms and went back into the dressing room.

Lily dropped into the fireside chair and wrestled the wool stockings onto her legs. Thank God Emma had shown her how to tie up the damned things so they didn't end around her ankles in the first fifteen minutes. She pulled her nightgown off over her head then shimmied into the chemise. The petticoats took some wiggling, and even if they were the kind that closed in front, the stays still confused the hell out of her.

"Let me." Emma marched out of the dressing room with a dark green wool dress, a bonnet in her hand, and a swath of beautiful plaid over her arm. She dropped a pair of black ankle boots at Lily's feet and placed the bonnet on the tea table. She crammed Lily into the stays to the point her boobs looked ready to bail over the top. Then the maid tossed the dress over Lily's head and snatched it into place. Emma spun Lily around, fastened the dress, then spun her back around to adjust the square, low-cut neckline. Lily had had dates where guys didn't manhandle her boobs the way Emma did. Lily stepped into the boots and laced them up.

"Is there a point to all this?" she finally asked. "Or does everyone at Rosemount Manor know my business?"

"Not everyone."

"If I had my damned phone, there'd be no need for passing notes and sneaking around. I'm beginning to think Eleanor has all our phones stuffed in her stays or up her—"

"She doesn't keep them with her. She...." Emma bit her bottom lip and went back to fussing with Lily's hair.

"We will continue this conversation when I'm not in such a hurry," Lily said.

Emma turned Lily around so she could herself in the

antique, full-length stand mirror. Whilst she stood there, the maid draped the blue, green, and black plaid over Lily's shoulder. It hung just below her knee in the front and the back. Emma pinned the front to Lily's shoulder with a silver broach in the shape of a thistle. Then Emma belted the entire outfit with a simple leather belt around Lily's waist.

"Oh." It was a lame thing to say, but she couldn't come up with much else.

She looked like something out of one of those portraits in the gallery. The bodice of the dress buttoned up the front and the neckline made her look like a 1950s pinup. Emma went to work with those instruments of torture Regency women called hairpins and piled up Lily's hair, twisting the ends into a small bun on top, but leaving the hair loose in the back.

"I don't know who Wentworth has doing hair for this film," Lily said as she turned back and forth to take in the entire look. "But I'm going to make him hire you to do mine."

"Oh, really?" Emma returned the brush and paper of hairpins to the dressing table in the corner. "And how do ye plan to get me to take the job?"

"I'm going to have him pay you a ridiculous amount of money." Lily grabbed her little silk ridicule, reticule—whatever—from the blanket chest and headed for the door.

"Aye," Emma said with a grin. "That might do it." She picked up the bonnet.

"You really think I'm going to ruin this Highland lass look with that ugly bonnet? If Lachlan asks me to help with his birds, I don't think they'd like me in Regency headgear." She narrowed her eyes at Emma's completely fake innocent expression.

"But you knew that, didn't you?"

"Knew what, miss?"

"That I'd be spending time with Lord Lachlan today."

"I didn't cram ye into that dress for nothing. The young master and that lad, Tommy Burke, are setting up the demonstration in front of the mews. Miss Witherspoon and the others will be headed there already. Even some of us below stairs are going. This is the first time Lord Lachlan's done something like this with his birds since he came home."

"Let's hurry. Maybe I can avoid the Regency police if we cut through the back gardens." Lily grabbed Emma's arm and dragged her down the hall to the stairs.

They made good progress through the house as footmen pretty much ran to open the doors for her. They crossed the gardens and the bridge over the ha-ha, then backtracked up the path toward the stables and the hill that led to the mews. Lily saw the others, led by Eleanor, Danny, and Samantha, climbing the hill in the distance.

"Emma, can you tell me something?" Lily asked as she lifted her skirt and slogged up the hill.

"What would that be, miss?"

"I'm not complaining," Lily said as she grabbed Emma's helping hand. "But why are the servants suddenly so nice to me? I'm not the easiest person to work for, ask anyone who's ever worked for me." She tried to make it sound like a joke, but over the time she'd spent at Rosemount Manor she'd not really made an effort to endear the servants to her. Not like Danny Arneaux or some of the others.

They reached the top of the hill. Abercrombie stood and pointed to where he wanted each wooden folding chair placed whilst the footmen hurried to do as he instructed. Samantha, Eleanor, Anna, and the other ladies had already seated themselves in the front row of chairs.

Lachlan strode out of the mews with Morgana, the eagle owl on his arm. He took the bird to one of the half-circle ground perches and settled her there.

"'Tis because of him," Emma said quietly. "Ye went out in

the storm and found him. He's a bit better because of ye. That's why we do a little extra for ye. Even if ye can be a snooty pain in the arse at times." Emma laughed so loud the people seated in the chairs heard her and turned to stare. Great.

"This is your fault," Lily muttered as she and Emma made their way to the rows of chairs. When they reached the others, the maid sauntered off to join the rest of the servants who stood at the back behind the chairs. The only seat available was next to Arneaux's Regency coach.

"You look amazing," the author said softly.

"I have to agree," the snooty costume mistress said. "Very authentic Highland lady."

"Thank—"

"Nice of you to join us, Miss Randolph," Samantha said. "Mr. Arneaux is going to show us what he's learned about falconry."

"He is?" Lily clasped her hands to her bosom in an exaggerated way that had Teddy Rousseau snickering. "I'll try to contain my excitement."

"Must you always be so catty?" Samantha asked softly.

"Must you always be so condescending?" Lily replied. "I realize I don't have a dozen college degrees, but I'm not nearly as stupid as Arneaux would have you all believe."

Damn, damn, damn! Do not engage. That had been her mantra since she'd fired her mother and taken complete control of her life and career. Do. Not. Engage.

The Regency coach's face turned a few shades of red. "I don't think… I mean, I daresay no one here thinks—"

"Don't worry about it, *Dr.* Higgins. We heartless bitches don't have feelings. A woman as educated as you should know that."

Lily faced forward and forced herself not to look at the rest of the spectators. Fortunately, Tommy Burke, dressed in formal Highland gear, stepped forward and began to talk about the history of falconry.

Lachlan stood back in his boots, white shirt, and traditional kilt of Innes plaid with his hair tied back with a strip of leather. He had Morgana on his gloved hand. Young Tommy might be the one speaking, but Lily only had eyes for Lachlan. He, however, had apparently picked a spot somewhere behind everyone assembled for the demonstration. She doubted the others picked up on it—neither the pallor beneath his tan complexion, the flat effect of his stare, or the tiny beads of sweat on his upper lip.

How could Eleanor ask him to do this? He hated large gatherings. He hated being on display. Lily caught his gaze in the most unobvious way she could. They locked eyes, and she tried to convey all her belief in him into the meeting of their gazes. The shift in him was miniscule, but his shoulders relaxed a little. The hard lines of his face smoothed. He gave her a nod.

At Tommy's word, Lachlan launched Morgana into the air. She soared and dipped and put on quite the show. The rest of the spectators were in noisy awe. Lily's awe took a different form. She watched in rapt silence as the magnificent creature danced across the sky, catching breezes and undercurrents she could not see. Lachlan let loose one of his long, sharp whistles, and the owl slowly worked her way lower and returned to his arm. The audience applauded in appreciation. Lachlan pointed at Danny Arneaux, then went to return Morgana to her perch.

A whispered thrill went through the rest of the group. Costumed in his Highland clothes, Danny appeared nervous as he strode up to stand next to Lachlan who had taken the peregrine falcon, Bannockburn, from his perch. After a few instructions only Lachlan and Danny could hear, Lily's fellow actor took the falcon onto his gloved hand. He strode away from Lachlan, out into the open area between the chairs and the mews buildings, then sent Bannockburn flying.

The falcon shot from Danny's glove to Lachlan's like a rocket. They continued to step farther apart and send the falcon back and forth between them. The bird's incredible speed drew gasps from those who watched. Lily had to admit the falcon's flight this close was nothing short of spectacular.

After about fifteen minutes, Danny returned Bannock-burn to his perch. Lachlan retrieved another bird, the kestrel named Bonny Lass. Lily knew her to be a little fussy, but Danny took her from Lachlan without much trouble. She did snap at this glove a few times, but she finally settled. Smaller than a pigeon, kestrels were fierce hunters—or so Lachlan said. This time, Danny sent her into the sky. Bonny was small, but so graceful it took Lily's breath away every time she watched her fly. While the kestrel showed off her flying skills, Tommy spoke about her incredible ability to hover, and of course her speed.

"Call her in," Lachlan said after about ten minutes.

The rumble that went through the people seated on the lawn had a lot more to do with the fact the duke's brother had spoken than it did with Danny's skill at whistling the bird down from the sky.

Once Danny secured Bonny Lass onto her perch, he turned and gave his audience an exaggerated bow. They laughed and applauded. Lily rolled her eyes. Danny returned to his seat among back slaps and praise from the group.

"Miss Randolph?" Lachlan stood, hands on his hips, and nodded in her direction.

Talk about a way to silence a crowd. She could have heard a pin drop. On grass, no less. Lily slid her palms down her skirts and hoped everyone thought she did it to straighten them out instead of to dry her hands that were suddenly sweating bullets. She filed past the rows of staring Regency boot-campers and the stone-faced duke to stand next to Lachlan as he lifted the magnificent golden eagle onto his gloved hand and arm. When Lily slipped a thick leather glove on, the chatter from the spectators grew exponentially.

She loved it.

Lachlan made certain the eagle gripped her arm securely before he bent down to whisper in her ear. "Ye have him, love?"

"Aye," she whispered back in an exaggerated brogue.

He snorted softly and shook his head. With a wave of his hand, he signaled Tommy. The boy grinned.

"I'll let our Miss Randolph tell ye about The Bruce," Tommy said as he stepped back and to the side.

His back to the others, Lachlan gave her a wink. Lily took a deep breath and walked to where Tommy had stood.

"This is a golden eagle," she said as she gazed at the spectators head on. She was an actress, and despite the scramble of emotions this group provoked in her, she'd be damned if she'd give anything less than the performance of her life. "His name is The Bruce, and he is nearly twenty years old." She stepped closer to allow them to see him more closely. He rustled his feathers, clicked his beak, then settled. "They're indigenous to the Highlands of Scotland where they hunt rabbits, foxes, and can even bring down young deer."

The group all stared at her in disbelief at first. Then with the disdain they'd shown her throughout boot camp. Now they appeared to be paying attention.

"The Bruce weighs a little over ten pounds, and his wing-span is nearly seven feet. He is considered a rare bird. Oh, and the golden eagle mates for life."

She stepped back into the clear space in front of the mews and turned toward Lachlan who had moved several strides away from her. He gave her a slow nod. Lily took a deep breath, emitted a short whistle between her teeth, and flung her arm up and out. The Bruce launched himself so powerfully she rose on her toes to prevent him from taking her arm with him.

The rest of the guests gasped. Over it all the whoosh of the eagle's wings and the sound of the wind created a unique music. She'd never paid much attention to the wind unless it was too damned cold or, in California, too hot. Now, she listened for every nuance. The Bruce rode every gust and stream like a cyclist on the track or a surfer on the waves. She followed the eagle's flight as he soared into the clouds. He dipped and wheeled and dropped from one current to the next with no more effort than a sports car changing lanes. In her mind, she flew with him, free with no worries or thoughts of anything beyond the moment. Lachlan and his birds had given her this. She understood now why he preferred their company to that of humans.

A shiver went down her spine. Lachlan stood behind her and pressed something into her hand. She wrapped her fingers around the soft fur of The Bruce's lure as Lachlan tucked a small plastic bag into her pocket.

"Are you sure?" she muttered out of the side of her mouth.

"Aye," he said in perfect imitation of her outlandish brogue.

She took half a step forward, and he caught her elbow. "Don't use my birds for your revenge, Lily."

"Not even on your brother?" She turned away from the crowd and gave him a wink.

Lachlan warned Tommy back with a quick nod. The young man took several steps toward the end of the open space closest to where the others sat. The gamekeeper strode across to the other side of the flight area. Lily took a deep breath and marched halfway between the two of them. She dropped the lure at her feet and measured out several feet of the line attached to it by letting the line slip through her fingers. Just as Lachlan had shown her during her lessons, she worked to set the lure in motion around her, whirring it higher and higher and gradually feeding the line until the piece of heavy canvas stuffed with cotton and covered with rabbit fur flew several feet above her head in a wide circling arc. She pursed her lips and gave three shrill, short whistles.

For a moment, The Bruce continued to wheel above them, nearly out of sight. Lily whistled again. The eagle turned abruptly and banked downward. She knew the instant he saw the lure. She continued to spin it above her head. A thrill went through her as he emitted a piercing shriek and appeared to plummet feet first from the sky. She took in the line, rolling it between her fingers until the lure spun just above her head in a slightly smaller circle.

The moment he struck the lure the spectators gasped. She braced herself and dropped to one knee to allow the eagle and his prize to land without The Bruce dislocating her shoulder. Something he'd done to Lachlan about a year ago, according to Tommy. Once the bird's attention turned to plucking at the lure, Lily stood and walked toward him. She reeled in the line until she was close enough to extend her glove to him. The minute he focused on her glove, she pulled the lure free and tucked it into the pocket of her dress.

"Come on, handsome," she murmured. "Come to Mama."

She reached into her other pocket with her ungloved hand and fished out a piece of meat from the plastic bag. She placed the meat in the space between her thumb and forefinger. The Bruce immediately stepped onto her glove and began to feast on his reward. Lily tucked his jesses between her fingers, turned and walk toward the seated and standing audience.

They actually applauded. Lily nearly stumbled. She

stopped in her tracks and glanced over at Lachlan. He stood in that fortified way of his, arms folded across his chest and booted feet planted wide. His face was unreadable, but his eyes spoke volumes. Pride and confidence shone in their light gold depths. She basked in that light for a moment longer then turned to offer the others a shallow curtsy. A curtsy she hoped was at least a little sincere. After which, she beat a hasty retreat to return The Bruce to his perch.

For the next hour Lily had a blast. No other way to describe it. She flew the various birds—some in free flight and some back and forth between Lachlan and her. She even, after a one-or-two-word argument with the stubborn Scot, flew the kestrel and the hen harrier with Arneaux. All the while, dear Tommy did all the talking in his lovely brogue and sounded like a cross between *Outlander* and a zoology professor.

Even better, not a single member of their audience left. The servants appeared fascinated and thrilled in turns. Her fellow Regency boot-campers and the duke expressed shock, awe, and an appreciation that had Lily nearly jumping out of her skin. Once the demonstration was over, Lachlan disappeared into the mews with Morgana, leaving Lily and Tommy to answer questions from those who crowded around them to get a closer look at the birds.

"I am impressed, Miss Randolph," the duke said as he stood, hands clasped behind his back. Lily opened her mouth to reply. "Sincerely." He glanced at the mews where Lachlan stood braced in the doorway. "Thank you. For what you've done for him." Before she could say a word, he inclined his head and joined Mr. McGinty and some of the servants as they made their way back to Rosemount Manor.

What the hell?

Samantha Higgins and the rest of the Regency crew of women stood around Tommy and asked him questions about falconry and its history. Although the dear doctor kept tossing curious glances Lily's way.

"You were magnificent, my dear," the dance master, Mr. Goode, said as he squeezed her arm. "I am in awe of your courage."

"That's very sweet of you, Mr. Goode. I'm so glad you enjoyed the demonstration." She meant every word. The short, round dance instructor was one of her favorite people Wentworth had ordered to boot camp. He was an excellent teacher and a sweet person.

Teddy gave her a curious look, but she detected nothing catty in his expression.

"Come along, Rousseau," Mr. Goode said as he dragged the younger man away by the arm. "We have time to warm ourselves by the fire and perhaps drink some of the duke's brandy before luncheon."

They headed toward the manor.

Eleanor and the other Regency ladies made their way toward the house. Danny looked as if he wanted to join them, but he and Tommy strolled over to where she stood next to the line of ground perches.

"I'll help you take the birds in," Danny said.

"Aye, me too," Tommy said even though he gazed longingly at where the boys from the stables discussed a walk to the village for a visit to the pub for lunch and a pint.

"Go on, Tommy," Lily said. "You did most of the work this morning. I'll take care of this." She ignored Danny and extended her glove for The Bruce to step up and grasp her arm.

"Himself might not like it." Tommy glanced to where Lachlan still stood in the doorway.

"Himself will get over it," Lily said as she passed close enough to Tommy to elbow him gently in the back. "Go on. Live a little." She didn't have to tell him twice. He waved at

Lachlan and ran toward the others like he'd been shot out of a cannon.

"Lily." Danny hurried to catch up with her. "You were amazing out there. Everyone was really impressed. I was really impressed."

"Even Dr. Higgins?"

"I—"

"Forget it." She stopped walking and faced him, trying not to unsettle the huge bird on her wrist. "Look, Danny, I don't want you in this film." Her brain told her to *shut up!* but her mouth was in fourth gear with no brakes in sight. "I think Wentworth casting you is a huge mistake. No matter how big an expert your personal Dr. Higgins is, she will never make you Mr. Darcy. And we both know it."

Shitshitshit!

She didn't know which was worse—that she'd put it all out there so clearly or that Lachlan watched the entire thing from just inside the mews. What was it about Danny Arneaux that made her act like a—

"Total bitch. I keep telling myself it's because of everything your mother put you through and that it's not your fault," Danny said when she finally paid attention to the fact he was speaking. "I have apologized six ways to Sunday. You may think you have to screw your way to the top. You're wrong. And I don't screw women to advance my career, Lily. I wish you believed that. All of it." He threw up his hands and strode down the hill after the rest of the guests.

Lily put her head down and pushed past Lachlan to take The Bruce into the main aerie. She settled the beautiful bird onto one of the lower branches attached to the tree built in the center of his huge cage, then backed out slowly. By the time she returned to the entrance to the mews, Lachlan had gone out to the perches and retrieved one of the other birds. Every time they passed each other, a bird resting on their arm, Lily had to brace herself against the powerful current that arced between Lachlan and her. He watched her with an intensity that both frightened and thrilled her.

The two of them worked in silence until every bird had been brought inside and secured. Lily wasn't ready to return to the house. Everything about Eleanor's Regency boot camp set her teeth on edge. She truly wanted to enjoy the experience, but as soon as she was with the others, she was…*on.* As automatic as breathing, she slipped into her Lily Randolph suit and did everything she could to put people in their place. Away from her. When it came to bitchery, she'd been trained by an expert.

Thanks, Mom.

She gathered the gauntlets, checked them for stains and damage, then put them on their individual shelves before she grabbed a cloth and wiped down the food prep and kitchen area. The door to the kitchen closed behind her. She turned and leaned back against the counter as he propped against the closed door and stared at her. A heartbeat thundered in her ears—his or her own, she didn't know which. She licked her lips. Swallowed. Took a breath.

"Thank you. For letting me fly the birds with you. For letting me show everyone I'm not just a self-absorbed, airhead actress. I think even your brother was impressed. And Danny looked like an—"

"Stop." Suddenly, Lachlan stood right in front of her, his kilt brushing against her dress. "Don't talk about my brother." His brogue made *about* sound like *aboot.* She'd discovered this happened when he was angry or…

"I—" She couldn't breathe.

"Don't talk about Arneaux." Lachlan's voice, deep, dark, and rough, scraped over her skin and set every nerve on fire. "Ever."

"Ever?" Good thing he stood so close. The word came out as a breath of air with some syllables attached.

"Especially when I'm about to do this."

He took her into his arms, lifted her onto the counter, and kissed her as if his life depended on it. His lips seared hers with an intensity just short of punishing. She nipped at his lower lip, and he gentled his kiss, but only a little before he plunged his tongue into her mouth. She wrapped her tongue around his and sucked as she tugged at the piece of leather that tied his hair back. They traded control back and forth. Lily's blood thickened and crawled through her veins. She ran her fingers through his long, dark, silken hair and tugged him back until he broke the kiss.

Useless effort on her part. He trailed his lips along her chin and down her throat to the edge of her wool dress where he ran his teeth across the tops of her breasts. He reached around to loosen the ribbon tapes at the back of her neck. The front of her dress fell forward enough for him to scoop her breasts free of her stays. Lily gasped as he drew one nipple between his teeth to tease with his tongue. She cupped the back of his head to hold him to her. He groaned and suckled hard. He massaged her other breast and rolled the nipple between his thumb and forefinger before he finally switched his lips to that one. All the while, Lily could only pant and arch her back to absorb every ounce of pleasure.

"What…brought…this…oh God, yes…on?" she asked as she positioned her legs on either side of his and hooked her ankles across his kilt-clad ass.

He raised his head. His eyes blazed an almost iridescent amber. He gazed at her with hunger and something more powerful, more thrilling than any sensation she'd ever known.

"You. Only you, Lily." He kissed her eyebrows, her nose,

the corner of her mouth. "Ye were magnificent with the birds. Dressed like some fey creature out of my dreams." He nipped the top of her breast.

"What kind of dreams?"

He raised the skirt of her dress and gave her the sexiest, most wicked grin she'd ever seen. "Wet dreams, love. Verra wet dreams." He rolled up the dress, petticoats, and everything else and clamped her hands over the roll once it reached her waist. When he saw she'd gone Regency commando he growled. "Yes!"

"Wait. Lachlan, what are you doing?"

Lily suspected she knew. A shiver went through her and vibrated between her legs where she was already wet and hot, and more than ready for him. Whatever his intentions.

He pushed her gently so her back rested against the wall at the back of the counter. With kisses pressed to the inside of her each thigh in turn, he lifted her legs to drape over his shoulders. He slid his palms beneath her butt and squeezed as he dragged her closer to the edge of the counter. The first stroke of his tongue sent a shock through her body so powerful she could swear it blew the top of her head off.

"Lachlan!"

He laughed, and the sound tickled her labia. He was relentless. She was torn between pushing him away and pulling him closer. It didn't matter. He was a man on a mission. Her legs shook. The heels of her boots dug into his back. Her hips rose and fell and set up a rhythm, especially once he began to alternate between deep licks inside her and light tortuous flicks to her clit. Once her orgasm started to build, she held her clothes with one hand and tried to grip the counter with the other. She was trying her damnedest not to fly onto the floor.

Suddenly, he latched onto her clit and sucked hard. Lily came in waves. Her screams and moans sounded so loud in the quiet of the little kitchen she imagined the birds in the aerie next door flying away in fear. Then she didn't think at all. She shuddered and gasped as each new stab of tremors shot through her. Lachlan braced his hands on either side of her on the counter.

He rested his forehead against her and lapped at her nipple at random intervals—a deep hum rumbling from his throat each time she shivered. She rested a hand against the back of his neck and stroked the spot beneath his hair.

He smelled of wool and the icy Highland air. Not to mention sweat, sex, and the evergreen cologne he wore. The cotton of his shirt brushed against her skin and created little fissures of sensation up and down her nerves. She leaned up slowly. Lachlan raised his head and pressed kisses to the underside of her chin and behind her ear.

"Ye'r beautiful all the time, but ye'r gorgeous when you come," he whispered.

She laughed softly. "How sturdy is that chair?" Lily nodded at the leather padded chair against the wall.

Lachlan glanced back. "I didn't bring any—"

Lily pressed two fingers to his lips and worked her hand into the pocket of her dress, still bunched at her waist. She pulled out her little silk reticule. Lachlan grinned. He shoved his hands under her butt and lifted her off the counter.

"Lachlan!" Lily threw her arms around his neck and locked her legs around his waist.

He lowered himself into the chair with her straddling him. Releasing his neck, Lily struggled to open the reticule. Lachlan didn't help, too busy continuing to caress her bare bottom and lick her breasts. She finally pulled a condom out of the silk bag and dropped the bag to the floor. Mercifully, he wore his kilt in the old style, which made it easier to drag apart at his waist. Thank God the man was a true Scot.

She must have made a sound of appreciation as his thick

erection sprang free. Lachlan chuckled. "See something ye like, love?"

Lily scooted back to perch on his knees then bent to run her tongue around the head of his cock. He jumped with a wordless shout and grabbed the arms of the chair. She raised her head to roll the condom down his shaft before she rose on her knees, planted on the outsides of his thighs. With a grin, she braced her hands on his shoulders. Lachlan fitted the head of his cock inside her and she sank down slowly, savoring every inch as she took him inside. They groaned in tandem. Lachlan rested his forehead between her breasts, his hot breath bathing her skin.

On a gasp, she threw back her head and raised her hips. When she lowered herself again, the sense of fulness, of completion overwhelmed her. Being with this man was different from anything she'd ever experienced. She opened her eyes and locked onto Lachlan's face. He gripped her hips, and his chest rapidly rose and fell as if he struggled to keep control. She leaned closer and pushed up again. The slide of his cock against her clit was perfect. Then, as if a bomb had been set off, she gripped his shoulders and set up a furious rhythm.

He helped her—raised and lowered her even as his hips surged up from the chair to meet her. The room filled with the scent of sex and their heavy breathing, punctuated by her gasped pleasure and his rumbled words of encouragement. The sounds their bodies made as they came together only urged Lily to go faster and harder. Her orgasm built like a freight train, and all the while, Lachlan's voice pushed her higher and higher to the point she was flying, soaring like one of his birds and riding the waves of passion he built under her.

"Aye. That's it, love. Ye'r...so beautiful. My wild, lovely lass. So...damned...

good. Don't stop."

"I can't...I can't...Lachlan. Lachlan." Her entire body shuddered so powerfully she felt it in her bones. Her mouth opened, but no sound came out. Her throat burned and tears stung her eyes.

Lachlan surged up once, twice—the third time he shouted her name. His grip on the arms of the chair turned his knuckles so white she thought he'd break the arms or his knuckles or both. She had to brace one hand on the back of the chair to keep from being thrown to the floor as his body went taut then finally shivered and collapsed back into the chair.

Lily draped herself over him. She'd been burning with heat a moment ago. Now the Highland cold tried to creep around the warmth being in Lachlan's arms always brought her. He wrapped his arms around her and buried his face in her hair. He kissed the side of her neck, her earlobe, her cheek. She'd never known a man this strong, this sensuous, this kind, and good in her life. How would she ever—

"Tha gaol agam ort, Lily. Tha goal agam ort."

Her heart stopped. Anna used several Gaelic phrases in *A Matter of Honor*. Lily had translated them all.

She was in serious, serious trouble.

Chapter Fourteen

LILY HAD LOST HER MIND. SHE'D OFTEN WONDERED WHAT IT would take to drive her into full lunatic mode. Apparently, all it took was mind-blowing sex with a hunky Scot and a declaration of love from that Scot in Gaelic, no less. That was all, and that was what had driven her to corner Emma and beg the poor woman to tell her where Eleanor kept everyone's phones. That was also the reason Emma now loitered at the end of the hall while Lily broke into Eleanor's bedroom to steal her own phones back.

She had to talk to Derek. Now.

Lily had left the mews a little over an hour ago. She and Lachlan had dressed each other between kisses and caresses. They'd almost ended up back in the chair for an encore performance. The entire time, that Gaelic phrase had flashed in her head like some kind of demented neon sign. He had no clue she'd understood what he'd said. She was nearly one hundred percent sure of that. He'd been loving, gruff, and sweet. Just like he always was. When she told him she probably needed to get back to the manor for lunch, he'd taken her in his arms and given her one of his soul-searing kisses.

"Will I see ye tonight?"

"Aye." She'd grabbed his butt under his kilt and squeezed. She'd even managed to walk slowly to the top of the hill and turn to wave at him. After that, all hell had broken loose, inside her at least. He loved her. What the hell was she supposed to do with that? What did she want to do with that? With him?

"Tha gaol agam ort, Lily."

"I love you, Lily." He'd actually said the words. In Gaelic, no less. He wasn't the first man to say those words to her. But he was the first man she believed in a very long time. She sat on one of the benches just over the hill where the view of Rosemount Manor and the fountain was lovely and peaceful.

"Okay, Lily," she muttered. "Figure this out before you freak out about it."

Men said those words all the time, especially in the middle of great sex. Really great sex. Then they regretted it later or worse, denied ever saying it at all. Lachlan Innes was not that kind of man. He didn't say things he didn't mean. Did he?

She closed her eyes and remembered his expression, the sound of his voice, everything about those moments. Nothing sounded fake or put on. Nothing felt fake. Nothing had ever shaken her so, body and soul deep.

"Shit!" She jumped up and started down the hill toward the manor house.

Damn Eleanor for taking her phone. She needed to talk to Derek and Rafael in the worst possible way. This was the stage where she always screwed things up. She either went all in or she pushed the guy away. Hard. She didn't want to do either with Lachlan. She wanted…. Halfway down the hill she stopped. She wanted this to work. Didn't she?

Oh sure. Her life was halfway across the world in Hollywood when she wasn't on a film set in God knows whatever country some director asked her to go. His life was here. No matter his issues with his brother, this place kept him sane. Kept him grounded and safe. She turned and looked back toward the top of the hill and beyond. The mountains and sky blended into the sheep pastures and raced toward the house just as they had done for over five hundred years. He was a part of this place and Rosemount was a part of him.

He was fast becoming a part of her. She wanted him in her life for all kinds of reasons that had nothing to do with sex. Her heart raced. Suddenly she couldn't breathe. This wasn't her. She didn't need this. Not now.

Fuck this on a cracker!

She dragged in breath after breath as she hurried to the house. She was about to hyperventilate dammit. She needed her phone, and she had to track down the maid, Emma, to help her get it. Lily cracked one of the front doors open and checked out the foyer. The coast was clear. She grabbed her skirt and raced up the stairs.

Lily hadn't come to Scotland to find the love of her life.

Shit! Stop saying that!

She needed help and the kind of advice only someone who knew her and refused to allow her to bullshit herself could give.

LILY'S HEART POUNDED AS SHE GRIPPED THE DOOR HANDLED TO Eleanor's room. It was locked—the door turned easily. Lily released a half breath half laugh, gave Emma the thumbs up, and slipped inside the room. The room was gorgeous. Full of antique furniture and knickknacks and a nice big fireplace. Clothes lay scattered everywhere, and the desk in the corner had an avalanche of paperwork and folders stacked on it. The canopy over the massive four-poster bed stretched close to the ceiling. It and the bed drapes were heavy gold brocade silk. The whole room was very stately home elegant. Except for the huge glass case stretched across the wall on the far side of the room.

"Damn," Lily said as she drew closer to the case. "That is one big snake."

Eleanor's unusual pet stretched from one end of the case to the other under a series of electric heat lamps. Hell, the damned thing had its own personal tanning bed. Apparently, the snake was not participating in Regency book camp. As fascinating as the fat orange creamsicle of a reptile was, Lily crept closer to the enclosure for an entirely different reason.

And there it was.

The velvet bag into which Eleanor had thrown all their cell phones sat nestled in the middle of the snake's coils like some kind of magical egg. *Hell!* Okay. She could do this. She ran her hands up and down her skirt. Fortunately, the sliding glass door on the front of the cage wasn't locked, just latched. It took a minute, but Lily figured out the latch and slid the door open. She shifted her gaze back and forth from the snake's head to the bag so quickly, she was afraid she'd sprain something. Slowly, she reached for the gold cord drawstring at the top of the bag. Sweat pooled in her stays and dribbled down her back.

"Okay, snakey, let's remain calm and nobody gets hurt."

She curled one finger around the cord and pulled up. The snake started to move. *No, no, no, no, no!* She really wished she'd worn drawers because she was about to wet herself. Though her hand shook, from her neck to her ankles her body was as steady as a rock. Good thing too. Once the snake started to uncoil and turn its head her way, Lily had had enough. She snatched the bag free, stumbled back a step, and after a couple of attempts, slid the glass door closed.

She stood there a minute, eyes closed, and waited for

her heart to drop back down from her throat. When she opened her eyes, the snake had pressed her nose against the glass.

"Oh, kiss my ass," Lily muttered as she fiddled with the latch. She made damned sure it was secure. Next time the snake decided to bed-hop, she might end up in Lily's bed. The bedroom door clicked open behind her. She froze a second then turned slowly. Relief flooded her.

"Emma, thank God it's you. I—"

"Miss Witherspoon is coming up the stairs." Emma strode toward the wall just beyond the snake's enclosure. She waved Lily over then pressed one of the individual squares that made up the paneling. A click sounded, and the paneling slid open. "This way."

This way? What the hell?

As soon as she stepped through the opening behind Emma, the panel slid closed behind them. The maid had a tiny flashlight, and she shone it just ahead of them. They descended a flight of stone steps. When they came to a landing Emma, took a sharp right, then went along a cold, damp hallway that led to another staircase going up. After a few more turns and another click, they passed through another section of paneling into Lily's room.

"Are you frickin' kidding me?" She glared at Emma, who shrugged.

"There are passageways and hidden stairs all over Rosemount Manor."

"For what?"

"So servants and the occasional mistress could move about the manor unseen."

Lily emptied the velvet bag onto her bed. She scrambled through the pile, but her phones weren't there. *Damn Eleanor!* One particular phone caught her eye. The case had an LSU logo on the back of it. Danny's phone. She hesitated for the barest of seconds, then knelt next to her bedside table and reached under the back of it.

Emma stepped closer. "What have ye got there?"

Lily looked up. "My secret weapon. One of them at least." She held up a mini power strip into which she'd plugged several portable cell phone power banks. "I had two copies of *Pride and Prejudice* in my luggage. One was real. The other is a storage box that looks like a real book. I hid these in it before the Regency police could search my luggage."

Emma grinned and shook her head. "Too clever by half. That's what they're all saying about ye."

"They, who?"

"The servants. Luncheon is in an hour. Best not miss it if ye don't want Miss Witherspoon to be suspicious."

"Thanks, Emma. I owe you."

"Aye. Ye do." Emma grinned then left.

Lily plugged one of the battery packs into Danny's phone. Maybe after lunch it would be charged, and she could go somewhere to get a signal. She smiled in satisfaction, then realized the phone might be password protected.

She turned it on.

It wasn't password protected.

Just about to put the phone down, she hesitated. One minute passed, then another. After a third minute, she accessed his text messages.

Jacqueline St. James. Danny's agent. She'd blown up his phone with text messages. Maybe it was something about the film. Maybe Wentworth had already fired him.

Lily opened the first message, the one with the earliest date. She read it. Then the next one. And the next. And the next. The more she read, the madder she got. He'd told her he wouldn't screw someone to advance his career, and yet his agent had told him to do exactly that as if they'd planned it all along.

Did sweet little Dr. Higgins have any idea?

And Danny had warned Lachlan about *Lily*? Lily, the Hollywood whore who screwed men to get ahead? At least that was what Danny had implied.

A red, hot flush swept over her. She'd had the most wonderful morning. Everyone who were there to see the falconry display had all looked at her with amazement and even respect. Lachlan had told her how beautiful she was and how amazing she was with his birds. All that praise and respect threatened to turn to ash in the storm of hurt, confusion, and rage that burned in the middle of her chest. It threatened to suffocate her.

Damn him!

She snatched up the phones and stuffed them into the velvet bag. Lily had had enough. She flung her bedroom door open and stormed down the stairs toward the dining room. She'd give Danny Arneaux something to chew on and it damned sure wouldn't be Mrs. Gordon's cranachan.

LILY STOOD IN THE MIDDLE OF THE DOWNSTAIRS DRAWING room with Eleanor's velvet bag hanging from her fingertips. She ignored the broken vase that lay in pieces on the expensive carpet—the vase she'd accidentally broken when she'd bumped into the dainty table the vase had sat on. Probably priceless with her luck.

"I hate these clothes," she ranted. "I hate using a chamber pot. I ate eel for God's sake. Eel. I want my phones. I want electricity. I want Netflix!"

"You signed up for this, Miss Randolph," Eleanor the Regency Nazi said under her breath.

Like hell she did!

"I want to wear makeup and my stilettos. And I don't care

what you're in charge of; you have no right to hide my phones away from everyone else's."

"When did we eat eel?" Danny asked. "What's wrong with eel?"

Lily wanted to punch him. He hadn't listened to word she'd said. Worse, every eye in the room was on him. One of the French doors that led out onto the front terrace cracked open. Lily was aware someone had stepped just inside the room. The breeze that followed this person stirred the flames in the giant drawing room fireplace. A log shifted and sent sparks up the chimney. Lord Lachlan. He'd come in from the terrace and was staring at Lily. Her entire body went cold. Fortunately, everyone else continued to stare at Danny.

"What? I'm from Louisiana," the fool said, as if that explained everything. "We eat gator and snake. Hell, we eat crawfish and barbecued nutria on the fourth of July."

"What the devil is nutria?" Teddy asked. He sat in one of the high-backed armchairs by the fire with a glass of brandy in his hand.

"Well, it's a sort of…it's…actually, it's a big rat, but don't take that personally, Teddy.

"Bugger off, Arneaux," Teddy snapped.

"There are ladies present, Mr. Rousseau." Lachlan's brother used his duke voice. Never a good sign. That meant he was about to play lord of the manor on someone. God help him if he tried it on her. She'd had enough.

"I don't give a damn about any of that. I want my phones, you red-headed witch." Lily stepped closer to Eleanor but hid the bag behind her back. "Now."

"You signed a contract just like everyone else, Lily. Give me the bag so we can all go to lunch. It's roast beef today, not eel."

"That's *Miss Randolph* to you, Eleanor." Lily glanced

around the room. When she saw Danny whispering to Samantha, an eerie smile twisted Lily's lips.

"Fine." Eleanor folded her arms across her chest. "Miss Randolph, give me the fucking bag of phones so we can all get on with our lives."

"You were saying something about ladies, Your Grace?" Teddy said.

"Shut it, Teddy." Samantha stepped closer to Eleanor, and Danny followed.

"I want my phones," Lily shouted so loudly everyone in the room jumped, except for the duke's silently watchful brother.

"Oh, for God's sake, Lily," Danny had the nerve to say. "Stop playing this tired old cliché. Child actress has a terrible life and becomes a spoiled diva so difficult nobody wants to work with her. Give it a rest. Grow up."

Grow up? Grow up? She'd tell him to kiss her ass, but she didn't want him anywhere near her.

"A cliché? A cliché? How about the cliché of the Hollywood bad boy who screws every hot actress in town but walks away when they get too serious? What can you expect from a guy raised by his grandmother who ran the most infamous whore house in New Orleans?"

Whoops! She didn't mean to go that far. Even she drew the line at grandmothers.

Samantha gasped and put her hand on Arneaux's arm. Little did the poor doctor know.

"You leave my grandmere out of this," he said in a dangerously low voice. "At least she didn't pimp me out to every director and actor in the business to boost my career like your mother did. And then run off with most of your money and your latest boyfriend when your career crashed and burned."

Now he'd done it. Out of deference to his grandmother, Lily had almost decided not to out him in public. Almost. Lily dragged the velvet bag from behind her back. She rifled through it and pulled out Danny's cell phone.

From his expression, he knew he was trapped in a train wreck of a nightmare with no way out. Whether he'd read the texts or not, he knew what they said. *Damn him.*

"No, your agent is the pimp," she said in a loud voice.

She tossed the phone to Samantha who caught it and stared at it. Her forehead wrinkled. She turned it over and brought the screen to life with a touch. Danny opened his mouth. Samantha raised her hand, palm out. Danny snapped his head around and glared at Lily, but she didn't care. She wasn't the one who had started this.

"Miss Randolph, this has gone far enough. You had no right to come into my room. Give me that bag," Eleanor said, the breathy edge of panic to her voice only made matters worse.

Lily couldn't help herself. Danny had ruined her beautiful day, and she'd seen red. Now, she just wanted to ruin him. "You really should call your agent, Danny. She's anxious to know if you've managed to get our Dr. Higgins into bed."

"Shut up, Lily."

Shock pulled up a chair and sat in the middle of the room like someone's drunk uncle at a wedding reception. Lily held her breath. That was until she looked at Lachlan's face. Her heart twisted. She commanded the pain to let go, but that only made the pulsing ache worse. Why was he here?

Samantha kept staring at Danny's phone as if it held the answers to every question in the universe. Lily saw the hurt she'd caused as if from far away—which made it far easier to twist the knife.

"We've been deceived, ladies and gentlemen. It seems this

is little Miss Higgins's very first job running the show. Her boss wouldn't take it."

"Lily, for God's sake, shut up," Danny said.

Eleanor rushed forward like a harpy and tried to get the bag back. With Lily's attention diverted, the duke stepped in and took the bag from her. "I suggest you end this, Miss Randolph." He handed the bag to Eleanor and rested his hand on Lily's wrist.

Lily threw him off. "And Wentworth has so much faith in her, the final decision as to whether Danny-boy gets the part of a lifetime lies in her amateur hands. Danny wasn't supposed to know that, but his agent tells him everything, doesn't she? That Amazon bitch ordered him to seduce the lovely teacher to make sure he got the part. Even if it means sleeping with her. Who's the pimp now, asshole?"

"Enough."

The whispered word in the dark, stony baritone barely touched her ear before Lily was lifted and slung over a broad, familiar shoulder. She inhaled to protest, but a breath of evergreen, sandalwood, and cold Highland air filled her lungs. By the time she shook off the rush of sensual awareness only Lachlan's scent evoked, his long legs had carried them both out the French doors and halfway across the terrace. She planted her hands on his shoulder and tried to push up from her position hanging over his rock-hard body. He loped down the steps and bounced her diaphragm across his collarbone to the point all she could do was gasp.

His long strides carried them past the stables, but not so quickly Mr. Urquhart and half the men who worked with the horses didn't get an eyeful—and send up a cheer.

Lily grabbed handfuls of Lachlan's shirt. "Put me down, asshole! This is not The Quiet Man, and you are not John Wayne."

"If I were John Wayne, ye'd be over my knee. There's still time for that if ye like." Even with her over his shoulder, Lachlan neither missed a step nor struggled for breath as he continued up the narrow lane beyond the stables, along the shores of the loch, and past the ruins.

"Where are you taking me?"

"Somewhere safe from the villagers Elle is no doubt arming with pitchforks to come after ye as we speak."

Lily dropped her head to rest her forehead against his back. Away from the drawing room, Lily struggled to maintain the level of hurt and rage that had fueled her attack on Danny and the rest of the Regency boot camp attendees. She didn't want that. She wanted to keep the white-hot burning alive and in motion. The sensation helped her to block thoughts of herself.

He stopped long enough to open a gate, then in a few more steps, the door to his cottage. The scent of a peat fire in the hearth and tea invaded her senses, so too the scramble of canine toenails on the rugs scattered across the stone floor.

He dumped her without warning onto the bed in the corner. Leonidas jumped up beside her while Lachlan went to stir the fire and add some wood.

"To come after me? What did I do but tell the truth?" Lily untwisted her dress and tried to fix her hair.

"The truth?" Lachlan turned, arms folded across his chest, and stared at her with a mixture of incredulity and almost sadness. "Is that what this was all about? Ye eviscerated poor Arneaux. What did he ever do to deserve that little performance?"

"What did he do? Why are you defending Mr. I-don't-screw-people-to-advance-my-career?"

He threw up his hands. "And Dr. Higgins? What about her?"

"She needed to know."

"Like that? In front of everyone?"

Lily's mind went blank. She didn't know what to say.

"Tell me ye did it for her sake alone. I'll try to believe ye." He stepped closer, took her hand, and gazed down into her eyes. "Tell me ye didnae do it to get back at Danny because he didnae love ye when ye needed him to."

Damn him. How dare he? How dare he spout this bullshit about her as if he knew her.

"Does it matter why I did it?"

"It does to me." He ran his thumb across her fingers. "Ye spend so much time worrying about who did or didnae love ye in the past that ye dinnae see who loves ye now."

"No one loves me now. No one ever has."

He shook his head, backed away, and released her hand. He turned and stared into the fire. The crackle, shift, and burn of the fire grew louder and louder. When he finally looked up at her, his eyes blazed, but not with passion.

"Bloody hell, woman. What do ye think I've been saying?"

Her heart raced so fast she had no hope of distinguishing individual beats. Her skin went cold and clammy. Her stomach turned to stone. "You don't love me, Lachlan. You don't even know me. Not the real me."

"Who have ye been all this time with me?"

"An actress. Playing a part to get laid by a hot guy." No knife-wielding movie villain ever sliced a victim like Lily's words sliced into her own heart.

"Then ye fucking deserve another Oscar, Lily Randolph. Because I believed ye. With all my ignorant Scot's heart, I believed ye."

Her breath sawed in and out like broken glass. Lily lost contact with her face, her eyes. She had no idea what her expression revealed. Every tool in her acting arsenal blew to hell and evaporated like smoke in the wind. Lachlan shook his head. He moved silently to his desk, typed something into the computer there, then snatched up his heavy wool coat and went to the door.

"Ye'll not find a latté for a hundred miles, but ye can check your messages, talk to yer friends, and watch Netflix to yer heart's content. If it's possible for yer heart to ever be content. Goodbye, Lily." He studied her face for a heartbeat and was out the door.

"Lachlan, wait."

She shot to her feet and grabbed the door before it slammed shut. He didn't look back. In moments, he disappeared. Not that it mattered. She had no idea what to say to him. No idea what to say to anyone. She hardly glanced at the computer he'd fired up and unlocked for her. His eyes. His eyes as he'd told her goodbye—the color of gold tarnished and dulled by time and wear, flat...cold as if they'd never be warm again. Not for her.

She stood in the doorway unable to move and unwilling to mark the time. When her legs threatened to give way, she stumbled to the bed, his bed, and crawled under the covers. Leonidas scratched at the closed door a few times. He whined. Lily wanted to join him. Finally, the little dog jumped up next to her and settled himself against her chest. She rested her hand on Leo's back and tried to concentrate on his breathing.

No amount of staring at the door made it open. She blinked and fought against the burn and itch of her nose. That odd scent of lavender and earth swept over her from somewhere. Not until a few wet, hot drops landed on her arm did she realize she was crying. A soft feminine sigh of commiseration sounded from across the room. Lily tried to find the source, but her vision was so blurred, and her heart ached so badly, she didn't care.

Something vital had walked out that door with Lachlan

Innes. She was in love with him. This very minute she realized that impossibly, irrevocably, and probably for the first
time, she was wholeheartedly in love. She'd not meant a
word she'd said to him. Then why the hell had she said it?
Try as she might, she couldn't make herself understand. Or
perhaps she didn't have the guts.

Chapter Fifteen

THE ADVANTAGE TO BEING THE BROTHER OF THE LOCAL DUKE, if there was any advantage at all, was that people tended to leave you alone, even when you'd spent all night in the corner of the local pub getting shitfaced. When Lachlan left his cottage three nights ago, leaving Lily access to his computer, even if she no longer wanted access to his heart, he hadn't had much of a plan. Kind of hard to make a plan after the American actress had snatched that heart right out of his chest and ground it under her stiletto.

He vaguely remembered hopping onto the Harley he kept parked in Knox's garage and throwing out a request to fetch Leonidas to Cook in the kitchen, then riding all over the estate until the idea of getting falling down drunk struck him. He was damned sure not ready to return to the cottage or even to Rosemount at this point. Fortunately, the apartment over the pub was still vacant. Urquhart's sister had always had a soft spot for Lachlan. She'd handed him the key that first night without a word. First night. How much longer would he have to stay away before the urge to run back to Lily and do something really embarrassing went away?

"Another, my lord?" Sarah McAfee asked. "Or perhaps something to eat? Gert made beef pasties tonight." The young barmaid smiled as she cleared the collection of ale bottles Lachlan had amassed this evening.

"Sounds good, Sarah. Bring me another Guiness and a pasty. The way Gert's eyeing me if I refuse, I might end up chucked in the bin behind the pub."

"Too right you are. Can't have that, can we? I'll be right back."

Sarah wasn't fooling him. She'd been sent over by Gert and her husband, Hugh, to persuade him to eat because they knew he'd be less likely to turn down a lass of not quite twenty. He wasn't at Rosemount, but the people of the village considered him every bit as much family as the people on the estate. Which meant they'd do their best to make sure he didn't die. Not that he intended to. He hadn't survived Afghanistan to throw in the towel over a love affair.

"Well, Innes, word is the leggy American actress threw you over." Robert Gordon dropped onto the bench next to Lachlan and set his mug of draft onto the table. "My condolences."

"Bloody fucking hell. Who told you? Let me guess, your wife. Which means everyone in the county knows by now." Lachlan propped his chin in his hand and tried to make the crowded room come into focus.

"Wife's aunt told wife's mother who told my wife who told her sisters."

Lachlan groaned. Robert's wife had eight sisters, all married to local men.

"Hell, lad, what did you expect? You've been here going on three days now from open to close. You were riding your bloody motorcycle around and around the square at four in the morning 'til constable finally took your keys."

Bollocks! He had a vague memory of a couple of policemen chasing him and driving him back to the pub before he staggered up the stairs and made it to the settee and passed out. Sarah returned to the table with his beer and pasty. She acknowledged Robert with a nod and went back to the bar.

"How's your brother?" Lachlan asked.

Robert shrugged. "About the same. Has good days and bad. I never thanked you for bringing him home alive, Innes."

"No need. We brought each other home."

"Likely that's true. Which is why I'd rather you didn't kill yourself, even over a woman that looks like the American."

Lachlan slumped back against the wall, pasty in one hand and Guiness in the other. Robert picked up his beer and copied Lachlan's pose. The rest of the pub grew noisy with the jeers and cheers at a darts tournament on the other side of the room.

"She's more than a pretty face, Robert. That's the trouble. There's so much more to her than looks. She's kind and thoughtful, though she fights like hell not to show it."

"What happened then?"

"I have no bloody idea." Lachlan put down his bottle and rubbed the center of his chest with his fist. "I'm in deep trouble, Robert. I used to be able to tell the difference between fucking for fun and…" He shook his head and bit into the pasty. Not that he tasted the normally delicious offering from Gert's kitchen. Everything he tasted, everything he smelled, everything he saw had turned grey and flat.

"Making love," Robert finished for him. "That is a problem. Love her, do you?"

"I'm afraid I do, but she doesn't love me. Told me so. I was entertainment."

"Ouch!"

"No shite," Lachlan agreed and then polished off the pasty. He looked over at the bar to see Gert smiling at him. At least he knew how to please one woman.

"Do you think she was telling the truth? When she told you that you were just a fuck? Was she telling the truth?"

"Lily's not the type to lie about something. She's honest to a fault. Dammit."

"Sorry to hear that. You're fucked then, aren't you?" Robert emptied his mug and waved Sarah over from the bar.

"Did Gert and Hugh send you over here to cheer me up? Because you suck at it."

"The wife's aunt rang from the manor. Said your brother's looking for you."

"You didn't tell her, did you? The last thing I need is His Grace showing up."

Lachlan didn't have the patience or the strength to deal with his brother at the moment. Not with the image of Lily's face in his mind every time he closed his eyes. Lily laughing. Lily smiling. Lily swearing like a sailor, driving the phaeton like a maniac, flying his birds. Coming apart in his arms. A cold chill went through him and he wondered if he'd ever be warm again.

"Lucky for you I was the only one home when she rang. Told her I hadn't seen you. Bring us a bottle of Innes whisky, Sarah. There's a good lass."

Lachlan gave him a sideways glance. "You lied to Mrs. Gordon?" Robert's aunt-in-law was Rosemount's cook, a woman who had known Lachlan since he was a small boy.

"Didn't lie. I hadn't seen you when she called, had I now?"

Sarah arrived, whisky and two glasses in hand. She set them on the table.

"Good point. Thank you, Sarah." Lachlan opened the bottle of whisky and poured two hefty glasses.

"Thank you for nothing," she replied. "If Gert finds out I brought this over to you two, Hugh and I both will be in the soup. Behave yourselves."

Lachlan leaned up to raise a glass to Gert's husband who shook his head and waved a dismissive hand at him. Robert touched his glass to Lachlan's.

"To the women we ought to forget."

"Aye." He Said it, but he didn't mean it. Lachlan wondered if he'd ever forget Lily Randolph. She'd dragged him out of the hell Afghanistan had made of his mind before she even really knew him. Had she lied when she told him she didn't love him? What exactly had she said? He'd been so pissed off and…hurt, dammit, he had tried to erase her last words with alcohol and mindless rides in the middle of the night.

A few of the lads called to him to join the darts game as he had the first night, but he couldn't force himself to enjoy the fun. Playing darts with a group of laughing carefree men and women no longer held any appeal. Even now he watched the players and then allowed his gaze to wander around the pub to where couples sat huddled at tables in the alcove close to the fireplace that had warmed this tavern for the last four hundred years.

He couldn't really visualize Lily in a place like this. Oddly enough, she struck him as the sort of woman who preferred the comfort of her own home. Curled up in bed with a book or watching television. The thought stole his breath away. He poured himself another glass of whisky.

What a fool he'd been. She was one of the most beautiful women in the world. She was a famous movie star. She could have any man she wanted. Lachlan wasn't a vain man, but he wasn't unaware of his looks either. He and his brother had been chased by women from the time they were teenagers and their titles and money weren't the only reason. His ability to detect how she really felt about him might have failed him, but he bloody well knew when a woman was faking it in bed. She'd enjoyed sex with him just as much as he'd enjoyed sex with her.

"Was that all it was? Sex?" he mumbled as he finished off that glass and poured himself another.

"That's the question, isn't it?" Robert held up his glass for Lachlan to fill. "We men say it to women all the time, or at least we do before we find the one. When women say it, they shock the hell out of us, don't they?"

"The right one? How the hell do you know? I thought…" He sighed and leaned his head back against the wall. "Well, what the hell do I know? Apparently, nothing."

"Aye, and if ye keep telling yerself that, one day ye'll believe it, won't ye?"

"You sound more Scot the longer we sit here, Robert."

"Tis the whisky."

"That makes you sound more Scot or that makes me hear more Scot?"

"Both." Robert laughed and poured them each another glass.

"I miss her." Lachlan put his phone on the table and stared at his screensaver, a picture he'd taken of Lily, head thrown back laughing at him as she drove the phaeton.

Robert leaned over and looked at the photo before he eased back against the wall. "Only been three days."

"I know. I miss her."

"Then go find her."

"And say what?"

"Tell her how ye feel."

"Tried that. She broke my heart." Lachlan considered what he'd said. He was in love with Lily Randolph, very much so. Worse, he probably always would be. This was bad. "I'm going for a walk."

He tried to stand up. After three tries and a helping shove

from Robert, he managed to hold an unsteady upright position. The floor shifted from side to side. He made his way to the door before he realized Robert had signaled a few of the dart players to join them.

"I don't need an escort," he grumbled as the cold night air hit him. He took a moment to get his bearings and then headed down the cobblestoned street toward the center of the village.

"Not an escort," one of the young men called behind him. "We've a wager going on how far you'll go before you fall down."

Lachlan grabbed Robert's arm. "Who was that? Tell me Robbie and Dougal from the manor aren't here."

"Nae," Robert assured him. "Tis Duncan, Robbie's cousin. Gert already swore him to secrecy."

Lachlan felt his jeans pocket. Yes, the key to the apartment over the pub was still there. "Here." He pulled the key out and handed it to Robert. "In case I do fall down."

"Jesus, Joseph, and Mary. My wife is going to kill me, Lachlan Innes."

They made it to the fountain in the village square. Lachlan sat on the edge of the fountain and splashed some water in his face. He gazed up at the stars and wondered what Lily was doing at this exact moment. Was she thinking about him at all? Had she called her friends and laughed about the big dumb Scot who loved her?

What she'd done to Samantha and Arneaux was cruel and uncalled for. Was that who she truly was? She was striking out in anger because she'd been hurt. She'd been hurt as a little girl and never got over the hurt. Then she'd been hurt as a young woman. Hurt piled upon hurt only festered and waited for someone or something to take a shot at in the hope of finally putting that hurt to rest.

He and Knox knew all about that kind of hurt. Knox got

over his hurt by acting like it never happened. Lachlan had gotten over his by going to war. And Lily? She hurt people before they could hurt her. Was that what he little speech about using him was all about—hurting him before he could hurt her?

"Awright, then?" Robert asked. "Looking a bit green in the gills, yer lordship?"

"Fuck you." Lachlan swatted at him and missed.

"Right, lads. Time to fetch him back to Gert's before he falls down. I'm not hauling his big ass down the pub again tonight."

"There's a barrow down the street in front of Sewell's Hardware," Duncan Wallace called out.

"Fuck you too," Lachlan called.

"Yer awful ambitious for a man who can't keep an American lass in his bed," one of the other lads said.

Lachlan came up swinging. For no good reason except he ached for Lily to his bones, and he didn't know what he was going to do without her in his life. Robert and Duncan wrestled him still and guided him staggering up the street. A car drove by slowly, radio blaring.

"Oh, Jayzus," someone groaned. The strains of the song Loch Lomond echoed in the quiet night.

Lachlan threw back his head and began to sing.

'T*WAS THERE THAT WE PARTED, IN YON SHADY GLEN,*
  On the steep, steep side o' Ben Lomond,
  Where in soft purple hue, the highland hills we view,
  And the moon coming out in the gloaming.

O YE'LL TAK' THE HIGH ROAD, AND *I'*LL TAK' THE LOW ROAD,
  And I'll be in Scotland afore ye,

But me and my true love will never meet again,
On the bonnie, bonnie banks o' Loch Lomond.

"WHICH ONE OF YE LOT TOLD HIM HE COULD SING? YER IN FOR a beatin' from me," Robert said.

A dog howled in the distance.

"There he goes," someone shouted.

"Lily," Lachlan mumbled before everything went black.

Chapter Sixteen

LACHLAN WAS DEAD.

He'd often imagined what it might feel like to be dead. Apparently, death involved having every bone in a man's body beaten with a battalion of hammers while his skin shifted from chilled and clammy to afire and clammy and someone stuffed cotton soaked in ale and shite into his mouth. Curious as to *where* he'd died, Lachlan made a feeble attempt to force open one eye.

Didn't happen.

He dragged his arm from beneath his chest and jammed his finger against his eyelid—which managed to open the eye but didn't do a damned thing for his ability to focus beyond a blur of light and colors. A pair of brogan boots moved past him. The clatter of rolling bottles and a couple of Gaelic swear words told him he had not died alone.

"At least ger 'im off the floor, Dickie," a raspy feminine brogue ordered. "Sprawled on Aunt Kate's rug like 'e is 'tis beneath 'is dignity."

Dickie? Urquhart?

"I'm afraid his dignity left around midnight when the lads

fetched him up here to sleep it off, Gert." Hands slid under Lachlan's arms and hoisted him with surprising strength onto a piece of furniture upholstered in a scratchy wool fabric. "Try to sit up, lad. Cup o' tea might help."

"Right. I already put the kettle on," Gert said.

Lachlan wobbled his head over his shoulder and watched Urquhart's sister, Gertrude, waddle behind the flowery curtain that led to the kitchen of the little apartment over the pub she owned. He scrubbed his hands over his face in slow, jerky movements. Hell, even his hair hurt. Urquhart dropped onto the settee next to him.

"Take it the lass is done with ye then?" The old man drew his pipe from his pocket, clamped it between his teeth, and fired it up with an old silver lighter embossed with a Scottish regimental crest.

"Aye," Lachlan muttered, his head in his hands. "Turns out she always was."

"Hmm." Urquhart drew on his pipe and sent the smoky scent of cured tobacco swirling around Lachlan.

"Here ye go, yer lordship. Get this in ye." Gert handed him a heavy brown mug of tea with milk and sugar, unless his sense of smell had deserted him. Lachlan wrapped his hands around the mug and allowed the heat to warm his hands. For a few minutes he simply held the mug and breathed in the steam. Finally, he took a sip and let the tea send tendrils of warmth into his veins. He hadn't realized how cold he was until he began to thaw.

Gert patted Lachlan on the shoulder. She shuffled to the end of the settee and bent to whisper something into her brother's ear. "I'm for home," she said when she straightened. "Stay as long as ye need, yer lordship." With a wave and the echo of heavy footsteps on the stairs, she was gone.

Gert and her husband shared the large eighteenth century cottage across the cobblestone village's High Street from the pub. Her husband would be looking for his breakfast before he went off to work at Rosemount's distillery at the far end of the village.

"I've got to be getting back," Urquhart said, though he made no effort to move off the settee. "Ye coming?"

Lachlan shook his head and winced. Rosemount was the last place he wanted to be right now, but he wasn't about to share that information. Not that he needed to share it with his brother's horse master. Urquhart's ability to read man and beast at a glance was well known on the estate.

"He's asked after ye." The stable master had a knack for making a statement into an accusation.

"He?" Lachlan glanced at the old man, who rolled his eyes in response.

"I told him ye'd gone for a walk. Over a woman."

"Oh?"

"He said we best give it a day." The old man drew on his pipe. "Told him for a woman like that best give it two."

Lachlan smiled despite himself.

"It's been three days." This time Urquhart stood and stepped toward the door that led down to the pub. "What do ye want me to tell Himself?"

"I doubt he's noticed—"

"He's not yer father, lad. His Grace notices everything." The stable master's expression grew hard, censuring with a touch of pity.

"Tell him I'm fine."

"And are ye?"

"When I suss that out, I'll let ye know." Lachlan finished his tea and placed the mug on the low table in front of him. He collapsed against the cushions of the horsehair settee, tilted his head back, and closed his eyes. "Can ye check on Leonidas for me?"

"Likely yer wee dog is right where ye asked Robbie to drop him off before ye embarked on this bacchanalia."

Had that been Robbie in the garage when he got on his Harley?

"Poor thing skulks about the kitchens all day and sleeps in front of Mrs. Gordon's hearth at night," Urquhart said. "Tries his damnedest to escape the house to look for ye. He isn't the only one." The chair he sat in creaked.

Eyes still closed, Lachlan strained to hear Urquhart leave. The last three days had all run together. Bits and pieces of his last argument with Lily. Memories of her with his birds. Dreams of her in his bed. Perhaps the curse of the Innes Witch was real. He'd loved and lost in Afghanistan, and the loss still haunted him years later. How long would Lily Randolph haunt him?

His limbs grew heavy, as if to move them required herculean strength. A shroud of weariness wrapped around his brain. He reached out with his senses, but they had all blunted themselves against him. Life had emptied him of everything save one—an ache that hammered in his chest and made it hard as hell to breathe. He needed to rest. For a bit, just a bit, then he'd figure out what to do.

The familiar scent of heather, lavender, and freshly turned earth surrounded him as he floated from the edge of awake into sleep. The way he sat he'd have a kink in his neck when he woke up.

"Ye know, Elsbeth, if ye want to kill me, kill me. Otherwise leave me be."

The sound of faraway feminine laughter followed him as the deep gray of dozing gave way to darkness and rest.

LACHLAN WOKE WITH A START, SAT UP TOO QUICKLY, THEN immediately grabbed his neck. *Damn!* He hadn't had a kink this bad since the last time he'd slept with his helmet as a pillow in Afghanistan. While using one hand to massage the place where his throat met his right collarbone, he rubbed at his eyes with his free fist. The sky outside the windows had turned gray and slate blue. Earlier, when he'd awakened to Gert and Urquhart's conversation, full daylight had lit the room. The sun had not set, but the fading light said mid-afternoon had come and gone.

How long had he been asleep? He blinked a few times and squinted at the old bracket clock on the mantel. Four in the afternoon already. Time to go home. Lachlan rocked forward and forced himself to his feet. Shower. He needed a shower. He stumbled toward the washroom and wasn't surprised to find a fresh shirt, a plaid, and clean socks placed on a chair just outside the washroom door. Towels and a flannel sat on a stool next to the shower. *Gert. Bless her.*

Lachlan made quick use of the shower, and in twenty minutes, he was washed, dried off, dressed, and clattering down the back stairs out into the alley next to the pub. His motorcycle stood where he'd left it. Elle wouldn't be happy he'd made use of a modern conveyance in the middle of her Regency boot camp, but as he was most definitely *not* one of her recruits, she'd have to get over it. The sun had begun to set, and he didn't fancy walking back to Rosemount in the dark. Besides, a ride on his motorcycle usually cleared his head.

Not so today, though. He sped down the country lane toward the estate, his thoughts as tangled and knotted as they'd been when Urquhart had jerked him upright on Gert's settee hours ago. Lachlan would like to believe his brother worried about him. He'd like to believe Lily was looking for him, perhaps wanted to talk to him. Yes, and if wishes were horses, beggars would ride. He'd never wanted to be a beggar, but where Lily Randolph was concerned, he might. Beg, that is. He slowed his motorcycle and nearly turned back to the village on that thought. Didn't matter. He gunned the engine and soon passed through the gates of Rosemount.

His begging was rather a moot point. Lily had made it perfectly clear she didn't share his feelings. He wanted to fight for her, for them, but damn he was so tired of fighting. Fighting his childhood, fighting his memories of Afghanistan, fighting the love he'd lost, fighting the night-mares. He didn't know if he had any fight left.

He pulled around the fountain and parked his motorcycle next to one of the large stone lions on either side of the front doors and dismounted. Speaking of a fight, now that he'd returned to Rosemount, he stood between the fountain and the doors and contemplated his next move. Walk to his cottage and hibernate there until the entire bloody Regency experience was over? Or go inside the manor in search of his brother, and perhaps accidentally run into Lily? A lavender and heather scented breeze swept behind him and raised the hair on his arms where he'd rolled up his flannel shirt.

"Screw it," he muttered, and strode across the drive.

He stepped into the entrance hall to find an odd quiet settled there. He shrugged and headed for his brother's study, which when Lachlan entered was anything but quiet.

Knox stood at his desk with McGinty and Urquhart. The three of them were all talking at once and looking at something spread across the surface of the desk. Elle and the author lady, Miss Chase, stood to the side and shouted at Lachlan's brother. Lachlan hung back at the doors and delayed announcing his arrival because he enjoyed anyone who tried to take the starch out of His Grace.

McGinty spotted Lachlan. "Where the devil have ye been?" he demanded.

That tore it. Every gaze in the room was on him in an instant.

"Down the pub." Lachlan raised his chin to keep from wincing. Not his best answer.

"For three days?" Knox asked in that annoyingly calm, quiet way of his. Made Lachlan want to punch him.

"What's going on here?" Lachlan ignored his brother's question and crossed the room to get a look at what was spread across the desk. A map. A map of the estate grounds and beyond.

"I just found out mesel'," Urquhart said quietly.

"We've lost the American woman," McGinty snapped. "Because of ye and yer trip *down the pub.*"

"McGinty." Knox raised his hand to silence the older man.

"He's right." Elle turned to stand toe to toe with Lachlan. "You took off and stayed gone so long His Grace actually got off his ass to look for you. And then Lily—"

"Where is she?" Lachlan's blood turned to slush in his veins. The room threatened to recede from view. "How long—"

"Since yesterday afternoon, you big idiot." Elle poked him in the chest, though he hardly felt it. "She took your little dog and went to search for you, and no one has seen her since. What the hell were you thinking?" She poked him again.

Knox pulled her hand away from Lachlan and guided her back to Miss Chase. The two women stared at Lachlan, which finally set his feet in motion. He turned and headed for the French doors that led onto the back terrace.

Lily. Where are you—

"Lachlan."

His brother's voice barely registered. Lachlan flung open the doors with such force the clatter of glass breaking followed him down the steps into the gardens.

"Start at *Cnoc damh Brackans Aonach*," Knox called after him.

Lachlan stopped mid-step and glanced over his shoulder. Knox stood at the top of the stairs. Only then did Lachlan take in his brother's disheveled, dirty, haggard appearance.

"We've searched the grounds, the fields, and all the way to the far side of the loch. McGinty and Urquhart are taking some of the lads into the hills. We'll find her." He tossed Lachlan a military grade flashlight.

"She's been out there all night." Even as he said the words Lachlan's voice nearly failed him. He closed his eyes against the images that raced through his head.

"We'll find her." Knox started to turn back to the house but stopped long enough to offer a slight grin. "Don't you get lost again. Aye?"

"I wasn't…. Aye." He gave a curt nod.

By the time he reached the bridge across the ha-ha, Lachlan broke into a run. The ridge his brother directed him to search was a few miles from the manor over some rough terrain. The distance indicated they'd searched everywhere close to the house. What the hell was Lily thinking? Why had she wandered so far? Why had she even bothered to search for him? Anyone would have told her Lachlan often disappeared for days at a time. Also, she didn't care about him. She'd made that perfectly clear.

He tried to concentrate on his pace. Years of forced marches in full gear lent speed and endurance to his efforts. A strange calm came over him the faster he ran and the closer he came to *Cnoc damh Brackans Aonach*. He'd pointed the peak and the ridges around it out to Lily on one of their driving lessons when he'd taught her to drive the sturdy pony cart. Did she remember how much he loved the view from the ridge?

His lungs burned. The sky turned dark slate, and the little

bit of sun that remained shot through the clouds in slivers. He reached the ridge. Had he been running that long? A quick pat down of his kilt and a search of his sporran revealed he'd left his cell phone somewhere. Did he even take it with him after his fight with Lily? He'd walked out that night and never looked back. The three days that followed were a blur, but he did remember that some of the lads from Rosemount had come into the pub and announced that Danny Arneaux and Samantha Higgins had run off to Gretna Green to get married.

"What did you think of that, Lily?" Lachlan asked the vast empty valley below him. "Is that what set you off? Are you even looking for me?" He leaned against an outcropping of rocks, hands on his knees.

She'd taken Leonidas. Of course, she was looking for him. Didn't mean anything. Guilty conscience. She'd broken the heart of the poor fucked-up ex-soldier, and she wasn't completely heartless. That was all. Or perhaps—he straightened and thumped his chest with his fist. *Not going there. Not now.*

He paced the top of the ridge from one end to the other. On the side farthest from Rosemount lay only steep mountains and stony crags. He prayed Lily hadn't gone that way. An image of her lying on the rocks with broken limbs or a gash to her head flashed before his eyes. He slid down the ridge toward the mountains.

"Lily! Lily, where are you?"

The wind beat against his back and carried a faint, familiar sound to him. The sound came from the other side of the ridge, the side away from the mountains and toward Rosemount. He climbed back up the ridge and listened again.

"Lily!"

Silence.

Then the wind gusted past him once more and brought with it— Yes! He'd heard a dog bark.

"Leonidas! Again, lad. Bark again." Lachlan half ran and half slid down the grassy side of the ridge.

Night had essentially fallen. He switched on his flashlight and listened. The wind picked up, but it came from farther up the valley, farther into the open moors of the estate. A blast of lavender and heather practically slapped him in the face.

"You'd better be right, Elsbeth," he muttered as he loped away from the ridge.

He shone the flashlight at his feet. It had been a while since he'd wandered the moors, but he remembered the ruins of several old crofters' cottages along the valley. There was something else he needed to remember, but desperation and fear made quick work of his memory. He narrowly missed tripping over the remains of a cottage wall, reduced to a half meter tall line of flat rocks.

"Lily!" The rocky terrain did its best to trip him up. "Leonidas! Come on, lad. Where are you?"

The temperature had dropped considerably. The wind smelled like rain. And all the while, lavender and heather danced on the breeze and led him deeper onto the moors. Another cottage wall, perhaps a meter in height, rose so suddenly he had to veer sharply to avoid it.

"Lily!"

A spate of furious barks and feminine shouts erupted out of the darkness. A mixture of relief and fear washed over him. Lily was close, but a weird sort of warning tapped at the back of his mind. Something about this place, something from his childhood. He ignored the warning.

"Lily, where are you?" Lachlan panned the flashlight ahead of him as he jogged toward the place where he'd last heard her voice.

"Here! We're here!"

He raced across the rocky ground, which smoothed from time to time as if paths had once lain beneath the undergrowth. He'd found her. He'd found Lily.

"Lachlan, look out for the—"

"Shite!"

The ground disappeared. For a moment, Lachlan ran on thin air, then he fell arse over teakettle into the dark. The fall took a while, or so it seemed, until he landed on his back with a bone-rattling *thud*. His flashlight, still lit, shone on curved rock walls that climbed at least fifteen feet above him. Beneath his hands lay cool, damp earth. His ears rang. Suddenly, his face was covered with wet slobbery kisses.

"I hope that's you, Leonidas." Lachlan gritted his teeth and groaned as he sat up—only to be immediately flattened by a warm body, damp heavy wool, and the scent of gardenias.

"Are you okay?" Once she'd hugged him, Lily planted a hand on his chest and pushed herself to her knees, then patted up and down his arms and legs. "Is anything broken?"

"I don't think so." He tried to sit up, then gasped when her hand landed between his legs where his kilt had exposed him. "But perhaps you should keep checking."

She snatched her hand back enough to tug his plaid down to cover him, then grabbed his face in her hands and kissed him until he saw stars. After which, she pulled away and punched him in the chest. Hard.

"Damn. What was that for?" He rubbed the spot with the heel of his hand for a long moment, then retrieved his flashlight.

"Where the hell have you been? You just walked out and left me sitting there. Then you disappeared. I've been out here looking for you for days. I thought...I thought...." Her voice caught, and she shook her head.

He put his arms around her. Her limbs trembled, and a

few errant sobs escaped her. That tore it. Now he felt about two feet tall and a real horse's *arse*.

"Hush now." He pulled her closer and stroked her hair. "Ye found me, didn't ye? Sort of."

She gave his chest a half-hearted punch. "This isn't funny, you big Scot doofus. We're both lost in a big frickin' hole in the ground and no one knows where we are and"—thunder rumbled in the distance—"it's going to rain."

Lachlan laughed. He lifted Lily into his lap and scooted back until his shoulders met stone wall. Leonidas trotted over and crawled under Lily's arm.

"Knox knows where I am. We have fallen into a cistern, and it is not going to rain. Much."

"What the hell is a cistern?" Lily wiggled around and drew something warm, woolen and slightly damp across both their legs. She wore his coat. Suddenly, despite the temperature and the wind, heat infused Lachlan's body.

"It's a sort of well, but instead of water coming from the ground beneath it, rainwater collected in it and filled it for the use of the crofters who lived here."

God, he sounded like a history professor. Understandable considering half his brain tried to comprehend why Lily would look for him in his coat in the dark, and the other half tried to devise a plan to get them out of their current predicament. Lachlan hadn't nearly the confidence in someone rescuing them as he wanted Lily to believe.

"Oh. It's a big frickin' hole built on purpose to fill with water when it rains. Great. I knew I shouldn't have followed that ghost." Lightning lit the darkness above them. A rumble of thunder followed. "I hope you can swim. Wait. You *knew* about this…cistern?"

"Actually, I'd forgotten all about it."

"When did you remember?"

"About halfway down."

Lily did laugh then. "What are we going to do?"

Lachlan sighed and gently wiggled out from under Lily and Leonidas. "I was afraid ye were going to ask that."

He stood up too quickly and groped for the curved wall to steady himself. He trolled his flashlight slowly around the cistern. As he suspected there were few handholds or footholds, and the spots bare of the large flat rocks used to line the well were—

"Ye followed what?" He shone his light on Lily, who raised her hand to shield her eyes.

"Please tell me you can scramble up that wall with some special forces G.I. Joe technique before we drown, and they have to drag our bodies out of this well with a hook."

Lachlan took in the nearly white color of her skin and the dark circles under her eyes. Her eyes glittered and her chin trembled the slightest bit.

"Ye'v given this a lot of thought, haven't ye?" He returned to his spot against the cistern wall and pulled her back into his lap. He rested the flashlight, still on, at their feet, which created a sort of halo of light around them.

"I've had plenty of time. I've been down here since last night. Where were you?"

She rested her head against his shoulder and tucked Leonidas inside the coat she wore over one of her simple wool Regency dresses. It was too dark for him to tell what color of the dress. At least she'd worn her sturdy leather ankle boots instead of her stilettos.

"Are we going to talk about the ghost?" He tightened his arms around her and tried his damnedest not to read too much into how she curled into him and wiggled her fingers between the buttons of his shirt to rest over his heart.

"I'd rather not."

"Then I'd rather not talk about where I was last night."

"Asshole."

"Flattery will get ye nowhere."

"We're already nowhere."

Thunder clapped close by, and Lily nearly jumped out of his lap. Leonidas poked his head out of the coat and gave a little bark.

"There, there, lad." Lachlan patted the dog's head. "Naught to fret over. Knox will find us." *Eventually.*

"Don't you *there, there* him. He's the reason we're in this ditch," she said.

"Leonidas is?" Lachlan looked down at her until she tilted up her face to meet his gaze. He tried to put some steel into his expression, but her narrowed eyes and firmed lips told him he was wasting his time.

"He ran ahead, and I lost him. I *might* have gotten a little hysterical. I knew you'd never forgive me if I lost your dog. I smelled heather and lavender. Then I saw… something or someone, and I followed." She swallowed hard.

"Something or someone?" He rubbed his thumb along her jawline.

"I don't even believe in ghosts dammit. But I saw a woman, and she kept waving me on, and the next thing I know, I'm flat on my back in the dirt with Leonidas licking my face."

Had she stood up at all since he'd fallen in the cistern? He grabbed the flashlight and began to shine it up and down her body as he patted her down.

"Are ye injured? Did ye break anything?"

She grabbed his free hand and took the flashlight away from the other. "You keep that up, and you'll owe me dinner and a movie if we ever get out of here."

"Done. Are ye sure?"

"About dinner and a movie? Yes."

He snorted and pulled the coat closer around her. "Ye'r

being a regular pip about this, Lily. Most women would be shrieking like a banshee by now."

"I'm tougher than I look."

"I know. Ye'r tougher than me to be sure." She was, but he hadn't intended to tell her.

A rumble rolled across the valley until it swept over their heads accompanied by a flash of lightning that held for several counts before it disappeared.

"I don't think—"

"I was afraid." She raised her head and stared directly into his eyes.

"Ye'v been trapped at the bottom of a cistern for a full day. Of course, ye—"

"That's why I said what I said."

She wasn't talking about today or tonight. She was talking about three nights ago. She didn't say it. She didn't have to. The chill that crept through him had nothing to do with the damp earth beneath his *arse*. Did he want her to keep talking?

No.

Yes.

Mother Nature let loose a long volley of deep rolls above them. The sky lit up like mortars going off one after the other. His every sinew began to tighten. He couldn't catch his breath. His vision spiraled down until her face was all he could see. She placed her palm along the side of his neck and stroked his pulse with her forefinger. Her strokes matched his heartbeat at first, then gradually slowed. His lungs filled and slowly emptied. He opened his mouth to speak with no idea what words might spill out.

"Stop." She slid her fingers up his jaw to his lips and gently pressed. Lily slid off his lap and knelt next to his hip. Leonidas crawled from under her coat and settled across Lachlan's knees.

"I've rehearsed this the entire time I've sat in this hole and planned to either kill you or kiss you if you ever showed up to rescue me like some John Wayne in a kilt."

Lachlan's mouth tilted up against her fingertips. An odd banshee-like cry carried on the wind. The noise and light show continued, but he didn't go where his mind screamed at him to go. Here was where he needed to be, wanted to be. No matter what Lily said next.

"You told me you love me," Lily said, a tremor in her voice. "Lots of men have said those words to me. You aren't the first."

Well, this wasn't going the way Lachlan expected. The howl of the banshee joined with the coming storm. It echoed the fear and doubt settled against his chest.

"I believed them all at the time, but none of them meant what they said. Not one of them. Ever."

Great.

"But you're the only one who scared the hell out of me when you said it."

Maybe he needed to sign up for Eleanor's Regency boot camp. Apparently, he sucked at romance.

"Because I know…" she closed her eyes tight and took a breath "…I know in my heart you mean it. And I didn't know how to deal with that. I still don't. I've never—I think I've never really known how to— You scared me, and I said whatever I had to say to push you away because I'm terrified that I'm in love with you too, and I'll fuck it up, and that would kill me worse than walking away because I don't think any man will ever look at me the way you do, and—"

"Stop."

Lachlan's heart pounded so fiercely he was convinced she had to hear it, see it pushing out of his chest. He palmed the back of her head and kissed her. Hard. When he finally broke the kiss, he touched his forehead to hers while they both fought to catch their breaths.

"Say it again," he said once he managed to make his voice work.

"The whole thing?" She gripped his biceps so tightly he'd wince if he didn't love the way she held onto him so much.

"Just the part about being in love with me."

"I am, damn you. Stop grinning, you idiot. The last girl you loved was a soldier. I'll bet she was beautiful and normal and wasn't afraid of anything, especially not loving you. I'll bet I am nothing like her."

Her words stabbed at his heart for all kinds of reasons. One day he'd tell her all about the love he'd lost in Afghanistan, but not today.

"Ye'r right. Ye'r nothing like her." She gave a tiny gasp. "Ye'r gorgeous, frustrating, wounded, and angry. Ye'r passionate, gifted, tough as nails, and one of the bravest people I know. Yer soul speaks to animals and ye dinnae suffer fools."

He ran his thumbs across her eyebrows, across her cheekbones, and caught the tears that floated on her eyelashes. He kissed her again—a slow, soft savoring of the sweetness she hid from the world.

"Lachlan." Lily shook her head. "You don't understand."

"No, Lily Randolph. *Ye* dinnae understand." His brogue grew thicker as he spoke. "If ye'r truly in love with me, ye cannae fuck it up. Not with me. Not ever."

Her eyes widened, impossibly wide. Her lips moved soundlessly. She swallowed and shook her head. "I don't—"

"Ye make me mad as hell sometimes. Ye make me want to throw up my hands. Ye probably always will. Ye try yer damnedest to convince people ye'r a terrible, selfish bitch, which is a lie, but ye do it to keep yersel' safe. Ye don't need to anymore. I'll keep ye safe, even when ye don't want me to.

But there is nothing, nothing ye can do to make me stop loving ye, Lily. If that makes me daft as hell, so be it, but where ye'r concerned, I don't know how to be any other way. I—"

"Shut up," she half sobbed. "Just shut up and kiss me."

Lily threw her arms around his neck and sank against him in a wave of heat that consumed all else. He framed her face between his hands and devoured her mouth as if he lay dying and her kiss was his last chance of salvation. She loved him. He tasted it on her lips, heard it in the soft sounds she made, and felt it as her pulse danced beneath his fingertips. In a small corner of his mind, Lachlan sent up prayers the moment might never end.

The storm brewed closer above them. It wailed and howled. Any other time he would remember the war, but now the storm was Lily and love, and he'd fight heaven and earth and the entire army of his demons to hold onto her and how she made him feel.

He fumbled under the coat she wore and reached for the buttons down the front of her dress. She ran her hands under his kilt. Thunder shook the entire valley. Lachlan gasped and grabbed her hands.

"Wait. Wait a minute." He gazed at her face. He'd probably never forget the way she looked at him as lightning illuminated the cistern. "We will *not* be making love in this hole. I may be a brute, but even I know there is nothing romantic about worms and mud."

She started to laugh.

"Thank God for that," a familiar voice called above them in the dark. "I'd really rather you didn't, at least until I'm out of earshot."

"Knox, is that you?" Lachlan tried to get to his feet but couldn't let go of Lily because she was laughing so hard.

"Well, it's not the Almighty. What the devil are you doing

down there? Never mind. I don't want to know. Are either of you hurt?"

A vociferous baying let loose from next to his brother's shadowy form.

"We're fine," Lachlan shouted back as he and Lily finally stood.

She had Leonidas tucked under one arm. When she tilted the flashlight toward Knox, he threw his hand up to fight the glare. In addition to His Grace, two bloodhounds in full cry leaned over the edge of the cistern.

Lily shrieked and dropped the flashlight.

"What?" Lachlan ran his hands over her and encountered something wet and slimy in her hair. He snatched his fingers back and shook them to dislodge whatever it was.

"Please tell me that is rain or mud in my hair." Lily practically moaned.

"I don't think so." Lachlan looked up. "Knox, please tell me you have a plan to get us out of here."

"Not exactly. Robbie, for God's sake move those damned dogs away before they pull you into the cistern as well."

"What do you mean, not exactly?" Lachlan exchanged a look with Lily

"I came to look for you. I didn't plan on finding you at the bottom of the bloody old cistern. How the hell did you both end up in there?"

"I'm going to kill your brother," Lily declared. "Duke or no duke, I'm going to kill him."

"Can we wait until after he gets us out of here?"

Chapter Seventeen

"Shhh," Lily said quietly. She glanced from the screen of the iPad over her shoulder at the monster antique bed that dominated the room she and Lachlan had finally escaped to after the chaos of their rescue. "You'll wake him up."

She wrapped her big shawl around her more tightly. Leonidas, from his spot at the foot of the bed, blinked sleepily at her, then with a little sniff closed his eyes again.

"You left him in bed to talk to us?"

Lily returned her attention to the screen in time to see Derek elbow Raphael and give her a dirty grin.

"Not to mention you stole a duke's iPad and Wi-Fi to make this call? She loves us, Rafie. She really loves us."

"Oh, give me a break. I didn't steal anything. The duke let me borrow it. And if the Regency Nazi finds out, he and I are toast."

"One of the perks of banging a duke's brother," Derek replied with a wink. "Are you sure you're okay, sweetie? You've had a rough couple of days."

"Tell me about it." She brushed her newly washed and dried hair off her face. "I had dirt in places I don't even want to think about, and I had to soak in a big metal tub in front of the fireplace to get rid of it." She shuddered. "I'd kill for a shower."

"Well, I'm sure your hunky Scottish soldier saw to it you didn't miss any spots. Was that a tub for one or two?" Derek elbowed Raphael again.

Raphael rolled his eyes.

"I plead the fifth," Lily said, but couldn't stop the little smile that curved her lips.

The long hot bath, even in the crowded tub, had been one of the highlights of the past several hours. Hours filled with lots of highlights. And very little time to think about the last few days, to think about what Lachlan had said—which was why, the instant she woke up, she'd hopped on the iPad his brother had slipped to her when Eleanor wasn't looking. She had no idea why the duke had done it. On the ride back from the cistern and all the while Mrs. Wallace and the rest of the staff had fussed over her and Lachlan, Lily had caught the stone-faced aristocrat staring at her and his brother. Weird. And a little disheartening.

"What is wrong, *mijita?* You didn't climb out of a nice warm bed to call us in the middle of the night for nothing." Raphael touched the screen with two fingers. Lily pressed her fingers onto the iPad to meet his. "Especially after the day you've had."

"He says he loves me," Lily said in a rush. She checked to make certain Lachlan was still asleep. So far so good. She grabbed her head with both hands and leaned closer to the iPad. "He says he's in love with me no matter what. He actually said I can't fuck it up. Who says that?"

"That's wonderful," Derek crowed.

"Do you believe him?" Trust Raphael to go straight to the source of her sudden need to talk to her two best friends.

Between the rush of being hauled out of the cistern by

way of a rope and nearly every male on the estate, including Teddy Rousseau and the duke himself, of all people, then being driven in a Land Rover back to the manor and being examined from head to toe by Mrs. Wallace and stuffed with food by Mrs. Gordon, Lily and Lachlan hadn't had time to talk. Once they'd taken their bath together, talking was the last thing on their minds. She had no idea what the morning would bring. Or even what she wanted it to bring.

"Well, do you?" Derek asked.

"I…." His words still echoed in her mind.

If ye'r truly in love with me, ye cannae fuck it up. Not with me. Not ever.

"I do believe him, and it scares the hell out of me."

"Good," Raphael said.

"Why?" Derek asked at the same time.

Lily rested her chin on her arms folded on the desk where she'd set up the iPad. "You both know why."

"Is he anything like the dozens of assholes who have declared their undying love until they showed their true colors?" Raphael asked.

"Nothing like them. I don't have anything he wants. He doesn't want money or fame or…anything. He'd never fit in in Hollywood. The only place he fits is here."

"Do you want him to fit anywhere else?" Derek asked.

Lily slowly sat up. She gazed out the window next to the desk. Sunrise was coming, but right now, the moon still shone bright and full. The light lit Rosemount's back gardens, the fields, and loch beyond. The ruins of the castle glittered in the distance.

"No. I don't." She didn't. Lily hadn't really considered what a future with Lachlan might mean.

"You do have something he wants, Lily." Raphael's words brought her attention back to the glow of the iPad's screen.

"The question is, what do you want and what are you willing to give him to get it."

"You two are not helping."

"Yes, we are." Derek, who never took anything seriously, pointed a dead serious finger at her. "You deserve to be loved, Lily. You deserve someone who sees you and still wants to take you on. I suspect any man who would fall headlong into a well for you can handle whatever you throw at him. And it sounds like he's hell bent on trying. Let him."

Heather and lavender. The scent was so strong Lily glanced around the room to find the source. Lachlan made a sound and shifted in the bed. The fire subsided then flared back to life. The iPad screen turned to snow for a moment. She tapped it with a torn and distinctly unpolished fingernail. The picture came back up.

"Lily, are you still there?"

"I'm here, Derek."

"That was weird," he said. "I thought I saw someone by the bed, then we lost the picture. Did we wake your hot Scot up?"

"No. It was nothing."

"Damn. We were hoping to get a look at him." Derek flinched when Raphael punched his arm.

Lily gave a quiet little laugh. "I hope you get to meet him some day."

What was she thinking? What was she hoping? There was a ghost in the bedroom, and she'd lost her mind. Or maybe she'd found something, and the Innes Witch wanted to make certain Lily knew what she'd found.

"When?" Raphael asked.

"Well, I'm sort of stuck here for a while, boys. After this damned boot camp is over, we'll start shooting the film here so—"

"Poor thing," Derek cut in. His voice dripped mock

commiseration. "Stuck in a mansion in Scotland with a Scot built like a brick shithouse who thinks you can do no wrong."

"Well, I widnae go that far," a sleepy Scot said behind Lily.

She jumped as an arm snaked around her just beneath her breasts and the brush of a day's scruff skimmed against her cheek.

"She does wrong now and again. I've even threatened to spank her."

Lily punched Lachlan's arm as Derek squealed and Raphael chuckled darkly.

"The bed is cold without you in it," Lachlan whispered in her ear. "Does Elle know you have Knox's iPad?"

"How do you—"

"The cover is Innes plaid. Whose else would it be? I'm Lachlan Innes," he said as he lifted Lily into his lap and dropped into the desk chair. "And you must be Derek and Raphael."

"Well, hello," Derek said as he straightened in his chair. Lily and Raphael rolled their eyes in tandem. "You didn't tell us he was so tall, Lily. Or so—"

Raphael clapped his hand over Derek's mouth. He pointed at Lachlan. "Afghanistan?"

Lily turned her head and realized Lachlan wore only a bedsheet wrapped around his hips. He touched the scar on his shoulder.

"Aye."

Raphael pulled the strap of his tank top aside and pointed to his own scar.

"Iraq?" Lachlan asked.

"Si."

The two men nodded solemnly, as if words between these two warriors were unnecessary. Lily blinked back tears. Sitting in the dark in the arms of the man she…loved and talking to the men who were like brothers to her, even if they were a world away, Lily wondered, was this what it felt like to have a family, to be home?

"Does anyone want to see my scar?" Derek asked.

"No!" Lily and Raphael shouted together.

"Shhh!" Lily pressed her fingers to the image of Raphael on the screen. "We'll wake up the whole house, and Eleanor will have me peeling Regency potatoes."

"That's the least of your worries," Derek said. "Regency ladies were *not* allowed to keep half-naked men in their rooms under any circumstances."

"Actually, this is my bedroom," Lachlan said. "Does that make me a Regency rake?"

"We are so not answering that question," Lily said. "We're going back to bed. It's not even dawn here."

"Definitely a rake," Derek said, then his smile faded. "Take care of her, Mr. Innes. She's very dear to us."

"I will. She's more than dear to me as well."

They all said their goodbyes, and Lily shut down the iPad.

"Am I?" she asked as she slid her arms around his neck.

"Are ye what?" Lachlan stood with her in his arms and carried her back to the bed.

"Dear to you."

Lily caressed his stubbled cheek as he tucked her under the covers and climbed in next to her. He lay on his side, his head propped on one hand, his other hand over her heart.

"I dinnae have the words to tell ye how dear ye are to me, Lily. But I'll keep trying to find them because I want ye to know and believe I love ye."

"Why do you love me?"

"I haven't the foggiest bloody idea." He drew the shawl from around her and bent to kiss the bruise on her chin. "I only know I do. With every breath I take, I do."

Lily could only smile and shake her head in wonder. She tried to turn onto her side to face him but hissed in pain when she pulled the throbbing muscle in her hip where she'd landed when she fell into the damned well.

"Still hurts?" he murmured as he started to massage his way down to her hip. "We didnae really take much time to recover, did we?"

"No, but we did compare bruises in the bath, if I remember correctly." She closed her eyes and sighed.

"Which is the reason we didn't take the time to recover." Lachlan laughed. He helped her onto her stomach and raised the hem of her muslin nightgown until she could help him take it off. "I promised ye a massage."

His long strong fingers started at her shoulders. The combination of strength and gentleness in his touch released the tension in her muscles, but it did more than that. Lily placed her body completely under his control, but little bits of her soul, her armor, the pieces of herself she used to keep safe, also gave way. She blinked against the sting of her eyes, the tightness of her throat.

"Do ye want to tell me what ye and yer friends talked about before I woke up?"

With her cheek resting on her arms crossed on her pillow, Lily smiled and shook her head. "Not particularly. Do you want to tell me why your brother gave me his iPad and Wi-Fi password like he and I were spies, and Eleanor was our arch enemy?"

Lachlan worked his way down her shoulder blades. He kissed the back of her neck. Lily shivered. "Elle *is* his arch enemy. He hates her being here. Hates this entire Regency boot camp and film location scheme. But he doesn't have a choice."

"Oh please. He has a hard-on for her that could cut diamonds."

Lachlan roared with laughter.

Lily reached back and pinched his thigh—which was like

pinching solid rock. "Stop laughing. You'll wake the whole house, and I want to enjoy my massage in peace."

"Yes, miss," Lachlan said contritely before he carefully worked on the painful spot on her hip.

"Those two just need to hook up and get on with it."

"Aye. I wish they would. Knox needs an heir. The last thing I want is to inherit Rosemount because my brother cannot be bothered to marry and have a child."

For a minute Lily couldn't think. Lachlan? A duke? What the hell? She'd never even considered his position at Rosemount.

"Hey," Lachlan said. He leaned down and kissed her cheek. "What happened? Ye were nice and relaxed and now ye'r tense as a post. What are ye thinking about?"

"Talking about your brother always makes me tense." She looked over her shoulder and gave him her most sexy smile. "I guess you'll have to start this whole massage over again."

"Ah. So that was yer wicked plan all along." He ran his hands up her back and caressed her neck and shoulders.

"You've caught me." Lily hoped her voice didn't shake.

Lachlan kissed up her spine and finished with a kiss to the sensitive spot behind her ear. "One day, I hope ye'll trust me enough to tell me everything that troubles ye."

How could a heart freeze and warm at the same time?

"Lachlan, I—"

"I know ye dinnae need me to solve all yer troubles, my love. But I hope ye'll at least let me share them."

"I will. I do. I trust you, Lachlan." She resettled her head on her pillow. Her ability to hide anything from him had dwindled to nothing. "Now how about my massage?"

He rested his hands on her shoulder blades. Lily counted her breaths as he stayed that way, his knees on either side of her thighs. His rough palms pulsed against her skin. Finally, he started to knead her muscles once more. He didn't speak.

He didn't have to. Every touch, every caress said what words could not—which made the doubts and what-ifs circling her brain like a pack of Hollywood paparazzi vultures all the more ominous and scary. And they stayed there until the sound of Lachlan's *I love you, Lily Randolph* and the scent of heather and lavender lulled her to sleep.

THE SCENT SHE AWOKE TO WAS VERY DIFFERENT. BACON, EGGS, and a pot of strong tea. Lily rolled over, stretched, and opened her eyes to find Emma setting a little table in front of the fireplace. Leonidas sat attentively to one side of the table while Emma plumped a pillow in a comfy looking chair on the other side of the table. Lily could get very used to this. That was until she plonked her hand onto the other side of the bed and found it empty. She glanced around the room as surreptitiously as she could.

"His lordship came down to the kitchens to eat a few hours ago," Emma said with a grin. "He and the dog. He asked me to wait until now to bring your tray. The lads will be bringing up the tub and water for a bath in a bit."

"The *lads* are going to hate all of us in Miss Witherspoon's Regency Army before this is over. Hauling all that hot water up a couple of flights of stairs every day has got to be a pain in the ass." Lily swung her legs over the side of the bed. Emma held out a man's dark blue velvet robe and helped Lily into it.

"Don't worry about the lads. They've taken to betting on who can carry the most buckets at one time and who can fill a tub in the fewest trips." Emma strode to a beautiful old wardrobe and fussed over a dress and various other female garments she'd hung on the open door.

"You aren't serious?" Lily slathered a piece of toast with

some of Mrs. Gordon's strawberry jam, then added a few pieces of bacon before she took a bite and sighed. Bliss. Almost took her mind off why Lachlan had left her in bed without saying anything.

"Of course, I'm serious. They're men. This bunch will bet on who can fart the loudest."

Lily snorted and nearly drowned in her cup of tea.

"Are ye all right, miss?" Emma hurried over to Lily's chair. "Ye gave us a fright, ye did."

"I gave myself a fright, Emma, but other than a few scrapes and bruises, I'm fine. Really."

"His lordship was frantic when he found out ye were missing. And Himself was beside himself."

"The duke? Probably just didn't want it to get in the papers that he'd lost an American."

Emma laughed. "We're glad ye and his lordship weren't hurt."

"I'm kind of glad of that myself." Lily wiped her mouth with the silk embossed napkin and shoved out of the chair. "What did you bring for me to wear? And can I get away without stays or a corset with it?"

"Did ye really think Miss Witherspoon would have mercy on ye because ye spent a night in a well?"

Lily snorted. "The Regency general? Not a chance in hell."

She headed to the wardrobe and reached out to touch the dress. It was a heavy satin dress in a blue, black, and gray plaid. The sleeves were elbow length, but they ballooned from the shoulder to the sleeve. It was actually kind of elegant.

"We'll go with the front closing stays and leave off the corset if ye don't say anything to Miss Witherspoon," Emma said as she helped Lily out of the robe and into the petticoats.

"I won't tell if you don't. What's on the schedule for

today? Curtsy lessons or needlework practice while riding side saddle?"

"I'm not quite sure. Ye'r supposed to be dressed and at the mews in an hour."

Emma pinned Lily into the dress then dragged her to the chair in front of the desk. The maid produced a brush, several pretty tortoiseshell combs, and a handful of what passed for bobby pins in the Regency from her apron pockets. While Emma worked on putting Lily's hair up, Lily took the opportunity to study the bedroom. She hadn't paid all that much attention last night.

It was an elegant room done in masculine colors—all blues, grays, and dark, rich woods. But it was still a soldier's room. Not a lot of frills or decoration. Framed photos of Lachlan with Knox sat on the mantel and Lachlan with what might be his parents. Very formal and stiff looking. The room was nothing like his cottage—which made her wonder, which place was where he belonged.

"Ha'penny for them," Emma said as she jammed the last hair pin into place and patted Lily on the shoulder to indicate she was finished.

"For what?"

"Yer thoughts."

Lily turned in the chair to face her. "What is the legend of the Innes Witch, Emma? I really want to know."

She'd surprised the maid, no doubt about it. But Emma didn't frighten easily. In fact, she kind of smiled. She dragged a leather futon over and sat down in front of Lily.

"There are a lot of stories about the Innes Witch and why she comes to people. Mr. Urquhart's people have worked on the estate for hundreds of years. His sister owns the pub in the village. Most people say the Innes Witch cursed the marriages of the Innes family for all time so no Duke of

Turra or any of the men in his family will ever have a happy marriage, but 'tisnae true."

"What is true?" Lily couldn't believe she'd asked or that she was listening to such a silly superstition.

"The Innes Witch appears to those who are in love. She tests them, and if they fail the test, their love will also fail."

"What's the test?"

"There's the rub, isn't it? No one knows."

Lily threw up her hands. "I need to talk to Lachlan. Do you know where he is?"

"He was in His Grace's study the last I saw him." Emma gathered up Lily's nightgown and the hairbrush. "Don't forget ye'r to be at the mews in an hour." She walked to the door. "Miss Randolph?"

"Yes, Emma?"

"Good luck."

Lily stood for a minute and stared at the closed door. This day just got stranger and stranger. Or maybe it was Lily. Her head and her heart had decided to take off in two different directions. Neither had let her in on where they were going or why. And the voices in her head, the memories of everyone in her past who had used her, let her down, or convinced her to set her value at the roles she'd won or lost, refused to shut up. Hell, no wonder she was seeing and smelling ghosts.

She crossed to the door and stuck her head out into the hallway, checked up and down the empty hall, then hurried toward the staircase. As she turned the corner to the floor above the duke's study, she spotted Lachlan and his brother standing outside the study doors. Like an idiot, she ducked behind the balustrade so she could see them without being seen. She wasn't close enough to hear them. Dammit.

It looked like they were arguing. Wonderful. Lachlan kept shaking his head. The duke had his *I'm-the-duke-and-I'm-not-*

putting-up-with-any-shit expression. Looking really serious, Lachlan finally nodded and walked away. His brother watched him until Lachlan left the house.

Lily slid to the floor. She wrapped her arms around her upraised knees—not easy to do in a full, floor length dress with a couple of petticoats underneath. Lachlan was fighting with his brother, and she could just imagine over what or over whom. The duke had expectations of his brother. Lachlan loved the Highlands. He was at peace here.

"Stupid. Stupid. Stupid," Lily muttered as she banged her forehead on her knees. How would his need for peace and the chaos of her career ever mix?

"Miss Randolph?"

Lily looked up. Anna Chase stood in front of her.

"Are you okay?" The quiet unassuming woman offered Lily her hand.

"Absolutely not," Lily said with a watery smile. She took Miss Chase's hand, and the writer helped Lily to stand. They descended the stairs together. "Miss Chase—"

"Anna. People who get lost in the middle of boot camp and fall in a well call me Anna."

"I am never going to live this down, am I?" To Lily's amazement the author hooked her arm through Lily's as they left the house and headed toward the stables and the mews beyond.

"I doubt it." Anna gave her a cheeky grin. They both laughed.

"I read your book," Lily said. "More than once."

Anna tensed. "You did?"

"It's a great book. I mean it." She did. Sometimes Lily surprised herself. She knew she'd shocked the hell out of Anna.

"Thank you…Lily."

By the time they reached the open place in front of the

mews, the other Regency boot campers and a fair number of the servants and estate workers had gathered. Lachlan spotted her from his place near the flight cage door where he stood with Tommy. He waved her over. Lily took a deep breath, excused herself from Anna and went to join Lachlan and Tommy. Almost the instant she arrived, Tommy made himself scarce—but not before he and Lachlan exchanged a weird look. Lachlan fitted the leather gauntlet onto her right hand.

"You want to tell me what's going on?" she asked.

Lachlan wrapped his hands around her upper arms. "Nothing is going on. Elle asked us to do another demonstration."

Lily shook her head. "You were arguing with your brother. I saw you."

"Oh. And what do you think we were arguing about?"

"Me, of course." She took a step back, forcing him to drop his hands. "Look, I realize last night was really intense for both of us. Your brother probably thinks I'm the last person who needs to be a duchess. And he'd be right."

"I see." Lachlan folded his thick arms across his chest. "I wasn't aware ye get to decide who the next Duke of Turra is."

"What do you mean?"

"I've already told Knox I don't want to be the next duke. I told him he has to marry and produce an heir because I bloody well don't want the job. We were arguing because he thinks ye'd be a *bloody good duchess*. His words. He's using you as an excuse for him not to marry, the arse. But even if he didn't think you'd make a good wife for me and a good duchess, it wouldn't matter."

"Lachlan, you belong here. You feel safe here. This is your home. I don't know if I can…that is…."

"I cannae believe we're having this discussion here and now."

"We can't have this conversation when we're alone. If we were alone, you'd get me naked, and I can't think when we're naked. Stop. Grinning. I'm trying to be serious."

"Ye'r trying to be a pain in the *arse* and ye'r succeeding. Do ye love me?"

She narrowed her eyes. "Did you just call me a pain in the ass?"

"Yes. Do ye love me?"

"Yes, dammit, you big, stubborn Scot. But that doesn't mean—"

"I left the Highlands to go to Afghanistan to have people shoot at me and blow me up. Do ye really think I'd not travel wherever ye need to go?"

Lily couldn't breathe. The whole idea of a future with Lachlan had been her fantasy, something she could control and therefore wouldn't ever hurt her. He'd actually been considering a future with her. What the hell was she supposed to do with that?

"You're right. I don't know why we're even talking about this." Lily threw up her hands and made herself turn and walk away. Everyone was looking at her, but she didn't care.

Don't follow me. Don't follow me. Don't follow me.

A long sharp whistle stopped her in her tracks. She turned in time to see Culloden dive out of the sky and head straight for her. Lachlan had called the beautiful bird, but she had no idea who had launched him into the air. Damn him, he knew she had no choice but to extend her arm to give Culloden a place to land. She braced her feet and assumed the position to catch the bird who dropped onto her gauntleted wrist like a single feather.

"Hello, handsome," she said softly as she stroked the soft feathers on his breast.

Tears sprang to her eyes. She glanced at Lachlan, his arms still crossed, but his expression one of fierce pride. Her finger brushed against an object that hung from Culloden's jess. The object caught the sun's rays that stormed the gray clouds overhead.

A ring.

A large, dark sapphire surrounded by diamonds set in a thick gold setting and band. Lily sensed rather than saw movement. Lachlan suddenly stood in front of her, his face completely solemn except for his eyes. To make matters worse, he slowly lowered himself onto one knee.

"What. Are. You. Doing?" she whispered.

"I'm either proposing to ye or I'm about to suffer the worst humiliation of my life since McGinty's nephew, Shamus, snatched my kilt off in front of the Sisters of Mercy in Aberdeen on Hogmanay when I was sixteen."

"Dammit, Lachlan, don't make me laugh. Not now."

He reached up and removed the ring from Culloden's jess. "This is my grandmother's ring, and the reason Knox and I were arguing was because he insisted I give it to ye instead of him waiting to give it to whatever woman decides to take him on. He said the ring needs to go to a woman who is loved beyond reason. That's ye, in case ye don't know."

She glanced at the crowd of people who stood on the little rise in front of the mews. The Duke of Turra stared at her expectantly.

"Lachlan." She couldn't say another word. Her entire body felt like it was about to float away.

Culloden pecked at her glove. It seemed everyone awaited her answer to a question she hadn't even been asked. Had she?

"Lily, love."

She had no choice but to meet his gaze. When she did, her chest did everything but burst open.

"It won't be easy. Nothing with ye is. And I'm not a walk around the loch in spring either. Whatever problems we have, we'll work out together. My home is where ye are. I'll do as much or as little as ye'll let me to keep ye safe. And I promise I'll let ye do the same for me."

A lavender and heather scented breeze rolled down the valley. Lily shivered, but not from the cold. A spiritual strength, an assurance, filled her.

"Lily Randolph, will ye marry me?"

"He snatched off your kilt in front of a bunch of nuns?"

"Aye. In January." The hint of a grin creased his lips.

"Well then, I really don't have a choice, do I?" Lily had never been more terrified in her life—and nothing in her life had ever felt this right. "Aye, Lord Lachlan Innes, I'll marry you. Now give me that ring before I change my mind."

He was on his feet and had her and a very angry Culloden in his arms in an instant. His hands shook as he grabbed her left hand and placed the ring on it as if he fully intended it to stay there forever.

"Tommy," Lachlan shouted. "Come and get Culloden, so I can properly kiss my bride to be."

The young Scot hurried over, smiling ear to ear, and took Culloden from Lily. A good thing too, as the crowd erupted into shouts, whistles, and applause. Lachlan swooped Lily into his arms and whirled her around before he seized her lips in a kiss that sent shocks of sensation to her toes.

"Ye said yes," he murmured against her lips without putting her down. "Ye'r stuck with me now. For better, worse, witches, cisterns, and everything in between."

"God help us both," Lily whispered.

"He already has, my love. He already has. You may have survived Regency boot camp so far, Miss Randolph, but I won the prize."

She was finally free. This man loved her enough to let her be herself. Was there anything freer than that?

SNEAK PEEK AT CRITIC WITH A CLAYMORE

A sneak peek at the next Rosemount Manor: Love Regency
Style novel
Critic with a Claymore

If Hadrian Cross had known his career depended on making nice with an oversensitive romance writer, he wouldn't have written that scathing review of her latest book.

Reviewing a *bodice ripper* is the last straw for journalist Hadrian Cross. He is a legitimate news journalist—not a romance novel reviewer. Spending time in Scotland at a Regency boot camp where the novel he trashed is being made into a movie is a small price to pay to gain his own byline. Charming Anna Chase out of the plot of her next novel so he can write an exclusive about that plot seems an easy assignment. Until he meets her.

Anna's introduction to Hadrian starts out with the unfortunate ice cream incident, segues into the accidental bonnet chase and goes downhill from there. He's intelligent, hot as hell, and completely unexpected. Damn him. She's stubborn, insightful, and too sexy for Hadrian's good. Hell!

Chapter One

Late March, 2021
Rosemount Manor, Scotland

HADRIAN CROSS WAS GLAD HE'D OPTED FOR THE FLANNEL boxer briefs. Going commando, even under a heavy wool kilt, didn't seem like a good idea in Edinburgh where he'd bought this Highlander get-up yesterday. Now, a guest at the Duke of Turra's brother's wedding, one hundred and sixty miles *north* of Edinburgh, even with underwear on, he kept watch to see if one of his balls had fallen off and rolled from the pew, then down the chapel aisle toward the dais. He'd sacrificed a lot to get this assignment, but nobody said anything about losing body parts.

The duke's private stone chapel was so old, King Arthur had probably served as an altar boy here. Maybe that was why Guinevere dumped him for Lancelot. Poor guy froze his nuts off wearing an altar boy dress in some duke's chapel. The ancient walls glistened with condensation. Stained glass windows were set high on each side of the small building, made to appear bigger by its vaulted ceiling.

But dukes were supposed to have money, right? The current guy must be spending his money on liquor and women. He damned sure hadn't spent anything to heat this ancient deep freeze.

Then again, everything in the chapel had to have been carved out of trees that grew right out of the floor. The pews, the altar, the pulpit, the railings had all been sculpted by a master carpenter in a medieval style he'd never seen outside a museum. And the accessories, candlesticks, crosses, chalices, very heavy and very expensive silver. Hadrian liked history and antiques as much as the next jaded New Yorker, but couldn't they forego a couple of candlesticks for some central heat?

"Care for a wee nip?" The elderly Scot who had picked Hadrian up from the train station in a damned horse and cart this morning asked quietly as he shoved a large silver flask at him.

"Thanks," Hadrian muttered.

He opened the flask and took a long swig. Mistake. He managed not to cough, but his eyes watered and his nose burned like someone had shoved a hot poker up his left nostril. He handed the flask back to...Urquhart, that was the little old man's name.

"What was that?" he whispered in spite of the four-alarm fire down his throat and into his belly.

The Scot chuckled. "Whisky. Distilled here on the estate."

"Good to know." Hadrian shifted on the wooden pew and checked the back of the chapel for the hundredth time in the last thirty minutes. "Any idea when they're going to get this party started?"

He sounded like a whiney bitch at this point, but he was jet-lagged, hungry, cold, and second-guessing this whole expedition. He wasn't here to cover the wedding about to take place. It was a good story, but he had bigger fish to fry.

Or at least fish his editor considered bigger. Hadrian had no such delusions.

"Our Miss Randolph does things in her own time," Urquhart said. He raised his flask toward the altar where two men in what had to be full formal Scottish attire stood and talked and glanced down the aisle every three minutes. "She'd best be here soon. His lordship looks ready to bolt."

"Which one's the groom?"

"The younger one. Longer hair. Military bearing."

Hadrian checked him out. Yeah. He looked a little nervous. "And the other guy is the duke?"

"Himself."

Hadrian had exhausted his arsenal of wedding small talk. He needed to get a bead on his real target. A story about the wedding of a washed-up child star to the brother of a Scottish duke was strictly tabloid fodder. Hadrian perused the pews ahead of him in search of the person he'd dragged his ass to Scotland to see. Men in kilts, shirts with lace at the throat, and knee boots. The women's dresses looked like something out of another century, dark wool with plaid sashes and plaid shawls. The plaid was all the same pattern, grey, blue, and black. None of these women looked like a bestselling author, especially not a bestselling *romance* author. Not a feather boa, red lipstick or tiara in sight.

"Here we go, lad." Urquhart elbowed him in the side and nodded toward the back of the chapel.

A quartet of young women in long colorful gowns stood just inside the doors. They were dressed like cover models on those historical romances his mother read. Ah! The Regency boot camp he was here to attend. Hollywood's latest big-name director, Erik Wentworth, had invited Hadrian to participate as he researched an article about the filming of *A Matter of Honor*, supposedly the greatest period film since *Gone with the Wind* or some such crap.

Lily Randolph, Oscar winner and former child star, was slated to play the female lead. Apparently, she'd come to Scotland and fallen in love with the brother of the duke who owned the estate that had been rented for the boot camp and location for some of the film. Instead of a big Hollywood wedding, she was marrying the Scot in a quick "private, simple" ceremony on the estate. Two words Hadrian had never seen associated with this particular actress.

A blond-haired man, typical California surfer type and a dark-haired body builder type stepped between the ladies. These two men wore the same fancy kilts and formal jackets as the groom and his brother. They didn't look nearly as comfortable in them. A couple of Americans playing dress up. Kind of like him. Each guy escorted a pair of ladies down the aisle. Hadrian recognized the author immediately. The photo in the back of her books had been glamorized. PR people did that. But he recognized her. She looked…different. He couldn't put his finger on how, but Anna Chase didn't resemble any romance author he'd ever seen.

Today she wore her auburn hair in a period film sort of updo. Behind delicate wire-rimmed glasses, her eyes were really green in the light from the stained-glass windows. She couldn't be more than five and half feet tall, nearly a foot shorter than him. How much of that sexy figure was a trick of costuming? He stared at her long after she and the rest of the group processed up the aisle and took their seats in the front pews. Nope. Not here for that, unless he had to be. This story was his ticket. He'd do whatever he had to do.

Hadrian flinched as the sound of bagpipes echoed and filled the chapel. Urquhart grabbed his elbow and half-hauled him to his feet. He didn't recognize the tune, but it was beautiful, haunting and as much as it pissed him off to think the word, *romantic*. The piper in full regalia came up the aisle and took a place in front of the raised pulpit to one side of the altar where he continued to play the beautiful tune. The groom and his brother turned to face the entrance of the chapel. Everyone, including Hadrian, followed suit.

Hadrian blinked. *Well, I'll be damned.*

In a simple white silk wedding gown with a plaid sash at her waist, Lily Randolph glided toward the altar on the arm of Danny Arneaux, America's most popular action star and her co-star in the big deal film. She didn't have a father or a brother or some other family member to give her away? She had a mother with a notorious reputation, but Hadrian didn't see the woman here. Too bad he had no intention of writing a gossip piece. This story had lots of fresh meat. Just in case, Hadrian pulled his pen and notebook out of his coat pocket and started to make notes. Once Arneaux handed the lovely Lily off to her long-haired Scot, the guy in the clerical robes told them all to sit.

Hadrian sat and kept writing. Hell, he could always sell the story under a pseudonym. He'd done it before, especially when he first started out and needed money for little luxuries like food and living indoors. A story about Lily Randolph marrying a Scottish lord she met at a Regency boot camp? Even *People* might be interested. But the story his editor had sent him after was the one that would get Hadrian out of the black hole that was his present position and into the world of real journalism. Which was exactly where he wanted to be, once he'd given up on—

A ripple of laughter bounced off the walls of the chapel. Hadrian glanced up to see a small white dog arrive at the altar and make himself at home on the train of the bride's gown. He turned around three times, scratched a bit and settled down, head on his paws with a doggy sigh. Hadrian tensed in readiness for the actress to pitch a fit. He didn't know a lot about her, but he'd heard she had a temper. Didn't happen. She bent and petted the dog's head, then straightened to gaze into the big Scot's eyes. Interesting.

A woman two pews ahead laughed a throaty sort of laugh, then looked over her shoulder at the rest of the guests. Anna Chase. His quarry. Her gaze paused on him. She frowned, eyes narrowed, not with recognition but with that *do-I-know-you?* expression. Once her gaze shifted to Urquhart she smiled, waved, and turned back around to watch the service. Good. She didn't recognize him. They'd never met, but his photo was next to his byline. This would work far better if she didn't know who he was.

Hadrian turned his attention back to the wedding. Might as well. He needed to figure out who all of these people were and what role they played in the boot camp and in the filming of *A Matter of Honor*. Wentworth had given him a list. On his arrival at Rosemount Manor this morning, the tall, striking redhead in charge of the *Regency Experience*, as she called it, had given him a handbook, which he had no intention of reading, and a schedule, which he'd use to get close to Ms. Chase.

The guy in the clerical robes slammed his book closed. The big Scot grabbed Lily Randolph, bent her over his arm and kissed the hell out of her. The guests burst into applause and jumped to their feet. Hadrian shoved his notebook and pen back into his coat pocket and hauled himself up as the bagpiper started up again. He led the *happy couple* down the aisle followed by the poker-faced duke, and the two Americans, each with a lady on either arm. Last came Danny Arneaux and a pretty blond. Wait. Arneaux had run off and gotten married a few weeks ago. To somebody involved in the film. Arneaux was married. Lily Randolph was married.

Hadrian grimaced. Best he didn't drink the water at Regency boot camp.

Hadrian followed Urquhart out of the pew. When he

started up the aisle with the rest of the small crowd of guests, the old man grabbed his arm. His expression as he looked up at Hadrian reminded him of some of the statues of Scottish warriors he'd seen in Edinburgh.

"I dinnae know why yer here, Mr. Cross, but if ye do anything to hurt her ladyship, ye'll not enjoy the consequences."

"Her ladyship?"

"Aye. Miss Randolph just married the heir to the Duke of Turra. She's Lady Lachlan now."

Hadrian needed to nip this in the bud and quick. "I'm here to write a piece about the making of the film, Mr. Urquhart. The director hired me. Ask the redhead in charge. Ms...." A little lie, but nothing nefarious. Not really.

"Witherspoon."

"Yes. Ask her."

The old man studied him pretty intently for several heartbeats. He finally nodded and started up the aisle out of the chapel. "Come on then. You dinnae want to miss the spread Mrs. Gordon has laid on in 'ta house."

Hadrian exhaled and followed the tough Scot outside in time to see Lily Randolph's new husband lift her into a weird looking two-seater carriage high off the ground pulled by two antsy looking horses. The guy climbed in next to her, handed her the reins and, in a flash, the carriage took off toward the big manor house at a speed somewhere between giddy-up and holy shit. There was more to this *Regency experience* than meets the eye.

He scanned the various groups that walked up the narrow cobblestoned road that led to Rosemount Manor in the distance. Quite a distance. Anna Chase walked arm in arm with the California surfer boy. She and the woman Hadrian assumed was Arneaux's new wife chatted and laughed as they walked. As if she sensed his eyes on her, the author looked over her shoulder. She squinted and her mouth quirked up in consternation, for lack of a better term. Hadrian smiled and waved. He'd been told he had a sexy smile. It worked. She suddenly smiled and gave a little wave back.

"Do I need to send 'ta cart back for ye or can ye make it this little bit?"

Hadrian suspected he was being tested. "I can make it if you can, Mr. Urquhart."

He took off in long strides up the road. The old man's hoot of laughter caught up with him. He smiled in spite of himself. It wasn't the distance of the walk that worried him. It was the damned icy wind blowing up his skirt.

FIREPLACES. FIREPLACES WERE GOOD. THE DRAWING ROOM OF Rosemount Manor had several. Hadrian wondered if anyone at the wedding reception would notice if he backed his ass up to the monstrous fireplace halfway down the drawing room and raised the back of his kilt. That little bit of a walk in the late March air chapped his cheeks to a whole new level. Even *with* his flannel underwear on under this ridiculous outfit.

As he checked out the other guests that milled around the loaded buffet tables, he picked out the Scots easily. They all stood perfectly at ease in their kilts and boots. Wentworth had hired a couple of Brits to teach weapons and dance. The only ones who looked more uncomfortable than them in the Scottish version of formal attire were the new Lady Lachlan's two American friends. Danny Arneaux surprised him. He appeared perfectly at ease, almost as if he'd grown up wearing a kilt. Weird, but the man was an actor.

Enough. He needed to find Anna Chase. The quicker he got his story, the quicker he could bail on Regency boot camp. A guy dressed in a kilt, black jacket, white shirt, knee socks, and shiny black shoes offered him a glass of champagne from a silver tray full of them. Hadrian grabbed two and emptied them back-to-back in quick succession before he returned the empties to the tray. The young men jerked his head toward a table in front of some French doors.

"Ye can get a pint of Guinness or something stronger," he said in a not-so-subtle whisper.

Hadrian clapped him on the shoulder. "Bless you."

He'd nearly reached the table when he sensed someone's eyes on him. He shrugged it off and asked the footman, that's what these young men were called, for a Guinness. It took a sip or two for him to adjust to the dark, bitter taste, but the stuff actually tasted pretty damned good. Or maybe he was desperate for something to warm him up and take the edge off being in this time capsule of a house dressed like an extra in *Braveheart*.

The hairs on the back of his neck stood up. He searched the room. The bride and groom stood at the far end with Arneaux, his probable wife, and the duke. The woman Ms. Witherspoon had introduced as the housekeeper stood with Mr. Urquhart and a big bear of a man in a kilt with a swath of plaid thrown over his shoulder. Where was she?

Oh shit.

In front of a table on which a huge cake and all kinds of desserts beckoned, Ms. Witherspoon chatted with Anna Chase. Chatted wasn't the right word. The author waved her hands in sharp small gestures. The woman in charge of this Regency adventure answered her just as quickly. Her hand gestures were not small in the least and a couple of times she pointed at the duke. Lucky guy. Then, at the exact same time, both women turned incendiary gazes at Hadrian.

Busted.

So much for his idea to engage the author in conversation *before* she recognized him. She knew who he was all right.

And by the look on her face, she'd read his review of her book in *The Times* right after the book came out. From the flash in her green eyes and the grim line of her lips as she marched across the expensive oriental looking carpet, she'd memorized that sucker. He hated it when authors did that. They never memorized the good reviews, and he'd written a few. Nope. Always the bad ones.

Best defense is a good offense. He'd gone to college on a football scholarship. Maybe that's why he started across the room to meet the woman in the gold striped dress. Or…if he met her in the center of room, she might be less likely to cause a scene. Especially during a wedding reception. A wedding to which Ms. Chase had been invited and Hadrian had attended by default.

Like a flock of steely eyed butterflies, several of the ladies in the room fell in line with her as she passed them and they met him next to a round table topped with an urn full of flowers nearly as tall as Hadrian. Which at six feet four was saying something.

Hadrian offered his hand as he stopped in front of the romance author. "I'm—" He flinched. Someone had elbowed him in the back. Before he could check to see who, Ms. Witherspoon raised a hand and stepped between him and Ms. Chase.

"Bow," a male voice muttered behind him. An American voice. Arneaux? "Bow and don't say a word."

What the hell? He gave a half-assed bow and shot a quick glance behind himself. Yes, it was the Cajun action star decked out like Sean Connery at the Oscars. Somebody cue the *Twilight Zone* music.

"Miss Chase," Ms. Witherspoon said. "May I make known to you, Mr. Cross of New York City. Mr. Cross, allow me to introduce Miss Anna Chase of Bangor, Maine."

This was some bizarre shit.

Ms., rather, *Miss* Chase, held out her hand like she was afraid he'd bite. Hadrian took her delicate fingers in his. A sensation of heat and light flared against his skin where their flesh met. Some sort of flowery scent blew through the room. All the arrangements for the reception.

"Bow, dumbass, then let go of her hand," Arneaux whispered behind him.

What the actual— An elbow to the kidney forced Hadrian to bow whether he wanted to or not. Anna Chase snatched her hand from his as he straightened.

"I'm pleased to meet you, Ms. Chase. I—"

"It's *Miss* Chase. Sir." She dipped into what he recognized as a female bow. What the hell was the word? Courtesy. "Good day," he said.

Just like that, in a loud shushing of long dresses, the author and her posse of women crossed the room to the table of desserts where the bride and groom and the duke pretended to examine the wedding cake. *Pretended* because everybody in the room had watched his introduction to the pissed off writer like it was a damned Netflix trailer. The minute she flitted off they all went back to their conversations.

"Have you read the handbook yet?" Danny Arneaux handed Hadrian a heavy crystal glass and stepped up next to him. Both of them watched the ladies interact with Lily Randolph and her muscle-bound Scottish lord.

"Haven't had the chance." Hadrian took a cautious sip of the liquid in the glass. Good thing too. It was the local whisky. He took another sip. "Do I need to?"

"If you're going to survive boot camp? Hell, yeah. In case you are wondering you were pretty much given the *cut direct.*"

"Is that bad?"

"It ain't good. Want to tell me what you did to piss off Miss Chase?"

"I reviewed her book."

"Uh huh."

"I'm a literary critic for the *New York Times*."

"Uh huh."

"I don't think she liked my review."

"No shit."

Hadrian sipped his whisky. "Did you really run off to Gretna Green and marry your Regency coach?"

"Why are you here, Mr. Cross?"

The welcoming good old boy disappeared. Hadrian couldn't blame him. Every magazine cover in the airport had a story about Hollywood's top action star marrying the woman hired to turn him into a period film actor on the cover.

Hadrian kept one eye on Anna Chase, but he raised his hands in surrender as he said, "I don't write gossip, Mr. Arneaux. My editor wants a piece on the filming of *A Matter of Honor*. Erik Wentworth gave me permission to join your little Regency boot camp and to observe the process. That's what my story is about." He despised lying, but his entire future in journalism hinged on this assignment.

"Kind of weird story for a literary critic," Arneaux observed.

"Not for one who is ready to move out of book reviews into serious journalism." That much at least was the truth.

The actor raised an eyebrow.

"If I get this piece right, my editor will promote me. Maybe that sounds kind of stupid to you, but—"

"Not at all. I understand better than you know."

Hadrian studied the man's face. He wasn't kidding. Interesting. But he wasn't here for Arneaux or anyone else involved in the silly period film of a ridiculous historical romance. He emptied his glass of whisky and looked for a place to put it down. A small table with a Fabergé looking egg on it stood between two chairs next to Hadrian and Arneaux. Before he could put the glass down the actor grabbed it.

"I wouldn't," he said. "That table is three hundred years old and that fancy egg is the real deal. Worth more than I made on my last movie." He waved the glass toward a group of young men in matching kilts and black jackets. One of them hurried over and grabbed the glasses. "Thanks, Robbie."

"Aye, Mr. Arneaux." The young man grinned and dodged in and out of the milling guests then disappeared into the wall, or at least that's what it looked like to Hadrian. What kind of place was this?

"Excuse me, Mr. Arneaux, I need to go and beg Ms. Chase's forgiveness if I'm going to survive this assignment unscathed." Hadrian took a step toward the dessert table.

The actor grabbed his arm. "Call me Danny. Call *her* Miss Chase. They didn't use Ms. during the Regency and Eleanor will rip you a new one if you do. And you *really* don't want to try and apologize to her right now. If ever."

"You know her that well?" Hadrian watched the dainty, auburn haired woman adjust her glasses and laugh at something the duke said.

"I know *women* that well. The way she looked at you? You're pretty close to number one on her shit list."

Hadrian laughed. "Did they have shit lists during the Regency? I've got this. I didn't put on this skirt in the middle of a Scottish winter for nothing. You coming?" He waved an inviting hand toward those admiring the wedding cake.

"Go ahead, *couyon*. I'll watch from here." Danny folded his arms across his chest and sat on the arm of one of the chairs next to the three-hundred-year-old table.

Hadrian didn't like the half-assed grin his new movie star friend wore. He didn't like it at all.

The author with the pretty green eyes didn't see him as he crossed the thin red, black, and gold patterned carpet. Miss Eleanor Witherspoon noticed him immediately. So much so, she glanced up at the heavy swords crossed over a shield that hung above the mantel of a monster of a fireplace. Hadrian flexed his shoulders and turned up the wattage on his smile. Miss Witherspoon stepped toward him. Hadrian sidestepped her like a running back dodging a linebacker and went straight to Anna Chase's side. He even remembered to bow.

"Miss Chase," he said quietly. "Can we speak privately?"

The look she gave him threatened to set his hair on fire. Kind of erotic to be honest. So long as she didn't go for one of the swords.

"Do we really have anything to say to each other, Mr. Cross?"

"This won't take long. I think I need to apologize." His face started to hurt. A pleasant expression wasn't his normal affect.

"Whatever for?" She went from furious to angelic in the blink of an eye. A really sexy, striking angelic. Weren't romance authors supposed to be frumpy and...ordinary.

He touched her elbow and steered her toward the far end of the dessert table, the end farthest from the fireplace. And the swords. The desserts at this end were arranged in trays of ice. Some sort of frozen dishes. Sorbet, maybe? The fireplace wasn't the only source of heat he needed to escape. The Witherspoon woman, Danny's new wife, Lily Randolph, and a couple of other women he'd seen at the wedding were staring a hole in the back of his head. He could feel it.

"I want to apologize. I'm afraid my review of your book may have been a bit—"

"Harsh? Condescending? Insulting? A condemnation of

the entire romance genre? A suggestion I should go back to Bryn Mawr and learn to write real books?" Arms crossed beneath her breasts and raised her chin in defiance, Anna Chase was an Amazon ready to cut him down. And he wondered what she'd look like naked. Damn, where had that come from?

Hadrian forced himself to ignore the twinge of what he guessed was regret that pinged into his chest. "I really am sorry if my review hurt your feelings, Miss Chase." She turned to examine the little glasses of frozen stuff. He stepped closer in spite of the fact she ignored him. "I'm more qualified to review serious literature than I am romance. I never would have been asked to review your book if it hadn't made all the bestseller lists. I never would have chosen to review a romance novel so—Miss Chase?"

She came at him with a big dish of frozen sorbet, smiling sweetly. Reflexes that had saved his ass on the football field more times than he could remember said, *"Screw this, buddy. You're on your own."* She shoved one hand down the front of his kilt and dumped the entire dish of sorbet down his boxer briefs.

He bit his lip to keep from screaming *"What the fuck?"* at the top of his lungs. Didn't matter. His surroundings suddenly became quiet as a funeral parlor and everybody in the Duke of Turra's drawing room stared at him. And he'd only thought his balls were cold before.

Anna Chase put her hand against his thudding heart and leaned up to get right in his face. "You can take your half-assed apology and shove it in there with Mrs. Gordon's orange ice." She pitched her voice so only he could hear and there wasn't the slightest hesitation in her words.

When she tried to move back, he trapped her hand on his chest. "How'd you know I was wearing underwear under my kilt for you to stick your hand down, sweetheart?" He wanted nothing more than to kiss her out of her mind. Or at least rattle that steely façade.

"Because if that's how your kilt looks when you aren't wearing underwear, I'd be sending your girlfriend a sympathy card. Have a nice day. Asshole."

Hadrian stood perfectly still as she strolled away. The Witherspoon woman, Arneaux's wife, a few other women, and even Lily Randolph followed her, each one stopping to smirk at him on their way across the room. The duke's brother stopped long enough to pat him on the shoulder and shake his head before he went after his actress wife. And all the while, Hadrian couldn't take his eyes off Anna Chase as she walked away.

"Welcome to the Highlands," the duke said as he handed Hadrian a heavy silk napkin.

"That must have been some review." Danny said as he came stepped up next to Hadrian. He handed him a glass of whisky. "How do you like Regency boot camp so far?"

www.scarsdalepulishing.com

Love Regency Style

Cajun in a Kilt
Sassenach in Stilettos
Critic with a Claymore
The Stuntman and the Swordmaster
The Duke the Witch and the Party Planner

Stay tuned for the next Rosemount Manor series
The Price of Love